365 Days

365 Days

by

KE Payne

A Division of Bold Strokes Books

2011

365 DAYS

ISBN 13: 978-1-60282-540-6

This Trade Paperback Original Is Published By
Bold Strokes Books, Inc.
P.O. Box 249
Valley Falls, NY 12185

First Edition: June 2011

Credits
Editors: Lynda Sandoval and Stacia Seaman
Production Design: Stacia Seaman
Cover Design by Sheri (graphicartist2020@hotmail.com)

Acknowledgments

My grateful thanks to everyone at Bold Strokes Books for all their help, especially Vic for her initial assistance and invaluable advice and, latterly, to Lynda for fielding all my daft questions with such patience!

Thank you too to BJ for reading and rereading endless drafts of *365 Days* night after night, and for offering so many brilliant and funny suggestions.

Dedication

To anyone who's ever found themselves
in Clemmie's shoes…

Monday 1 January

A new diary! Yay! I promise to keep this one neat, bearing in mind the mess I made of the last one. I also promise, after last night, NEVER to go out with my parents on New Year's Eve again! OMG! We went to Uncle Bob's annual shindig and I swear to God I'll not go to next year's. Yes, I know I say that every year, dear diary, but seriously…after the absolute tit Mum made of herself last night, I'm just going out into town next New Year, with all the other sensible people. I'm going to stand in the Abbey churchyard feeling cold and just a little bit miserable, and wait for the Abbey bells to bong at midnight. I'm going to kiss the nearest person standing next to me, whether or not they're a stranger (although I'd prefer it if I knew them) and be back home in my bed by 12:30. Why be out with all the drunks, freezing all night, when I could be curled up in my warm bed?

Mum did her usual party trick last night, yes, you know the one—downed Campari frappés like they were going out of fashion—and tottered home at 4 a.m. with a 'prize'. And what did she surprise us with this year? A pair of boxer shorts!! *Men's boxer shorts!!* Ugh!! What's worse, they're a pair of USED boxer shorts! Double ugh! She claims she has no idea who they belong to, although I did catch a glimpse of her shortly before midnight, getting *very* cosy with some poor man whom she had pressed up against the wall-mounted electric can opener in Uncle Bob and Aunty Marie's kitchenette, and who looked as if he wished the floor would open up and take him away somewhere safe, away from this mad woman with a bright red tongue (the Campari).

It wouldn't be so bad if Mum was a seasoned drinker, but she only ever drinks on New Year's Eve. One sniff of anything remotely alcoholic and she's on her back with all fours in the air. It's most unbecoming of a teacher; I often wonder what class 7MA would make of it if they ever had the misfortune to catch my mother, tanked up on cheap alcohol, in full throttle at two in the morning.

It remains to be seen if she can reunite aforementioned underpants with owner once she deigns to rise from her bed and greet us with her presence [/sarcasm/].

Tuesday 2 January

Alice rang me at 8:20 a.m. and wished me a happy new year. I told her she was 24 hours late and that she should have wished me a happy new year actually on New Year's Day. She sounded a bit upset, even though I was joking [/hormones/]. Anyway, we met up in town at lunchtime and had a Starbucks, and I told her about the mysterious boxer shorts (which are now, thank God, residing in the bin) and she laughed at my telling of the tale, so that made me feel good. We're going to the cinema tomorrow night to see some Russell Crowe movie: I wanted to see *Over the Hedge* but I was too embarrassed to tell her that. I *am* sixteen after all, so I suppose I ought to be maturing in my movie tastes. She'd probably laugh at me for wanting to see a cartoon…

Alice told me that a new girl's starting in our class next week. I'm pleased. I like sitting next to Charlotte but she picks at her fingers *constantly* and it makes me feel sick. I swear one day she's going to be there picking at the skin on her fingers and she's going to peel a whole stretch of skin off, right up her arm. Gross! It would be good to have someone new to sit next to. I'll speak to Mrs. Schofield, our form tutor, next week and see if I can be moved next to the new girl, on health grounds. Or maybe on the grounds of me having my human rights violated by having to sit next to Charlotte. Or something.

Alice talking about school got me thinking about J again. I hadn't thought about her that much (although she's always on my mind, lurking in the background) but I suppose I've been so caught up in all the Christmas festivities that I've not really had much time to, well, *think.* I'm going to try so hard not to be so involved with her (in my head, I mean…chance would be a fine thing to actually BE involved—ha ha!) so that I can concentrate on more important things. Like schoolwork! And a life!

Wednesday 3 January

I asked Mum today why she still hadn't opened up the new mobile phone me and my sister bought her for Christmas. She said she had opened it, and it had looked too complicated to use, so she'd put it back in its box again. She said she was worried to use it in case she pressed a wrong button and started a war with Iran or something. She laughed as she said it, but I noticed that she had a nerve twitching in her cheek. I told my sister we should have bought her what every other sensible daughter buys her mother (saucepans) but would she listen? Nooooo! So that's my half of £50 completely bloody wasted!

Went to see the Russell Crowe movie with Alice. It was crap. I knew I should have gone to see *Over the Hedge* instead!! Cute animated creatures or posturing, hairy Antipodean? Hmm!

Thursday 4 January

Such a boring day! Dad went back to work today. My sister (Her Royal Bloody Highness) went out shopping in the sales with Mum, so I spent the day at home on my own. I don't actually mind being on my own 'cos it gives me time to *think*. Guess what, or who, I thought about? Yup, J! It's not as if I actually fancy J, well I don't think so anyway…it's just that I like being around her. Does that make sense? I'm happy when I see her, and even happier when she speaks to me (not that it happens very often). I think I just want her as a friend…I want to be her friend, even though I have Alice as a friend, it feels different with J. Maybe I do fancy her? I just dunno. All I do know is that it's driving me crazy and I don't know what to do.

No one at school has any idea how I feel, and I'd dieeeeeee if they ever found out about these feelings I have. I can't even write her full name in my bloody diary, for God's sake, in case someone should read it! What a mess!

Friday 5 January

It snowed a bit today! Barbara got hideously excited at the sight of white flakes, peed on the lawn, then looked confused 'cos the snow turned yellow. Rained this afternoon so pure white/yellow snow now gone to mush. That's about as exciting as my day got today!!!!

Saturday 6 January

Ugh, my last weekend of freedom before school starts again! Had a lazy day today, got up late and watched some crap kids' programmes on the telly till Her Royal Bloody Highness walked in, then I turned over (she thinks me a baby as it is, without catching me watching Nickelodeon). Took Barbara out for a nice long walk in the woods with Dad, which was going great till she tried to kill another dog that she saw, so we came home.

Sunday 7 January

Was awakened by the sound of Mum going to church at 8 a.m.! Thanks, Mum! My last day to have a lie-in and I'm interrupted by you!! [/mad/]. Forgave her when she came home and cooked Sunday lunch, though!! I thought of all the calories in her homemade trifle and worried that I won't be able to get into the jeans Mum and Dad bought me for Christmas. But then I figured all the stress of returning to school tomorrow will help keep the weight off, so I helped myself to seconds.

Spent the rest of the day getting stuff ready for the return to school tomorrow. Next year we all take our final exams and I'm dreading it. All I want to do is English language and nothing else, but I suppose I can't do that. What's the point of Maths anyway? When am I *ever* going to need to know that $\pi = 3.14159$ or that $E = mc^2$ or whatever? Imagine, I'm down at Bob the Butcher's buying my sausages for tea, I get to the counter and woman on the till says 'that'll be $\chi - (\chi+\chi^2)$ please.' It's never gonna happen! Get real!

And what about French? What's the point of that?! Everyone speaks English anyway! As long as I can order a sandwich (*un sandwich*— er, hello??!) and find out where the nearest toilets are (*les toilettes*— er, hello??!!) then what's the point? Actually, reading back over what I've just written, if I was in France and asked for a sandwich, I'd better make damn sure I *did* know where the nearest toilets were! [/joke/].

Monday 8 January

Back to school. Ugh! Nothing had changed since we walked out of there on 20th December last year! I swear to God, it was like time had stood still! Mrs. Russell could still be heard clip-clopping down the corridor with her unfeasibly high stilettos (this is despite telling all girls that they must *not* wear high heels), Miss Mynett still couldn't teach a bunch of chimps if her life depended on it, and Mr. Banner still smelt of BO. So there you go.

The new girl doesn't start until next week, apparently. She's still on her Christmas holiday in Florida (!!!!), so Mrs. Schofield told us anyway. So I have to put up with Charlotte and her flaking skin till next flipping Monday!

It was good to see all the gang again, though. Ems came bustling up to me at break-time and squealed with delight at seeing all her chums again. Then we met up with Marcie, Caroline, and Matty at lunchtime and compared our awful Christmases. I recounted the tale of my mother and the mystery boxer shorts and everyone thought that was very funny. I didn't tell them that I found the whole thing revolting, and just laughed along with them as I told the sorry tale.

Aaaaaaaand the best thing of all was that I saw J again! Okay, well I saw her retreating back as she went down the corridor, but it was good enough for me. Man, I'm soooooo sad!! (not).

Tuesday 9 January

Had double Biology first thing this morning. The last thing I want to be looking at, at nine in the morning is a PowerPoint presentation about the male reproductive system. In colour! Felt well queasy but had a Mars Bar at break and felt a bit better, until Ems thought it funny to shout 'sper-MARS-oa' at me half way through eating it and I nearly spat it out on my shoes!

When I got home tonight Mum was already in, and doing her yoga exercises in the front room. She was lying on the carpet with her feet up on the sofa, watching *Deal or No Deal* upside down; she tells me yoga helps her relax, but I'm sure I heard her shout 'No Deal!' in an agitated manner more than once. Personally I think she uses yoga as an excuse to lie on the floor and do nothing (like cook my flipping tea). She looked comfortable where she was though—I didn't have the heart to tell her I'd seen Barbara wiping her arse on the carpet that morning.

Wednesday 10 January

J was sitting on the wall outside the gym with her chums at lunchtime today and she smiled at me as I walked past!! I was having trouble chewing a Werther's Original toffee at the time so I looked like something resembling a dribbling, grinning chimp as I tried to smile back. Just my luck!! Of course, I tried to remain as calm as I ever can when I see her, so I don't think any of my lot realised that my heart was going at about 1,000 beats per minute!

We're doing all about the Cold War in History this term. We've been given homework already!! In our first week back!! I mean, c'mon! We've got to write a short essay on some bloke called Stalin by next Monday, so I'll log onto the Internet tomorrow after school and see if there's anything on there about this here Stalin fellow.

Thursday 11 January

HRBH announced at the breakfast table that her music class are doing a trip to Italy this year, and can she have the £440 needed by next week please? After Dad had finished choking on his Fruit 'n Fibre he asked her how long she'd known about this trip? Her Royal Bloody Highness shrugged and said, 'a few weeks.' Dad just looked at Mum and rolled his eyes!! How does HRBH do this? If I'd asked my parents for that amount of money in such a short space of time I would get earache about it for weeks! HRBH mentions it casually and all she gets is rolled eyes!! She gets away with bloody murder. [/injustice/].

It's Alice's birthday tomorrow, so I went into town after school and bought her:

- A pencil case shaped like a carrot,
- A small china rabbit, with one paw raised and a quizzical look upon its face,
- A soft rabbit key ring. When you press its belly, it snores.

I also got her a birthday card showing two rabbits bouncing on a trampoline. The wording on it just said, 'bunny bouncers.' I thought about buying her some Maltesers as well but they look a bit too much like large rabbit poos for my liking.

(Alice loves rabbits.)

Friday 12 January

Alice's birthday!! I met her at her house this morning and nabbed a lift to school with her and her dad (he's just bought a new 4x4 and now takes Alice to school, like, every day just 'cos he wants to show it off to the other parents, I think). Dad calls him a 'sad bastard' and I'm inclined to agree. Gave Alice her presents and she seemed pleased with them; she squealed when she pressed the key ring rabbit's belly and it snored. She kept pressing it and pressing it to make it snore, and I must admit it was getting RIGHT on my nerves by the time we arrived at school. I'm pretty sure one time she did it just to mask a fart—either that or the air-conditioning in her dad's 4x4 needs adjusting.

Anyway, we're going out tonight, with the gang—meeting up at seven outside McDonald's, so I'm writing this in my diary now in case I'm too tired when I get home tonight!!

Saturday 13 January

Had a good night last night! Ems turned up with Ryan—he's okay but he reeked of cheap aftershave and kept putting his hand on Ems' arse all evening. That would drive me potty! I don't know why she lets him maul her like that! Anyway, we had tea in Maccy D's (I had a Whopper—won't touch chicken fillets since I heard the chicken cyst/mayonnaise story) [/queasy/].

Sunday 14 January

Remembered that I hadn't done my History homework (why does my mother never ask me if I've done my homework like everyone else's mother does?? Am I expected to remember *everything*?), so I logged on to the computer to see what I could find out about Stalin. There were *loads* of websites about him!! Result!! So I did a bit of copy and pasting, jiggled the words about a bit so it didn't look like I'd copied it, and wrote a sick essay in about 20 minutes! Well pleased with that!

Monday 15 January

The new girl started today. Her name's Hannah something or other. She seems nice, and she's kinda cute, if you know what I mean. Florida must have been hot, 'cos she had a cracking tan on her, but I figure one week of English January weather'll soon whip that off her!

She's not sitting next to me, despite me asking Mrs. Schofield if she could move Charlotte. No, she's sitting towards the back, next to

Aimee Tobin, who barely said two words to her all day, I noticed. If she'd sat next to me I'd have talked to her! Anything would be better than the constant sound of teeth nibbling on skin (Charlotte).

Tuesday 16 January

Ryan is trying to set me up with his friend Ben. Ems told me today in morning break that Ryan thinks I'm 'cute' and that it's a shame I don't have a boyfriend, and that Ben is 'cute' too and on the lookout for a girlfriend and that Ryan thinks we'd be a match made in heaven and that he's been trying to get my mobile number off Ems so that he can give it to Ben so that Ben can text me sometime.

Why do people do this? Why? I'm not interested in having a sodding boyfriend! I'm quite happy as I am. I told Ems as much but I think she's siding with Ryan 'cos she kept telling me how fit Ben was and that she could see us together and that I should at least send him a text to say hi 'cos it wouldn't hurt just to do that. She stuffed a piece of paper into my hand with his mobile number written on it and said, 'what do you think?' and cocked her head to the side and gave me that pitying smile that she's so good at. I smiled back and said I'd think about it. Yeah right! [/never-in-a-million-years/].

Now, if she wanted to set me up with J…

Wednesday 17 January

Got home from school to find HRBH wrapped round Ade on the sofa. They looked like they'd just been doing something revolting so I made sure I checked the chair covers for any funny stains before I sat down. I can't stand Ade. His eyes are too close together for my liking, he sniffs, like, *all* the time, and he calls me 'weeny' for some unknown reason, despite the fact he's only four years older than me. Patronising bastard. I know HRBH's only been going out with him for 3 weeks, but I really hope she's not thinking anything long-term with him. The thought of another year or so of being called 'weeny' chills me to my very core; it sounds too much like wiener for my liking and I don't want to be thinking about willies every time he speaks to me.

Thursday 18 January

We were sitting on the wall by the cemetery at lunchtime when Ryan and his mates came past. That Ben kid was with them. Ryan reckoned they were just passing but I think it was pre-arranged by Ems because I wouldn't let her give him my mobile number and I haven't bothered texting him yet, not even having so much as looked at the piece of paper with his number on it since Ems gave it to me. I took a good look at him anyway; he's fairly nice-looking but has sticky-out ears and lots of zits. He's quite tall too, with a mop of dark hair, which hangs over his eyes, but I didn't care for the way he stood there picking at a ripe spot next to his nose. He had neat trainers on, but he didn't say a word to me or make any kind of eye contact in the entire ten minutes it took for Ryan to arrange a date with Ems, and for his lanky streak-of-lightning sidekick Charlie to finish looking Caroline up and down.

I suppose it really is time I got a boyfriend, after all I *am* nearly seventeen, and everyone else I know has a boyfriend. I don't want people to talk. Perhaps if Ben asks me out, I'll say yes. After all, how bad could it be to go on a date with a boy?

He'll have to actually talk to me first, though.

Friday 19 January

A text! It said: 'Hey chk, howz bout u n me gttn 2getha sumtme???' After spending a good three minutes or so cracking the code (I think he maybe has something against vowels) I guessed this was Ben asking me out, so Ems must have given him my number even though I sodding well asked her not to! I'm not sure it was necessary for such a large number of question marks either, but I gathered my thoughts, read the message through again, checked the piece of paper with Ben's number on it to make sure it really was from him (it was) and sent one back that said 'sure'. I, unlike many others my age, believe in such unimportant matters like proper spelling and grammar (this is what comes of having an English teacher for a mother—either that or I'm shockingly old-fashioned) and of the importance of short punchy messages. Besides, I couldn't think what else to say to him.

Within 20 seconds (is he keen or desperate?) a message came back saying: 'Kool! Letz do 2moz @7 @ McDeez,' which I roughly translated as 'How splendid! Well then, let's dine together at seven o'clock at a local branch of an American-style diner-cum-burger bar. What say you?'

I suppose it's too early in our burgeoning relationship to point out that, amongst other glaring mistakes in his two messages, *cool* is spelt with a *c*, not a *k*?

Told Ems in afternoon break that I was meeting Ben tomorrow night and she squealed (rather too loudly, I thought) and said she'd lend me something to wear. [/insulted/]. I hadn't actually thought about what to wear, but my North Face trousers have just been washed so they'll be fine.

Saturday 20 January

Woke up and had a sinking feeling in my tummy because I remembered that I was meeting Ben later. I kinda wanted to just stay in and watch TV with Mum and Dad, but I supposed I ought to show willing.

Got a text from Ems (spelling marginally better than Ben's) wishing me luck and telling me to have a 'brill time'. We're only going to McDonald's.

Anyway, it's now 6:30 p.m. so I suppose I better get myself ready. Will write up results of date tomorrow!!!

Sunday 21 January

Well, it went okay I suppose. For a first date, I mean. It hadn't actually struck me that this was going to be my first proper date until I got into town and saw Ben standing under the big M sign, scuffing his foot along the ground, and picking at his zit (still). I had a momentary knot of fear in my tummy that was soon blown away when I was knocked sideways by a blast of cheap, acrid aftershave that hit me when I walked up to him. He looked nervous but did very well opening the door to McD's for me, which was sweet of him, I suppose.

It was kinda downhill from there, though. We ordered a burger and fries, each, and sat down, and that was about as interesting as the evening got, really. He wolfed his burger and fries down as if he'd never seen food before, barely said two words to me all night, then sat there with a globule of tomato ketchup in the corner of his mouth for the rest of the evening. I thought, bearing in mind he was in the company of a lady (me), he would have checked to make sure he had nothing round his mouth. But no! To add insult to injury, he asked me if he could finish the fries I hadn't been able to manage, then lunged across the table and grabbed a handful of them before stuffing those back in the same piggish manner he'd eaten his own. He then hiccoughed loudly for the next ten minutes without so much as one 'excuse me' [/unimpressed/].

Anyway, at about 10:30, I made up some excuse about having to get going home because my dad was picking me up and he was working nights (a great big lie) so Ben walked me down to the fountain in town where I'd agreed to meet Dad. We were walking down through town when Ben suddenly put his arm round my shoulders, so I let it stay there 'cos I didn't want to appear rude. He slowed his steps down when we got nearer to the fountain, then stopped altogether, casting a shifty glance down the road (to make sure Dad wasn't coming, I suppose). He started wiping his mouth with the back of his hand (the ketchup had gone by this point, thank God) then asked me if he could see me again. I said, 'sure' (why?????) and he seemed pleased. I said, 'Right. Bye then,' and he lunged at me with pursed lips!!!!! I jerked my head back, but not before I'd been engulfed by the taste of saliva, greasy burger, and stale Coke. Gross!!! Ben mumbled something inaudible, smiled weakly at me, then ambled off down the road. I took his mumble to be a good-bye and watched him disappear round the corner, face lit up by his just-flipped mobile phone.

Then my phone beeped! It was him!! It said, 'Soz wuz so quite wiv u. Wuz nurvus.' Assumed he meant quiet, not quite. Started to write a message but didn't know what to write, so stuffed my phone in my pocket just as Dad turned up in the car. Felt really depressed when I got home, I don't know why. Thought I ought to reply to Ben's text, but couldn't be arsed and anyway, my phone was going crazy with people texting me! Ems, Caroline, Marcie, AND Alice all texted me asking me how I got on. You'd have thought I'd been to hospital for some life-saving operation, not on a date!

I just replied to them all with a 'Yeah, good' text and switched off my phone.

Woke up to, like, 101 texts this morning. The most interesting one from Ben, asking me if I wanted to go out with him again on Saturday!!! Is the boy a glutton for punishment??? To my own amazement, I replied with a yes. I have NO idea what I'm doing, or why I'm doing it. We're meeting next Saturday in town.

Monday 22 January

Got my Stalin essay back today. Mr. Pritchard gave me a shit mark for it!! At the bottom of the page he'd written 'are you familiar with the term *plagiarism*, Clemmie?'

Must remember to look up what plague-whatsit means later. I'm thinking it means Mr. Pritchard wasn't happy with my essay; maybe it wasn't long enough (three-quarters of a page of A4). What more does he want? *War and Peace*??? [/sarcasm/].

Got quizzed about Saturday night but I was really cool about it all. Ems said that Ryan told her that Ben told him that he'd had a really good time. I wonder if he was on the same date as I was? He also said Ben was dead chuffed that I'd agreed to go out with him again; Marcie squealed like a piglet when Ems told the assembled group this. Me? I just smiled sheepishly and blushed, wondering for the hundredth time why I'd agreed to see him again.

Didn't see J all day today :o(I miss her, even though I don't even speak to her.

Tuesday 23 January

No sign of J all day again. Bit pissed off about that. English was *rubbish*! We're reading *Othello* and it's crap; we watched a movie of it made, like, about 100 years ago, with some ancient old actor playing *Othello*, and I thought he was dreadful! Really hammy! Mr. Harman told us we should feel privileged to watch 'such a classic' but all that ham on screen just made me think of bacon sandwiches and made my tummy rumble.

Wednesday 24 January

Had a good look at this Hannah girl today. She looks kinda funky; she has this jet-black hair and this well wicked belt with, like, studs all over it. I also noticed she was wearing a black sweatband on her right wrist, but she'd made sure it was well hidden under her shirt sleeve (Mrs. Russell is sooooooo strict on what she calls 'accessories').

She had lots of band names written on her bag, bands I'd not really heard of, and which I'd never listened to (this is what comes of having Abba fans as your parents). Sometimes I wonder if I'm a bit uncool 'cos there's lots of things I've never heard of, and things I've never done. If I ever get a chance to talk to Hannah, I'll ask her about them, although I'll have to get in line to speak to her—she seems *very* popular with a lot of the others in my class.

Text from Ben: 'cnt w8 2cu again'. I didn't know what to write, so just put 'See you Saturday.' I hope he can read non-text speak!

Thursday 25 January

We were all sitting round at lunchtime today talking about boys. I hate it when that happens 'cos it makes me feel soooooooo uncomfortable. We were talking about Monday night's *Prison Break* and Caroline said how much she fancied Michael Scofield and everyone else agreed. I didn't want to look the odd one out so I agreed as well, but I noticed Alice didn't say anything, so he's obviously not her sort. Then we got talking about our ideal men (groan), and what we look for in a man (groan again); Ems said her ideal man was, of course, Ryan and Marcie said she fancied Jason, Ryan's best mate, but said if he wasn't interested in her, then she'd have to stick with Jake Gyllenhaal, who she's fancied for, like, aaaaaaaages and didn't even stop fancying him when he played that gay cowboy (she said he looked cute in chaps).

Marcie said she also fancied Ben but that she wouldn't go after him 'cos she knew that we were an item now (huh?!). I smiled, picked at a loose thread on my jumper, and said nothing more on the matter, which I think they all took to be coyness 'cos then they all started saying stupid stuff like 'Clem and Ben sitting in a tree' and all that.

I really hate it when we have these conversations 'cos I have nothing to say, and have to make stuff up 'cos I don't want them to guess. So I agree with what they all say, telling them I like this actor or that actor and, I dunno, it just feels like some sort of act I have to put on—almost a betrayal. I can't explain it.

Friday 26 January

What a day!! I was walking down the corridor, on my way to double French (ugh!) when I bumped into......J!! We tried to pass each other, but you know how it is when you go one way, and the person trying to get past you goes that way too? Then you try to go the other way and the person also goes that way? J said, 'shall we dance?' and I just giggled. God how I wish I'd had the courage to actually *talk* to her but I was late enough for French as it was, so I just laughed (rather too loudly probably) and scurried off down the corridor like some frumpy housewife bustling off to the shops.

But!! It got better!! I saw her again later in the day and she said to me 'will you dance with me now?' and I said (off the top of me head, like), 'I'll show you my foxtrot if you show me yours,' and she laughed!!!!!!!!! I must have gone red 'cos she said, 'you're blushing—how cute' (!!!!!!!!!) Then Ems turned up so I had to look all nonchalant-like, in case she guessed. I walked down the corridor with Ems, but turned and looked back behind me, only to see J still standing there! When she saw me looking she smiled!!!!!!!!! Am on cloud nine!!!

When I got home I went straight up to my room to think about what had happened today. Why do I get this feeling in my tummy when I see her? It's like a thousand butterflies and I like it. I really like her and I want to get to know her more.

Why does it have to be Friday?? I'm going to have to wait a whole two days till I see her again.

Saturday 27 January

Went to bed thinking about J and woke up thinking about her! Aaaaargh! What is going on with me? Do I fancy her or what? I just dunno. I've never fancied anyone before, so I don't know how it's supposed to feel! I used to like Peter Scott when I was in junior school but I don't think I fancied him; I think I just liked him 'cos I thought he had funky hair and we both liked bananas. So I don't know what it is I'm feeling. Soooooooo confusing!

One thing's for sure—I don't feel like this about Ben! We went on our second date tonight and he got right on my twit. I wanted to come home after ten minutes, but didn't want to be obvious so sat with him in the park in the freezing cold while he drank a can of cheap beer which he kept offering me, and which I kept politely refusing. He had his arm round me and it felt alien; I wanted to tell him where to put his arm (not round my bloody shoulder!) but instead just sat there like an idiot, wishing I was at home watching TV with Mum and Dad.

At least he talked a bit more tonight. He told me about his family and how he played football for his dad's pub team on a Sunday and other stuff about school and things. I tried to sound interested but the truth was I was so bloody cold that all I could think about was going home.

We kissed again and it was slightly better than last time but I can't honestly say I particularly enjoyed it. It was a bit too wet for my liking; all I could taste was stale beer, and the little bit of bum-fluff that's struggling to grow on his face scratched at my cheek. I remember thinking that I should be feeling…I dunno…*something.* But I felt nothing. Not even a glimmer. Maybe I'm frigid??

Sunday 28 January

Dad asked us at lunchtime today where we'd like to go for our summer holiday this year. I said Paris (Gemma Davies went to Disneyland Paris last year and said it was sooooo cool), HRBH said Italy 'cos she wanted to practise her Italian (saddo) and Mum said Cornwall (!!!!!!!!) Err hello?? France v. Cornwall? No contest! Dad said he'd take our views into consideration and get some brochures, which basically means we'll end up going to Cornwall 'cos:

a. That's what Mum wants (he's sooooooo under her thumb!!!)
b. It's cheaper.

So looks like we're off to the land of the pixies in August. Hoo-bloody-rah.

Monday 29 January

We have a new Science teacher—I think he's a trainee. His name's Mr. Troutt (!!!!!!!!!) He looked very nervous today; he wears this cheap-looking signet ring on his middle finger and he kept fiddling with it, turning it round and round in an agitated manner. I also noticed he had a sweaty top lip. He kept forgetting our names and got very twitchy. The more agitated he got, the sweatier his top lip became, and the more he twiddled with his signet ring. I can't see him staying long.

Tuesday 30 January

Hannah has joined our little 'gang'. She does Philosophy with Ems and they've become friends, so now Hannah's our friend too.

Apparently Hannah's an atheist. Ems says she gives Miss Valentine, the Philosophy teacher, *such* a hard time in class, questioning everything. Miss Valentine's a bit fed up with her, so Ems says. I like the idea of someone questioning everything in class. I think Hannah sounds cool!

We asked her about being a Goth. She said she wasn't a Goth, but something called an EMO: we asked her what the difference was, and she said EMOs were more emotional than Goths. Apparently, even though EMOs are a kind of Goth, and they're all obsessed with death and everything, they are actually allowed to smile occasionally (or so Hannah reckons anyway).

I know *nothing* about this!! I live such a bloody sheltered life! Why does my dad have to be an accountant? This is his fault!

Wednesday 31 January

Met up with Ben in town after school. It was okay. Ben said we ought to vary our eating experiences, so we went to Burger King this time, rather than McD's. I didn't really want to go out with him, but kinda felt like I ought to so I did. I think I was really off with him though—it was almost as if I couldn't be bothered making the effort and I think it showed. Why am I such a cow?

Anyway, Ben walked me down to the fountain again to meet Dad and we kissed again. It didn't feel any better, or any easier, and I was aware that I was standing there, stiff as a board, hating every second of it. I looked down and saw he had a bit of lettuce on his trainer, and suddenly realised that I really didn't want to go out with him ever again.

Thursday 1 February

I lay in bed last night for ages just wondering why I felt so miserable. I was thinking about Ben and wondering why I feel so depressed when I think about going out with him. He seems nice enough, I suppose, but there's nothing there—with me, I mean. I feel... nothing. Not a flicker of interest. Nothing. Nichts. Nada. I have no interest in him, with him, or anything about him, and it worries me that I feel like this.

Sometimes I wonder if there's something wrong with me—with boys—with me with boys—with boys with me 'cos I just don't get it! I don't *dislike* boys, but they don't do anything for me, and I would have thought considering I'm nearly seventeen, they *would* do something for me. Maybe I'm emotionally immature as well as frigid?

Friday 2 February

Just realised today that I've not heard anything from Ben since he left me at the fountain on Wednesday. Cheeky sod. I bet that bit of lettuce is still on his trainer too. I was trying to picture his face in my head when I went to bed last night. I kinda thought if I spent some time actually thinking about him, then I might feel some flicker of feelings for him, or at least kick start something—ANYTHING.

I lay there thinking about him, thinking about our dates, thinking about what we'd said, whether he'd made me laugh or feel interested and I came up with precisely...nothing. In fact, every time I closed my eyes and tried to picture him, images of J kept swimming into my head and I ended up thinking about her instead.

Great! I'm trying to have something resembling a relationship with a boy and all I can think of is a flipping girl at school who barely knows I even exist!!

Saturday 3 February

What a day!! Me and Alice went into town this morning and guess who I saw?? J!!!!!

We were just coming out of the shopping centre when I saw her going into Game Zone on the corner (does this mean J is a gamer??) So I grabbed Alice by the arm and told her I wanted to look at Wii games; Alice said, 'I didn't know you had a Wii,' so I made some excuse and told her I was thinking of getting one.

So I lurked behind the games and watched J. Man, she's gorrrrrrgeous!! I felt a bit like a Peeping Tom, but I figured she wasn't getting undressed or anything, she was just browsing the PlayStation games, so I felt a bit better about watching her. Then she left and started walking through town, so I followed her (trying to act all nonchalant-like, in case I aroused Alice's suspicions). I think I managed to maintain an air of normality, despite the fact my heart was beating so hard I thought the whole street would be able to hear it! I made up some lame reason to keep walking up the street when Alice asked why I was walking so fast and ignoring all the shops. I was trying to concentrate on not losing sight of J, though, so I didn't reply.

I so wanted J to turn round and see me. I was too shy to call her name out (she probably wouldn't even know who I was anyway), so I watched her disappear into the cake shop on the corner and felt utterly miserable.

Still, I didn't see her with any boy so I still hold out the hope that she doesn't have a boyfriend.

Sunday 4 February

Replayed what had happened in town over and over in my head last night, imagining how it would have been if it had been different. I imagined me being all confident-like and calling out a breezy 'hiya' to her; then we'd get talking, and she'd suggest we went for a coffee (I'd lose Alice somewhere along the line). We'd get on like a house on fire; she'd find me funny and pretty and intelligent; she'd look intently at me, and cock her head at a quizzical angle, and I'd sense her wondering why it was she'd never noticed me at school before. Then we'd arrange to meet up again and…and…pffffff! It just ain't gonna happen.

Got a text off Ben but forgot to reply. Must remember to text him in the morning—too tired now!

Monday 5 February

The gang are arranging a big girls' night out (that is, the night will be big, not the girls, ha ha!) We thought we'd meet up in town next Saturday, late afternoon, see a movie down at the Odeon, then have a meal out afterwards. All very grown-up.

Should be good. Am looking forward to it.

Tuesday 6 February

Marcie asked today if she could bring a friend from her tutor group with her on Saturday. This is turning out to be a huuuuuuuuuuge night out!!

Still haven't texted Ben. Why are you such a pillock, Clem?? His feelings are probably hurt, but I really can't bring myself to give a toss.

Wednesday 7 February

The girl Marcie wants to bring is in the same class as J! I think her name's Rosie but I'm not sure. She's more Marcie's friend really. Ems wanted to bring Ryan but we pointed out, it's a girls' only night out—I think she was a bit peeved.

Texted Ben back (at last). Couldn't think of anything to say really, so just said, 'Hi—how are you?' No reply yet.

Thursday 8 February

Oh my God! Oh my God! Oh my fucking God!!!!!!

J has asked if she can come out with us on Saturday!!!!!!!!!!! Apparently this Rosie girl mentioned she was going out and J asked Rosie if she could come too and so Rosie asked Marcie and Marcie asked us and we all said yes!!!!!!!!!!!

Shit shit shit shit shit I've got nothing to wear!!! I was just going to wear my jeans and some random old top but this changes everything (J is sooooooo trendy). I need scarves! I need jewellery! I need things for my hair! Accessories, darling, accessories!

Ben asked me if I wanted to meet up on Saturday but I told him I was going out with the girls. So he asked me if I wanted to go out tomorrow instead but I said no (I have to get myself ready for Saturday). I told him I was visiting an elderly aunt tomorrow night (snigger) so I couldn't come out. He hasn't replied yet so hopefully I've put him off. Get the hint, pal!

Friday 9 February

Got all my clothes out last night and threw them onto the bed. They made a sorry sight. I'm just not that into clothes really. I spend half my time either watching TV or walking in the woods with Barbara—what's the point of having nice clothes for that?? I'm the sort of person who, when I approach trendy clothes shops, the assistants fling themselves behind their counters, sound an 'uncool person approaching' siren and make the sign of the cross at me.

I like walking trousers, fleeces, trainers! They're comfortable! I'm more As-Long-As-It-Fits Girl than It Girl.

Anyway, after much wailing and beating of chest (not literally, of course—that would be silly), I managed to cobble together something half-decent. I sooooooooo want to make a good impression on J tomorrow night.

Saturday 10 February

3 p.m.: spent the day making sure my clothes were clean, then had a bath and washed my hair. Writing this now as I'm supposed to be meeting the gang at 4 p.m. in town and I might not feel like writing when I get home. Am v.v.v.v.v. nervous. Wish me luck!!

Ben texted me to say have a good night tonight, which was nice of him.

Sunday 11 February

It's official. I'm in love with J, like, proper l-o-v-e…not just 'like'… but lovvvvvvvvvve, and it feels great!!

Last night was amaaaaazing! We all met up and went to see *Hot Fuzz* down at the Odeon. I wanted to sit next to J but ended up sitting between Caroline and Alice instead; I didn't want to arouse any suspicion so I didn't say anything. I could just *feel* her presence there, in the cinema, and that was quite enough for me! Movie was okay!

But! Then we went to the Far East restaurant next door (called F East—geddit??) and I ended up sitting next to J!!!!!!!!!!!! Sneaky manoeuvre, Clem!!! Anyway, I was soooooo nervous, but I needn't have been 'cos we got on great! I was on top form, even if I do say so myself, and was cracking loads of jokes and making everyone laugh. I just felt so happy! I was mucking about with the chopsticks and J was killing herself! Alice was a bit quiet, though: I wonder if she was unwell?

I think J could fancy me!!! We were very close all evening and she didn't make any effort to talk to anyone else. She seemed…wrapped up in me! I wonder if I should ask her out, or is it too soon? Maybe I ought to play it cool, see how things go? Would she be cool with being asked about by a girl? Hmmm.

Anyway, I practically floated home and I haven't stopped smiling since I got in.

I'm in love I'm in love I'm in love!!!!!!!!

Didn't think about Ben all night. Oops.

Monday 12 February

Wicked day at school today! J found me (she came to find me!!!!!) during break and asked if I wanted to go to the canteen with her at lunchtime: well, not just me, I mean, I was with Alice, Ems, and Marcie and she asked us all, but I'm sure she was directing her question just at me. So we had lunch with her (not Alice—she said she had some work to do in the library) and I couldn't take my eyes off her!!!! We made an arrangement to have lunch again tomorrow! It's a…date!

Maybe soon we'll be going on a proper date?

Was supposed to do Maths homework tonight but just wasn't in the mood. My head's too full of the lovely J to be bothered with such insignificant matters as x over bloody y = z!!!!

Tuesday 13 February

We had lunch with J again today and she started talking about her boyfriend.

I felt like my world had just collapsed around me. His name's Gareth, and he goes to King Edward's School (the nerd). I hate him.

Aaaaaaaaaaaaaaaargggggggggggggggggggggggggghhhh!

I really thought she might like me! So what was that all about on Saturday night, then? All that interest she was showing in me? Why is it that I finally start to think she might like me the way I like her, and then I find out she has a boyfriend?

Why me??????? Why is everyone fucking-well straight? Why is it I find someone I *really really* like and she's straight??? I'm sooooooo pissed off.

Texted Ben and asked him if he wanted to go out somewhere on Saturday. I figured if I go out with him loads, I might start to go off J a bit. It's got to be worth a try, hasn't it?

Wednesday 14 February

Valentine's Day. Did I get a card? Like hell I did! I bet J got one from Garrrrrreth, the cock! Even HRBH got a bunch of flowers from Ade!

Bet he nicked them from a graveyard, though.

Thursday 15 February

I've decided that I'm just going to be a friend to J. I'm going to stop all this shitty business and just have her as a friend—after all, that's got to be better than nothing, hasn't it? Anyway, this is just a phase I'm going through. Growing pains. I bet I'll read this in a year's time when I'm all sorted in my head and I'll laugh about it!!

Sat next to Hannah in Maths today. She has a wicked sense of humour and was making me laugh by doing a pretend commentary on Mr. Briggs' teaching methods (which are nonexistent!). I think I'd like to sit next to her in every lesson!

Got a Valentine's card off Ben. He thought Valentine's Day was the 15th, not the 14th. It had a picture of a crow (?) in a field of sweet corn, and the crow was saying 'It's kinda corny…' Then inside it continued '…but I'm sweet on you.'

I didn't get him a card—I hope he doesn't mind.

Friday 16 February

Had lunch with J again. She told us that Garrrrrrreth not only bought her a card on Wednesday, but gave her a bunch of roses *and* took her to Pizza Hut for a stuffed-crust extra-cheesy Milano. *How* cheesy is that??? While she was telling us all this, I kept telling myself she was just a friend and that I didn't fancy her. But she has such damn nice eyes and such a sweet smile and…and…

Shit.

Saturday 17 February

Met Ben in town at lunchtime and we went to Pizza Hut. All I could think of as I was munching away on my Italiano Supremo was that J had sat with Gareth in this very same restaurant. I felt miserable then, so didn't bother saying much to Ben. He seemed a bit grumpy with me, which only made me feel even grumpier. I ate six slices of garlic bread too, hoping that it might put him off trying to kiss me later, but no! He latched on to me round the back of the garbage bins and seemed undeterred by the whiff of garlic that, to me, was so strong it could have made a Frenchman cry.

Sunday 18 February

Went to church with Mum this morning!!!!!!!! Was wide awake at 6 a.m. and I heard Mum moving around at about seven so asked her if I could come with her. Church isn't my thing but I kinda thought singing some happy hymns might cheer me up a bit 'cos I woke up thinking about J and it made me feel like shit.

Mum looked a bit surprised but said yes, so we walked round there together. I didn't take communion, of course, me not being communed and all, so sat in my pew and ended up thinking about J again. Felt guilty about having Sapphic thoughts in church so switched my mind to something mundane, like the colour of our grouting in the bathroom, but no matter how hard I try not to think about her, she's always there, lurking in the back of my mind.

Monday 19 February

J keeps having lunch with us and I can't stand it! I can't stand knowing that I'll never be with her, that she'll never feel the way I feel and that it's just, well, hopeless! Oh, I sit there and laugh along with everyone else, but inside, my heart's breaking and I just can't stand it. Alice noticed I hadn't eaten my Pringles and asked if I was feeling okay. What could I say? I just smiled and told her I was fine. I'm not.

Tuesday 20 February

Bit depressed all day. Came home and took Barbara out for a walk up the fields as that's the only place I can think properly.

Started thinking about J and about how I'll never be able to be with her, and wondered how I'll ever get her out of my head. Then I thought about Ben, and about how I should be happy going out with him, but wondering why I don't feel happy.

Sat up on the hill and looked out across the city and before I knew what was happening, I was crying. Big hot tears plopping down my cheeks. I DON'T DO CRYING!!! What is happening to me? I feel like I'm in a big black hole and I'm just waiting for someone to throw me a spade so I can get out.

Sat up on the hill until it started to get dark, then hurried home. Mum looked at me strangely when I got in (could she see that I'd been crying?) and asked me if I was okay. I soooooooo wanted to talk to her about it, but I can't, 'cos a big part of me worries that she just won't understand.

If I tell her I'm cut-up about someone she'll automatically assume it's a boy and I don't wanna have to lie to her, but I don't feel ready to tell her that I'm having feelings for a girl.

Anyway, how could I even begin to tell her what's going on inside my head? I'm not even sure I really know what's bloody well going on in my head, so how can I try and explain stuff to Mum?

So instead I just told her I was fine, and went to my room. Was too depressed to eat more than four pancakes tonight.

Got a text off Ben but couldn't be arsed to answer it. He can wait.

Wednesday 21 February

Had the usual torture of eating lunch with J again today. Well, I say torture, but then I guess at least by having lunch with her, I do get to see her, and I figure that's got to be better than nothing! Besides, if I suddenly don't want to have lunch with her, the rest of the gang will wonder why, and I'll have to explain myself. So, to not draw attention to anything, I go along with it, even though inside I'm hurting like hell.

Caught Hannah looking at me across the table. She smiled at me when I looked back at her so I smiled at her too. She has a nice smile.

Thursday 22 February

Was walking down the corridor on my way to History when J came up behind me and put her arms around me!!!!! I jumped like a rabbit and felt myself going really red!! I wish she wasn't so touchy-feely 'cos it drives me crazy (with desire, not madness!). If only she knew that simply being in her presence makes me hot, she'd run a mile!!

Friday 23 February

Last day at school before half term!! I'm glad—I think I need a week away from this place 'cos it means a week away from J as well. It's getting on top of me, all this unrequited love. I'm even going off my food a bit: I turned down the chance of an extra helping of potato last night, which was sacrilege.

Played hockey in PE class. God, I hate hockey! I mean, what's the point of it? Hasn't Miss Robinson figured out yet that the only reason I always asked to play left back is because all I have to do is stand in front of goal and not do anything? That plus the fact it means I can watch Emily Wilson's arse wiggle while she runs down the left wing.

Saturday 24 February

Got a text off Ems first thing this morning telling me that Ben had told Ryan he was thinking of dumping me. Ems said I had to ring Ben straight away 'cos apparently he thinks I don't like him and he thinks he's wasting his time on me. I have to say I agree. I switched my phone off and went back to sleep.

When I woke up again, I switched my phone back on and Alice had left me a message asking if I wanted to go for a walk with Barbara. I rang her back and made up an excuse, telling her that Ben had dumped me and I didn't feel like going out. OMG! She started going on and on about coming over to comfort me and how she would help me get over it, but I told her I had a headache and wanted to stay in bed. The truth was I felt fine. I just didn't want to see her. I'm such a cow!

Moped around the house all morning, thinking about Ben and thinking that I should make the effort to contact him, make him think I didn't want him to dump me, but I just couldn't be arsed, which kinda tells me that I couldn't care less whether he dumps me or not. Watched a bit of MTV but even the sight of the Pussycat Dolls jiggling their bits about on the screen got on my nerves, so I logged on and looked at some silly clips on YouTube of dogs on skateboards, which made me feel a bit better.

Tonight watched TV with Mum and Dad. HRBH went out clubbing, so no doubt she'll crash into the house at 3 a.m. reeking of cheap beer as usual.

Sunday 25 February

Was awakened at 4:45 a.m. (!!) by the sound of HRBH retching in the toilet. It's so unladylike! How can she be so sanctimonious and tell me I'll never be a lady just 'cos I like wearing jeans and sweatshirts, then wake up the household heaving up the (liquid) contents of her stomach at some ungodly hour?

Was pleased to see she got NO sympathy from Mum when she eventually dragged herself out of bed at 3 p.m. Mum shoved a can of Coke in her hand and told her to take herself off for a bracing walk over the fields, 'cos she said HRBH smelt like a brewery and it was putting her off her crossword.

Monday 26 February

Went into town with Mum this morning to buy a birthday present for Dad. Why are men so hard to buy for? What is in the shops that's of any interest to men? Ended up buying him a pair of socks (yawn) and a CD of some old singer called String who apparently used to be a policeman or something way back in the 80s. Let's hope he likes it; if not, it's being eBayed!!

Tuesday 27 February

Had arranged to meet Alice in town today but she called it off 'cos she had a migraine. Decided to go in anyway, 'cos there was nothing else to do all day. Was rummaging through the DVDs in HMV when I spied J wrapped round some bloke who I can only assume is her boyfriend. Maaaaaaaaaaaaaan he's ugly!!!!!!!! He looks like he fell out of the ugly tree and hit all the branches on the way down. Oh, J, you could have done *so* much better than that (me!). Funnily enough, I felt a bit better for seeing him. It's kinda jolted me into reality and I feel…I dunno…different now.

It's good. No, it really is.

Wednesday 28 February

Met Ems, Caroline, and Hannah in town and went for a coffee in Starbucks 'cos Matty works there during the holidays. Matty sneaked us all a free muffin with our coffees—result!!

Ems left after about half an hour to meet Ryan [/rolls eyes/] and then Caroline got a call on her mobile from another friend asking her to meet at McD's so was left with Hannah. I've never really spoken to her properly before, 'cos I've only really seen her in lessons or with all the other gang at lunchtimes, so the conversation was a bit stilted to start with, but then we got talking and she's really funny! She was in full Goth mode; I've only ever seen her at school where she's got to be restrained so it was a bit of a shock seeing her in full 'gear'. She had loads of black eye makeup on which really showed off her eyes (she has very nice brown eyes), and she was wearing black lippy and black nail varnish!! She had this ultra-cool skin-tight pair of trousers on with zips all over them, and a pair of *fuck-off* biker boots. I have to say, she looked really cool. I felt quite dowdy in my jeans and fleece but she didn't say anything about it.

I asked her why she wanted to be a Goth—sorry, EMO—and she said it was 'cos she likes the look. She said she likes wearing all the black, and all the choke chains and all, and she said it was good 'cos she doesn't have to wash her hair as much as other girls 'cos it would spoil the whole look. She told me that EMOs are supposed to be depressives and obsessed with self-harming, but she said she had really nice skin and didn't see the point in spoiling it just to make a statement, and she said although she could do a good line in sullenness now and again, she wasn't generally as gloomy as most EMOs 'cos she had a naturally sunny nature and she thought life was too short to go around with a long face all the time.

I sat and listened to her and wondered if it was all worth it, this EMO lark. Her black hair and all her black makeup looks wicked, and she has some nice scarves and all, but I don't think being an EMO would be for me. All that talk of death and dying would get me down. Anyway, we sat and chatted about EMOs and loads of other stuff until about 5ish when we both had to get off home. I walked home feeling really happy for some reason!

Thursday 1 March

Went bowling at the Multi-Plex with the gang and it was a blast! I was mucking about as usual (ever the clown) and even Ryan (the miserable bugger) laughed at me. I don't like Ryan, I dunno why. He's a posturing little twerp but he's got no reason to posture. He's no looker, that's for sure. He's short and I'm *sure* he's losing his hair, even though he's only seventeen! And he's got funny-looking legs from all the football he plays; talk about bowed legs! Couldn't stop a pig in a passage, that one.

Felt a bit left out 'cos everyone turned up with their boyfriends except me (Ben couldn't come, even though he hasn't officially dumped me yet). I wished Alice could have come, 'cos she doesn't have a boyfriend, but she's still ill with her migraine. Hannah turned up with her bloke, some lad called Dan, apparently, but he seemed to spend the whole afternoon talking to a group of girls who were playing the alley next to us. Poor Hannah!

I caught her looking at me again and I wondered if she thought I was a bit of a show-off 'cos I was larking about, but she was laughing along with all the others so maybe I was just being paranoid as usual.

Friday 2 March

Got my long-awaited dump text from Ben and, dear diary, I didn't care less! He said that he really liked me but he thought I didn't feel the same and something else along the lines of life was too short to wait around when there were other girls interested in him. What a cock! I texted him back and said that he was right, that I didn't feel the same way about it, but thanked him for the few dates we went out on anyway. He didn't reply.

Everyone made the usual sympathetic noises when I texted them and told them me and Ben weren't going out with each other anymore. They kept asking me if I was all right and I kept telling them I was, and they kept telling me there were plenty more fish in the sea and stuff like that. Then Matty texted me and asked me if I minded if she went out with him 'cos she really fancied him!! The strange thing is I really *don't* mind!

Saturday 3 March

We all met up in town again today for our last Saturday of freedom before school starts again on Monday. I was glad that J didn't come 'cos I've come to the conclusion that the less I see her, the more I'm going to get over her. It's never going to happen (me and her) so it's best all round if I try to forget her. Try telling my heart that, though!

Dad's birthday today. He accepted his presents with a complete lack of enthusiasm and only a glimmer of anything resembling gratitude, which means he's probably pissed off at being old (43) and probably wanted something other than what I bought him. Next year he's just getting the socks.

Sunday 4 March

Me and Alice went out for a walk with Barbara over the fields. Alice has kinda adopted Barbara, as her parents don't like dogs. It feels sometimes like Alice's parents don't like a lot of things, and I feel a bit sorry for her 'cos everything she asks for, her parents tell her no. I think Alice needs to stand up to them a bit more sometimes; she's dead nice and all but she can be a bit…wet, really. Sometimes I just want to shake her by the shoulders and tell her to toughen up. Maybe I'm just hard, I dunno.

Alice asked me about Ben and whether I was upset that we weren't seeing each other anymore. I told her I was fine about it, and she said she was pleased I wasn't going out with him any more 'cos she thought he wasn't good enough for me! That was a turn-up for the books 'cos everyone else had been banging on to me about what a catch he was! I asked Alice what she meant and she just said, 'You deserve better than him,' and touched my hand, which made me feel a bit embarrassed. I was a bit taken aback by a rare show of affection by her (she's usually as quiet as a guy in a lingerie department), but it's nice that she looks out for me, I suppose.

Monday 5 March

Back to school (groaaaaaaan). We got told in History today that we have to choose a topic to do with all this Cold War stuff we've been studying and do a presentation on it. It all contributes towards our final exam mark apparently, which means I'm actually going to have to do some proper work. We've got to choose someone to do the project with, and we've got three weeks to write an essay on it, then we've both got to present it to the rest of the class. I'm shitting myself. I hate doing presentations 'cos I'm shy at standing up and talking to a group of people. Anyway, Hannah chose to do her presentation with me (she must be mad!), and we had a choice of subjects from:

- The Vietnam War (don't even know where Vietnam is, let alone what happened there!)
- The Korean War (they eat dogs in Korea, don't they?)
- The Space Race (eh??)
- The Cuban Missile Crisis (Cuba's famous for cigars, isn't it? Not missiles!)
- The Collapse of the Berlin Wall (couldn't have been very sturdy.)

Hannah chose the Cuban Missile Crisis, 'cos she said her dad would be old enough to remember it. Apparently it was, like, way back long ago in the 1960s, so I should be able to find something on the school computer library archives on it. Wonder if there are any veterans of the Crisis still alive that we could e-mail?

Me and Hannah are meeting up at lunchtime to start drawing up a plan. Hannah said it was better to start sooner rather than later… she's keen!

Tuesday 6 March

Met Hannah at lunchtime again today to discuss the presentation but we barely talked about it. Hannah asked me to tell her about myself; she said I didn't really ever say much when we're all having lunch together (too busy mucking about, probably) and that she wanted to know a bit about me. So I said, 'I'm lazy and lactose intolerant,' which made her laugh (even if it's not true—well, the second bit anyway.) I told her about where I lived, and about Mum and Dad, and HRBH and about our menagerie (dog/cat/rabbit) at home, then she told me that she lived with her mum and dad and her two brothers, Joe (eleven) and Dan (eighteen), who she said I met at bowling the other night. So that Dan lad was her brother!!! No wonder he wasn't paying much attention to her!

I've come to the conclusion that I like Hannah. We've got the same sense of humour and I can see us being good friends. She's kinda nice-looking too, and I had a brief 'coo, you're cute' moment but then felt guilty for betraying J.

Wednesday 7 March

We had cross-country running in PE today. I ask you! What IS the point of getting 30 big-chested girls to lumber round a freezing-cold hockey pitch, shouting at them to 'keep it up, girls'? It was dead cold and I kept getting a wedgie from my sodding gym shorts, so me, Alice, and Marcie snuck off to our usual hiding place behind one of the hedges and stayed there while Marcie had a smoke. She says it clears her head (but not her lungs) and makes her more able to cope with Miss Robinson's raucous hollering.

Thursday 8 March

Heard today from Marcie that Matty's going out with Ben. He didn't hang about, did he??

Got told off in English literature today by Mr. Harman. He said he appreciated that the poem that Lucy Freeman was reading was rather dreamy, but if I could concentrate on that rather than daydreaming about whoever my latest 'squeeze' (eh??) might be, he'd be grateful. I was daydreaming, it's true, but rather than dreaming about my latest 'squeeze' (chance would be a fine thing!) I was thinking about how marvellous it was the way J filled her bra. Shows what you know, Harman!

Friday 9 March

Caroline's having a party tonight 'cos it's her seventeenth birthday. I got her a soft dog plushie, which looks a bit like her dog, Pippin. She was very pleased with it. She's having a party at her house later; she lives with her dad 'cos her mum left them to go and live with a forklift truck driver in Liverpool when Caroline was ten. Her dad's going out tonight and has given her the run of the house! He's mad! My parents would *never* let me have a party at home, 'cos my dad would be worried that his precious CD collection would get trashed (probably would) and that various teenagers would be sick in his garden pond (definitely would). Anyway, it's going to be a late one, I think, so I'm doing my usual and writing this up now (5 p.m.) so that I can hide you away, dear diary, in case you fall into the hands of some evil ne'er do well (HRBH).

Saturday 10 March

Well, last night was a *disaster!* It started off okay, and I was having a laugh with all the gang and really enjoying myself. Everyone had turned up with boyfriends; Matty turned up with Ben, which was a bit awkward at first. He was all over her like a rash—all I kept thinking about was what an escape I'd made!!

J of course turned up with the awful Garrrrrreth. I thought I was okay seeing them together, 'cos I kept telling myself I was okay about her, that I was over her and that she's just a friend etc., etc., etc. I was doing really well for about an hour and a half, but then I saw them kissing in the conservatory and I burst into tears!! It was sooooooo embarrassing! I couldn't help it. So I ran out of the house crying and sat in the garden, in the freezing cold, with tears streaming down my face. I couldn't stop. So much for me being over her, huh? Anyway, Hannah and Alice came out to find me, and asked what was wrong, but what could I say? So I just blubbed and snuffled and snorted like some petulant toddler and said I wasn't feeling well. Alice started to say she'd walk me back home, but then Hannah stepped in and said she'd take me instead. She put her arm around me, kinda protectively. I didn't want to spoil Hannah's evening, but she said in a determined tone that she'd rather make sure I was okay. I was glad, actually, 'cos I didn't want to stay there a second longer. Alice looked a bit pissed off that Hannah said she'd walk me back after Alice had already offered, and I heard her mutter some comment about being capable of taking me herself 'cos she was my friend too. She was probably pissed off at me as well for accepting Hannah's offer and not hers, but I felt so crap that I didn't really give a shit.

So Hannah walked me home, which was really sweet of her. As we were walking back, I *so* wanted to tell her what was wrong with me, tell her all about J and how I feel about J and how confused I am about everything, but I just couldn't. How would anyone possibly understand what I'm going through?

Anyway, Hannah walked me right to my house; when Dad answered the door he looked a bit worried, but I just told him I was feeling ill and wanted to go to bed. He drove Hannah home, which was nice of him, while I crawled off up to my room, crept into my bed, and pulled the duvet over my head, waiting for sleep to take me.

Sunday 11 March

Cried myself to sleep last night, so woke up with eyes looking like two holes in a blanket. Alice texted me first thing to ask if I was okay, then other people texted me throughout the day asking the same thing. My answer was the same to all of them—I'm fine, ta. But I'm far from fine.

I've fancied J for aaaages, and last night's episode has pretty much confirmed that I'm madly in love with her now, and that's hit me almost as hard as the realisation that I must be gay. I don't know why it should have come as such a surprise to me when I consider everything that's happened to me over the last six months or so, though! It all makes sense—why I wasn't bothered about going out with Ben, why I wasn't bothered that he dumped me, and why I'm not bothered in the slightest that he's going out with Matty. I suppose I only went out with him because it was *expected* of me, like I just felt like I *ought* to show willing and at least *try* to have a relationship with a boy, even though I didn't want to.

Maybe I was in denial about everything, I dunno, but even I can see clearly that I'm gay. I've got no interest in boys at all—Ben or anyone else—and I spend every waking hour thinking about J. I mean, why would I deliberately go out of my way each day at school to try and see her, why would my heart beat faster every time I do see her, and why would I get so upset seeing her with someone else if I wasn't just a little bit gay?

You can't *not* be gay and fancy girls, can you? So, that's it. It's official. I'm a lesbian. Everything should be so much clearer, but it's not. I mean, I do feel a, I dunno, a wave of relief that I've admitted it to MYSELF, but I'm shit scared about what'll happen now. Okay, so I know nothing will happen *immediately*, it's not like I'll wake up tomorrow and find a badge pinned to my pj's saying 'welcome to the club' or anything, but what I mean is *something* has to happen next, right? I mean, 'cos, like, it's obvious to me that I'm gay, so does that mean it'll be obvious to other people?

I suppose at some point I'll have to tell Mum and Dad, and my friends of course, but how's everyone gonna react? Will they expect me to shave my head and start wearing dungarees? OMG, what if I suddenly start dancing like Ellen DeGeneres at inappropriate moments???

And what about Mum and Dad? What'll they say?? Are they gonna accept it??? Will they kick me out of the house? Maybe they don't want a gay daughter. Maybe they want an ordinary daughter. What's ordinary, anyway?

Oh God, this is just too confusing for words.

Monday 12 March

Couldn't sleep last night for worrying about stuff. I'm relieved that I've finally figured out what's going on with me, but then I lay awake half the night thinking about having to tell people. Just when it felt like my head would explode, though, I came to the conclusion that I don't *have* to tell anyone until I'm ready to. I mean, I'm happy that I've admitted it to myself, but think I want to let it sink in a bit before I start telling people. I felt a bit better once I'd decided that, at least.

I did, however, avoid J like the plague all day 'cos I felt embarrassed about Saturday (although she probably didn't even notice I'd gone, so busy was she chewing the revolting Garrrrrreth's face off). Was glad to get together with Hannah to do some work on our project (only two weeks to go—aaargh!) 'cos it took my mind off things, off thinking about J, off thinking about the fact I'm bent, and off thinking about what's gonna happen to me.

Hannah gave me her mobile number and asked for mine, 'cos she said she'd wanted to text me yesterday to see how I was (after Saturday's display), but she hadn't had my number. She also gave me her Hotmail address so that we can e-mail each other from home with ideas for the project. Her e-mail address was funky_munky something or other, which makes me laugh. Mine's just got plain old Clem.Atkins in it, which is hardly imaginative.

Texted Hannah when I got home, just to say 'hi'. My message said 'hiya, funky munky—how are you?' and she replied 'All the better 4 hearing from u. Been w8ing all day 4u 2 txt me!' She needs to get out more! Noted that she used text-speak but very pleased to see that it is at least decipherable! I suppose it's too much to ask your average seventeen-year-old to write everything out in full. I'm the exception to the rule in texty-speak land, but then I'm odd, I suppose!

OMG maybe that's another sign of my gayness??

Tuesday 13 March

Another text from Hannah—sent at 7:30 a.m.!!!!!!! She asked me if I wanted to get together again today to do more work on the Cold War project, so we met up and had lunch. As we ate, she asked me what Clemmie was short for, so I told her it was short for Clementine. She cocked her head and said, 'what, like the orange?' and winked at me. Her wink made me feel a bit funny inside, but maybe it was gas from the apple I'd just eaten. I think I blushed a bit. She said Clemmie was a nice name, and I smiled. Then she said it sounded a bit like 'phlegmy,' and I wasn't sure if she was taking the piss or not. But, really liked hanging out with her for the day, anyway.

The project is going really well, though! It's going to get an A*, I'm sure of it. I keep calling that Russian fellow Kalashnikov, rather than Khrushchev, but apart from that, it's pretty darned perfect.

Wednesday 14 March

I caught Hannah staring at me during break this morning!! OMG, what if she's sussed that I'm gay? She had this look of…I dunno… *knowing*, and I'm sure she's guessed my secret. Am I being paranoid? Is it because I've admitted to myself that I'm gay, I think everyone else knows too? Maybe it's obvious? I dunno. I mean, I'm cool about it now, but there are times when I still try to get my head around the fact that I am a bona fide gay person, and I sure as hell know I'm not ready for anyone else to know about it.

I'm being ridiculous. I know I'm not very feminine, but I'm not exactly butch, either. I know I don't dress like other girls my age, and I'm not into makeup and pink, fluffy things and stuff, but it's not as if I'm shouting my gayness from the rooftops. I don't wear 'sensible' shoes and I don't walk with my hands in my pockets (well, not *all* the time, and I don't even know if either of those indicate gayness in the first place). Granted, I don't wear skirts—only to school, and that's only 'cos I go to some la-di-da high school that insists we wear them—but it's not as if I've got 'poof' written across my forehead. I go out of my way to make sure I never arouse anyone's suspicion, so how could she possibly know?

Had lunch with Alice today. Felt a bit of a cow, 'cos I've been spending so much time with Hannah doing this project, that I feel I've neglected Alice a bit. I noticed that she's lost loads of weight; I think I've seen more meat under a butcher's fingernails. She didn't eat much at lunchtime either…I hope she's not got this dyslexia malarkey.

Thursday 15 March

Dad told me tonight that he's booked our summer holiday! We're going to France!! Wahay!! And there was me thinking we'd be going to boring old Cornwall again! We're going to Brittany in August, to a campsite, but we're staying in a caravan, not camping, thank God. I've never seen the attraction of camping: a flimsy bit of material over your head, hard ground to sleep on, and only a bush to pee behind. It's not exactly my idea of a break! Anyway, HRBH has already said she doesn't want to come 'cos she feels that, at nearly twenty, she's too old and sophisticated to be coming on holiday with her ancient mum and dad and younger sister. She's so sad! Dad says

I can ask Alice if she wants to come with us instead. I'll ask her in school tomorrow rather than texting her tonight 'cos I've only got 50p left on my phone and I want to text Hannah later.

Friday 16 March

School: boring as usual. Asked Alice if she wanted to come to France with us in the summer and she said she'd ask her parents tonight. She seemed pretty excited, though.

Logged on when I got home, and went onto MSN to see who was around. I noticed Hannah had added me as a contact, so I accepted and, two seconds later, my box was flashing with a message from her. It said 'hiya', so I said, 'hiya' back. Three hours later, when I was summoned for my tea, we'd talked about just about *everything* from *The X Factor* to the size of men's dicks!!! (Yeah, right—as if I know anything about that!!) She's very funny, and I found myself laughing out loud at the things she was writing. Alice came online and, I'm ashamed to say, I blocked her 'cos I didn't want to have to talk to her at the same time.

So I can't multi-task! Sue me! [/sarcasm/].

Saturday 17 March

Spent most of today catching up with homework and cleaning out Uncle Buck's hutch. Ems texted me and asked me if I wanted to meet her and Caroline outside Burger King later, but I made up an excuse and said I couldn't. I wanted to chat with Hannah on MSN 'cos she said she'd be around later this evening. Logged on around 8 p.m. but was disappointed that she wasn't there.

Watched TV with Mum and Dad, but didn't really do anything else this evening.

Oh, and Alice can come to France with us, which is cool.

Sunday 18 March

Switched my phone on first thing and had a text from Hannah saying she was sorry she'd missed me on MSN last night. Wanted to text her back and tell her I was really disappointed she hadn't been there but for some reason I didn't feel like I could.

It was Mother's Day, so took Mum down to the pub for lunch. I also gave her a card and a bunch of flowers that Dad had hastily bought from the petrol station last night. I thought I saw the tiniest hint of a tear in her eye when I gave them to her, but maybe the flowers had given her hay fever. Mum doesn't do tears.

Took Barbara out for a long walk in the woods this afternoon, to work off the lasagne *and* banoffee pie I'd eaten at the pub. I suddenly realised while I was out walking that I'd not thought about J for about three days now. Could this be it? Could I finally be getting over her? I think avoiding her at school has *really* helped. Maybe soon I won't think about her at all.

Monday 19 March

Only two weeks till we break up for Easter! I can't wait! I'm so sick of school it's unreal. We've only got one week left to get this bloody History presentation ready, so spent yet another lunch break making up PowerPoint slides and finding out information on the computers. I'd asked my parents if they knew anything about it; I figured they had to be around when it happened, 'cos they're both so old (43 and 42), so I assumed they'd know at least something. My dad said, considering he was only born in 1964, he'd missed it by two years so, no, he didn't have any newspaper cuttings from it. He's useless!

Tuesday 20 March

Got told in assembly this morning that some local dignitary will be coming to the school in May to officially open our new Art block. He's a Lord Someone-or-Other and is some distant relative of the Queen apparently. Mrs. Russell got very excited when she was talking about him. She has this rather annoying habit of letting her voice get shriller and shriller when she's whipped up, until she's practically squawking like a horny parrot! Apparently it's seen as quite a coup for our school, and the local TV and press will be here. We've all been told to look tidy and be on our best behaviour. I glanced across at Matty and saw a glint in her eye, which means she'll probably turn up with her hair dyed pink or something!!

Wednesday 21 March

Hannah asked me today if I wanted to go round to her house to get on with some more work on the presentation, but I told her I couldn't 'cos I had, like, a million lots of homework to get done. She seemed a bit disappointed, but I know that if my parents find out I've not been doing all my other work, they'll give me earache about it for the next fortnight. I told Hannah I could probably come over tomorrow or Friday and she seemed to cheer up a bit. I got home tonight and did my French, Science, and RE homework in exactly one hour and six minutes.

Ems told me today that Carrie told her that J and Garrrrrrreth have had a falling-out, and she's thinking about dumping him. Good! She's too good for that prat!

Thursday 22 March

A strange e-mail appeared in my in-box tonight from someone called lovesickpuppy; it said, 'u have no idea how I feel. I bet u don't even notice me do you?' Curious! I wondered whether I should e-mail lovesickpuppy back, but figured it had been sent to me by mistake, and didn't want to strike up an e-mail correspondence with some random person who could be, for all I know, an axe murderer. Well, you hear such horrible stories, don't you?

Friday 23 March

Had lunch with Hannah again today to finalise the presentation. We've had lunch with each other pretty much every day for the last couple of weeks instead of with the gang, and it's been great 'cos it means I don't have to suffer the pain of eating with J. Hannah asked me if I wanted to go to her house after tea tonight to do some last-minute tweaking to the layout of the presentation on her PC. I must say, Hannah's taking this project *really* seriously; every opportunity she has, she asks to work on it with me. This is going to be the best damned presentation in the history of St Bartholomew's School! I wish I could be as dedicated to my work as she is!

My fascist mother deigned to allow me to go over to Han's after tea, 'cos it was homework-related. Han's parents were out for the evening, so we were undisturbed all night. By the end of the evening, we had everything ready to go for first thing Monday morning, with some quite brilliant PowerPoint slides, natty pictures of the American President, JFK, and the Russian President, Kalashnikov—sorry—Khrushchev, in various poses which we'd superimposed over a map of Cuba. Pritchard's gonna be blown away (like Cuba nearly was—ha ha ha ha!!)

Saturday 24 March

A text from Hannah first thing! She asked me if I fancied bringing Barbara over so that we could walk her along with Toffee, Hannah's Shih-tzu. So I dragged a grumbling Barbara from her basket (Barbara doesn't do mornings) and walked her round to Hannah's house, then we went up to some nearby woods, which was really nice.

We started talking about boys (groan) and Hannah asked me if I was going out with anyone now that me and Ben were finished. What could I say? I could hardly tell her that I had absolutely *no* interest in the opposite sex, and would rather chew my own arm off than go out with a boy, so full is my head of J. Actually, my head is full of girls in general at the moment; I find myself looking at girls, on the street, at school, on the telly, and fancying the pants off them. Must be hormones!

So I told her, no, I wasn't going out with anyone, just stopping short of adding that I would give anything to go out with J. I asked Hannah if she was seeing anyone and she said she wasn't interested in going out with any boy at the moment. I figured as much. Judging by the amount of time and attention she's been giving schoolwork—and our presentation task in particular—over the last three weeks, she'd never have time to go out with anyone!

I told her that I'd thought her brother Dan was her boyfriend when we all went out bowling and she laughed and gave me this strange look. She looked like she was about to say something, but must have thought better of it, 'cos she turned her head away and whistled for Toffee. When we turned to walk back down the woods, the conversation turned to other things. I was glad; I hate talking about boys and everything to do with them. It makes me uncomfortable.

Sunday 25 March

Spent, like, FIVE hours on MSN with Hannah this afternoon. We were just talking and joking and sending each other silly pictures (I sent her one of Chairman Meow wearing a bow-tie), and it was FAB!

She also sent me some photos of herself cuddling Toffee, presumably taken in the summertime 'cos it was dead sunny and she looked really tanned, which I liked very much! She was looking right into the camera, sort of squinting, like you do when it's sunny, and I felt kinda weird and wobbly when I saw her, like how I feel inside when I see J down the corridor or something.

Hmm.

Monday 26 March

The day of the presentation! I woke up with my tummy churning and dreading the whole day, but in actual fact, it wasn't too bad!

Hannah and I stood at the front of the class and did our little piece, along with our slides and pictures. We'd done handouts for everyone, with bullet points giving a brief synopsis of what the Cuban Missile Crisis was all about. Mr. Pritchard said he was very pleased with the effort we'd put into it, and was especially impressed that we'd thought of the handout ideas. He gave us both a merit! Well chuffed with that!

Hannah and I left the lesson giggling and whooping, and I bought her a hot chocolate at break to say thanks. I told her I'd had a blast doing the presentation with her, and that I'd enjoyed working so closely with her for the last three weeks. She said she'd enjoyed spending time with me as well, adding 'more than you'll ever know', which puzzled me a bit.

And you know the best thing? Me and Hannah were laughing and hugging each other at break and J saw us and I'm *sure* I saw a hint of jealousy in her eyes, which pleased me greatly!

Tuesday 27 March

Was lying in bed, thinking about Hannah last night. I was remembering us hugging and laughing and I got this strange feeling! I *really* like Hannah, but I'm worried that it's going to turn into 'like' as in *nudge-nudge wink* like, and I don't want that. Trouble is, my head's so full of J that I don't think there's room for anyone else in there (I have but a small brain).

But whenever I picture Hannah in my head, it makes me smile.

Wednesday 28 March

Met up with Alice, Ems, and Caroline at lunchtime and we talked about how crap Mr. Troutt's lesson had been. Hannah came over and joined us; the gang were all pleased to see her, and I suddenly realised that *everyone* likes Hannah 'cos she's that sort of girl—hugely likeable.

Thursday 29 March

SUCH a boring day at school! My day wasn't made much better when I got in tonight to be confronted by Mum and Dad having an argument about peas, so I took myself off to my room. I texted Matty and told her about my stupid parents arguing over a pack of frozen bloody petits pois and then we had this silly texty conversation about *Lost*.

Friday 30 March

Thank Godddddddddd it's Friday! Aaaaaaand it's the last day of term, aaaaaaand it was Jeans for Genes day today which meant we could wear whatever we wanted, so long as it involved wearing jeans, of course. Get in!!

I wore my sweatshirt and jeans and Airwalks, and I think I looked okay. Other girls wore skinny jeans and off-the-shoulder tops and their ridiculous itty-bitty pumps, but that look just ain't for me! I can't imagine me wearing skimpy pumps, certainly not the way I stomp around all the time.

Alice wore her amazing over-sized jumper and a pair of skinny jeans. Hannah came dressed all in black and looked h-o-t, I do have to say! All the other girls were crowding round her, oohing and ahhing over her clothes and accessories: she was wearing a huge silver bangle on one wrist and a black sweatband on the other. She had her hair all gathered up in a black band and these wicked leather things round her neck!

She also had a whopping great skull (!!!!!) ring on one hand, and a Celtic band on the other. If that wasn't cool enough, she also had her fake lip ring in, which Mrs. Russell (boo-hiss) promptly spotted and told her to remove, even though it was bloody fake!

Wow! I was pleased to see that she was wearing a hooded top too, although hers was black and mine was purple. Ah, well...you can't have everything.

Saturday 31 March

I think I fancy Hannah. I mean, why else would I have spent all of last night thinking about how fit she looked yesterday in all her

Goth—sorry, EMO—gear? It's like, I was looking at her at school yesterday and I suddenly noticed how nice her eyes are, and that she has dimples; then I realised that her dimples make my tummy go funny when she smiles and you can see them.

I went to bed thinking about her and woke up this morning still thinking about her, just like I do with J, and now I kinda wish it wasn't the Easter holidays coming up 'cos I know I won't see her very much.

And I want to see her, like, all the time.

Sunday 1 April

Dad came rushing into my room at eight this morning to tell me it was snowing. I rolled over and mumbled, 'Good April Fool, Pa,' from deep beneath my duvet. He looked a little deflated. I'm sixteen (nearly seventeen!!), Pa! I think I'm a little too old for April Fools now.

Caroline texted me later this morning and told me that she'd seen Brad Pitt shopping for nappies in town, ha ha ha!!

I lay in bed before breakfast thinking that because I fancy Hannah as well as J, then I definitely have to be gay, right? I mean, how can I fancy two different girls and not fancy boys in the slightest, and not be, like, totally queer? So after everyone had got all their dumb April Fool jokes out of the way this morning, I decided to look up the definition of the word 'lesbian' in mum's dictionary, just to satisfy my own curiosity, and it just said, 'a woman who is sexually attracted to other women'.

That'd be it, then.

Mum came in while I was reading it and saw that the page was open on all the L words, and she asked me what word I was looking for. Once an English teacher, always an English teacher, huh?!

I told her (quick as a flash, like) that I was looking up the word leprechaun, and she rolled her eyes and said that, at sixteen, I should know what a bloody leprechaun was. She left the room muttering something about grammar school education being wasted on me. I didn't care. I was just pleased at my lightning-fast reactions!

So, I am a lesbian (not a leprechaun, thank God). It's got a name. I like that. Makes it, I dunno, somehow more manageable.

Monday 2 April

Hannah texted me first thing and asked me if I wanted to go over to her house today. I'd already promised Alice that I'd meet her, but I was sure she wouldn't mind if Hannah came too. I REALLY wanted to see Hannah so I texted her straight back and asked if she wanted to meet both me and Alice in town, but she didn't.

Met Alice outside the Virgin Megastore in town and we went for coffee in Starbucks. I kinda wanted to talk to Alice about everything I'm going through at the moment but I chickened out. Anyway, as I was sitting sipping my latte in Starbucks, I glanced out the window and saw J, with Garrrrrrreth. So they're back together! I watched them and didn't feel the awful stab of jealousy that I thought I would feel! It suddenly struck me that because I've recently been thinking so much about Hannah at the moment, I haven't been giving much thought to J. It's a relief actually. All this worry is beginning to bring me out in zits.

When I got home from town with Alice, I logged onto MSN, hoping that Hannah might be there, 'cos I fancied a chat. She wasn't there, just Marcie, so we chatted for a bit till I got bored, then I made an excuse and logged off.

Tuesday 3 April

Me, Mum, Dad, and HRBH all went down to the coast for the day to go and visit Great Aunt Kathleen. She embraced me, then HRBH in her usual vice-like grip and marvelled at how big we'd grown. (Well, I am nearly seventeen—I'd expect to be growing fast—durrr!)

We sat and chatted, and Great Aunt Kathleen got the sherry out and tried to foist it on us all, but ended up drinking most of it herself. When it looked like she was about to nod off, Dad made his excuses and said we had to get going so that we could get home in the light. She gave me, then HRBH a whiskery kiss, pressed a pound coin into each of our hands, told us not to spend it all at once, and off we went.

Dad drove us down into the town and we sat on the seafront, eating chips and fending off the seagulls until it was dark, then we drove home. Got back around 1 a.m., knackered, so nighty-night!

Wednesday 4 April

Went into town with Mum today, so that I could look out for some new clothes for me. Everything I saw was either too old for me, or too expensive. So that leaves me with not much choice! Saw some well funky stuff that I could imagine Hannah would wear and that got me thinking about her again. I felt too shy to look at all this funky gear properly, though, 'cos I had Mum with me and I knew she'd make comments about how inappropriate it was—like bloody mothers do.

Checked my e-mails when I got home and saw that I'd had another strange one from this lovesickpuppy person! This time it said, 'Ur driving me crazeeee.' Should I reply to it? I'm not sure what to do; I want to reply and tell this person that whoever they think they're e-mailing, it's the wrong person, but for all I know it could be from some Texan called Brad who's been on Death Row for the last 20 years for hacking his li'l momma's head off with a blunt knife. Perhaps I'll just leave it for now and hope whoever it is realises they've got the wrong e-mail address.

Thursday 5 April

Hannah texted me late last night to say good night, which I thought was really nice.

I thought about her again tonight before I went to sleep. About the way she looks, the way she dresses—and I was replaying our previous conversations in my head, remembering the bits that I said that had made her laugh. Then I thought about how cute she looks when she laughs.

I really, like, reaaaaaaaaally fancy her! Weirdly, it feels just like when I fell for J; I saw this girl walking down the corridor, laughing with her friends, she caught my eye as she passed me and...whoomph! That was it. I was hooked—and it seemed she was suddenly in my head 24/7.

I used to lie in bed thinking about J, reminding myself of every little incident that might have happened with her during the day—and feeling ever such a little bit cheated if I didn't see her on any particular day.

Friday 6 April

I'd made arrangements to go to town with Mum today, but Hannah rang me first thing and asked me if I wanted to go for a coffee with her. I debated whether I should say no, but I found myself agreeing to meet her in town at eleven, despite thinking (in my current frame of mind) that it might not be a good idea. I'm ashamed to admit, dear diary, that I found myself hideously excited at the thought of seeing her.

Anyway, we met up outside Starbucks and my tummy lurched when I saw her. I felt dead thrilled to see her. We had a really nice couple of hours just sitting and talking over coffee, and when it was time to for me to come home, I felt ridiculously happy—happier than I've felt for weeks, actually.

I decided I wanted to search for 'lesbian' on Google when I got in, just to see if it directed me to any websites that could give me some advice, help me out, that sort of thing, but Google just gave me links to a load of websites with pictures of large-breasted ladies that, like, TOTALLY freaked me out, so I logged off and went downstairs again. Had to excuse myself halfway through the news and went back upstairs to delete the browsing history on my computer in case someone (HRBH) hacked into it and discovered what I'd been looking at.

I gave it one more go while I was back online, and tried to find a definition of the word 'gay' instead. It gave a few, but the ones that struck me were these:

> *Gay (n): homosexual*
> *Gay (n): happy.*

I thought that was dead deep and would be a well good pick-me-up for whenever I'm getting stressed about it all, so I've written the two words down in the back of you, dear diary, and I'll sneak a peek at them and think about stuff whenever I'm ever feeling down.

Saturday 7 April

Up at eight today 'cos we went off down to Aunty Alison and Uncle David's house for Easter. When we got there, Aunty Alison was waiting in the doorway and she squealed with excitement at seeing us again. She hugged me rather too tightly and told me I'd grown so much since the last time she'd seen me. Why do adults always say that? I bet even when I'm 35 and 6ft tall in my socks, she'll be telling me how much I've grown!

After lunch we all walked down to the beach and watched as Barbara ran in and out of the sea, barking. My dad grumbled something about mucky wet dog paws but Mum shot him one of her special looks and he soon shut up and wandered off on his own to look at some rock pools.

Hannah sent me a text and asked me if I wanted to meet up with her tonight! I texted her back and told her I was down South on holiday. She sent me one back saying 'Oh! U never said', which I thought was a bit strange. To be honest, it had never occurred to me to tell her I was going away. So I texted her back and said more or less that I hadn't thought to tell her. It's now 11:30 p.m. and she hasn't replied yet.

Sunday 8 April

Easter Sunday! Went for a really long walk with HRBH, Barbara, and Uncle David. We went across the fields at the back of the house, along the cliff path and down to the beach. It took us two and a half hours and I was shattered by the end of it—though not as shattered as Barbara was!

Met up with Mum, Dad, and Aunty Alison in the pub afterwards and had an enormous Sunday lunch. When we got back, Aunty Alison gave me and HRBH an Easter egg each, which was nice of her. It was more than Mum and Dad gave us, anyway! They stopped giving us Easter eggs when we were about ten, saying Easter had become too commercialised. Sometimes I think my parents have no fun left in them at all.

Checked my phone on and off all day for a message from Hannah, but there was nothing.

Monday 9 April

Went over to Aunty Kate's house for lunch. My bloody mother insisted I wear a skirt, and no amount of grumbling from me would make her change her mind. I don't know why she does this! Whenever we go to see Aunty Kate, we have to dress up and be on our best behaviour. I'm sure this is only because Aunty Kate lives in a bungalow and votes Conservative. Aunty Kate talks like she has a plum in her mouth, and always gets her best china out when we go to visit, which always makes Mum shake.

When we got there, sure enough, Aunty Kate had laid out salmon and cucumber sandwiches, a tea tray, and a plate of shortbreads. Dad whispered to me that he wished he'd put on his suit 'cos he said he felt like he was having tea with the Queen, which made me giggle. Thankfully Aunty Kate had put out mugs for me and HRBH (she said she didn't trust the 'children' with her finest bone china. Children??) and Mum looked very relieved.

We talked about school and work, and then me and HRBH got asked (as we always do) whether we had boyfriends, so I shuffled nervously in my chair while Mum told her that 'Clem was seeing a nice boy for a while, but they're not seeing each other anymore'. Aunty Kate looked sympathetically at me and sighed and tutted, causing her false teeth to make a funny noise. I could feel a fit of the giggles coming on, so excused myself and went to the toilet where I had another fit of the giggles at the sight of the blancmange-pink crocheted doll which Aunty Kate had used to cover up her toilet rolls. Imagine if that doll ever got together with a boy doll—he'd have such a surprise when he lifted up her skirt!

Kept checking my phone for messages from Hannah, but still

nothing. HRBH asked me why I kept looking at my phone but I just glared and told her to butt out.

Why hasn't Hannah texted me? Is there anything in this world more infuriating than a textless phone??!!

Tuesday 10 April

Didn't do much 'cos it rained all day. Sat in and watched *Mary Poppins* on TV, then had fish and chips for tea. Thought Julie Andrews was fit. Does that make me kinky?

The rain stopped later in the afternoon, so HRBH dragged me and Barbara off for a walk down to the beach where we sat on some rocks until it got dark. I sat and looked up at the moon, which was shining really brightly in the sky, and found myself wondering whether Hannah was able to see the moon too, wherever she might be.

Still no text. Aaaaargghhh!!

Wednesday 11 April

Had a text off Hannah asking me if I was having a good time!! At last!! I texted her back straight away and told her about Aunty Kate's crocheted dolly and it made her laugh. I told her we were coming home tomorrow and she said she was looking forward to seeing me again.

It's been quite good being away from home and being busy 'cos I haven't thought about Hannah for a few days now, but exchanging texts with her has reminded me of her so I went to bed thinking about her again.

Thursday 12 April

Really nice out today, so we went to a pub for lunch that Uncle David recommended, and which he said was about 20 minutes from his house. Maybe it's 20 minutes the speed he drives, but Dad drives like an asthmatic cart-horse so we arrived 50 minutes after we set off, all starving hungry and a bit grumpy, to find Aunty Alison and Uncle David ensconced in the pub looking cheerful and asking Dad what had taken him so long.

Went up to the bar with Dad to buy drinks and he muttered at me that he wanted to go home. He can be so humourless sometimes!

Friday 13 April

Home again!

Left Aunty Alison and Uncle David's at around 11 a.m. Uncle David gave me and HRBH £10 each! I've always liked Uncle David.

Got home around 2 p.m. after stopping off for lunch at some crappy motorway café. Mum immediately started making noises about the amount of washing she had to do, so I took myself off upstairs and thought about ringing Hannah to tell her I was home. I sat on my bed looking at my phone for ages, wondering if I should call her; I finally made the decision, rang her…and her phone was off! Felt at a bit of a loose end, so rang Alice and asked her if I could come over. She sounded pleased to hear from me and said I could come over straight away.

Anyway, we went out for a walk along the disused railway line at the back of her house. It was nice, but I found myself kinda wishing that Hannah had answered her phone, and that I was out walking with her, not Alice.

Saturday 14 April

Tried Hannah's phone again today but it was still off. I felt really disappointed when it went straight through to voicemail, 'cos I'd psyched myself up to talk to her again and I could practically already hear her voice in my head as I was dialling her number. I like to think about the sound of her voice 'cos then I can picture her in my head and I really like the feeling it gives me.

Okay, so why's she not answering? I really wanna talk to her, just wanna hear her voice.

Sunday 15 April

Hannah's phone still off. Haven't heard a word from her since Wednesday. I hope I haven't pissed her off or anything. I wondered whether either Ems or Caroline or maybe even Matty might have her home number, but I didn't want them to ask me why I was so keen to get through to Hannah. Maybe they wouldn't think anything of it, but I don't want to take that chance!

I miss her.

Monday 16 April

Hannah rang me this morning! I tried to sound really laid-back but inside I was jumping with joy! I mentioned (casually, like) that I'd been trying to call her and she told me her phone had broken, that she'd just been out to buy a new one, and that she was testing it out on me to make sure it worked okay!! All that worry for nothing! Sometimes I think I'll be grey by the time I'm 20 with all the worrying I do.

She said her new phone had an awesome camera on it so I told her to take a photo of herself and send it to me (I don't know why I said that!). She said she would! Then she said she had to go to the supermarket with her mum, but would I like to go over to her house tomorrow? Of course I said yes! She rang off, but not before saying that she was looking forward to seeing me tomorrow, which was sweet of her.

About five minutes after our conversation, my phone beeped and there was a photo of Hannah poking her tongue out at me on my screen. I had, like, this major OOOOMG moment but reminded myself that my parents were downstairs so switched my phone off to stop myself from looking at Hannah's picture all the time.

Went downstairs and helped Dad plant some onion sets in the garden, but my mind was constantly on the picture on my phone.

Tuesday 17 April

Looked at Hannah's picture before I went to bed last night and went to sleep feeling ever so slightly naughty! The fact that I had this reaaaallly weird dream about her kinda proves that too!

In this dream, Hannah was a vampire, dressed head to foot in black, and I wanted to tell her how fit she looked but I was too shy. She had these little fangs, like dripping with all this blood, and I was scared but really turned on at the same time by the sight of her. Anyway, just at the point when I thought she was either going to kiss me or bite my neck (like vampires do) I heard all this running water and thought it was my blood, but it was Dad having a wee out in the loo which must have woken me up. Felt soooooo strange when I remembered what I'd just been dreaming, and I felt kinda freaked out all day 'cos of it. It didn't help when I went over to Hannah's and had lunch with her and her mum and her little brother Joe, either.

It was, like, sooooo weird sitting at their table eating with them, knowing that about eight hours earlier I'd been dreaming about her trying to bite my neck!!! Anyway, today was the first time I'd met some of her family, and they're all really nice. Her mum's great! She has a look of Kathy Bates (post-*Misery*) about her and a laugh that could start avalanches in Japan. She'd made scones and put them out on little paper doilies on a plate. We don't use doilies in our house except at Christmas; Mum says kitchen roll is quite sufficient for 51 weeks of the year.

Hannah's got, like, this huuuuuuuuge trampoline in her garden. It's got to be at least 100 feet across. It can take three people at a time, so we had a jump on it this afternoon with Joe. He's only eleven and quite small for his age. I was worried about jumping too hard in case I pinged him off the trampoline and straight over their neighbours' wall. We had such a laugh on it! Hannah showed me this trick where you jump, land on your front, then flip onto your back, then up to a standing position.

I had to try reaaaallly hard not to watch her jumping up and down 'cos I didn't want her thinking I was a perv or anything like that, but it was sooooo fucking hard not to stare at her jiggling up and down in front of me.

Hannah's obviously practised and done the trick before 'cos she was flipping back and forth like a dolphin. Me? I jumped, landed on my back, and floundered there like an injured pigeon caught up in netting until Hannah stopped laughing and flopped herself down next to me.

We lay there, side by side, and I felt really happy just being with her. I wanted to touch her but I knew I couldn't, and that was reaaaally tough. She was, like, right next to me, within touching distance and I could practically feel the heat coming off her. It took everything I had in me not to touch her hand or stroke her cheek. We were lying facing each other, like, inches apart. If I'd had my way I would have lazed with her like that all day, right next to her, taking in every single detail of her gorgeous face, but Joe was standing over us, threatening to slam-dunk us if we didn't move within the next two seconds. Shitty little brothers, hey??!!

Such a fabulous day.

Wednesday 18 April

Had another rude dream about Hannah last night!!! God, she's on my mind, like, 24/7 right now!! I dreamt we were at her parents' house and her parents were out and we were sitting in her dining room doing a jigsaw when she looked at me and said, 'I could fall for you in a big way, Clementine Atkins,' just as I was putting the last piece of the jigsaw in. I was busy looking at the completed jigsaw when she came and sat on my lap and started running her hands through my hair and kissing my neck!!!! Then her dog walked into the room wearing a pair of swimming trunks and started doing Scottish dancing while Donald Trump played the bagpipes and, of course, I immediately woke up!!

Hannah texted me around mid-morning and asked me if I wanted to go to town with her but I was still reeling from the dream and thought it best not to see her, so I told her Mum wanted me to do some chores round the house. I felt bad about lying, so I did some dusting while I watched MTV and didn't feel quite so guilty.

Thursday 19 April

Dad went back to work today, so he was in a foul mood this morning. FFS! Why do adults moan so much about having to go to work? I don't think they realise how hard it is for us teenagers, not only having to cope with raging hormones, but having to put up with the day-in, day-out grind of school, erm, 40 weeks of the year! [/indignant/].

Friday 20 April

Met up with Ems, Caroline, Matty, and Hannah in town for our last day of freedom before Monday. I was quite glad that Ems, Caroline, and Matty had come out with us 'cos I'm still freaked out over my latest naughty Hannah dream.

I don't think I said much to Hannah. She asked me if I was okay 'cos I was so quiet. I smiled and said I was just a bit tired 'cos Barbara woke me up to go out for a pee at six o'clock (I'm turning into an accomplished liar) and she smiled and said, 'as long as you're okay.' She carried on looking at me just a bit too long for my liking, and I could feel my heart starting to pound, so I looked away. She has such nice eyes! Brown, like pools of chocolate that I just want to dive into and devour.

She's so nice looking, and so sweet, and funny. It struck me as I was walking home from town, still thinking about Hannah, that I haven't thought about J for weeks now. So, if one good thing has come out of this—at least I seem to be getting over J. [/irony/].

Saturday 21 April

Felt a bit mean 'cos I've hardly spoken to Alice at all over the Easter holidays, so rang her and asked her if she wanted to come round. She came round after lunch and asked me if I'd gotten her postcard from Scotland (err nope!). I felt doubly mean 'cos I hadn't even noticed that she'd not been around.

Anyway, she'd been staying in a caravan for five days near Edinburgh and told me a really funny tale of how her mum had walked down a slipway and slipped (very apt) into the sea which luckily for her was just going out, and how she hadn't been able to get up again and how Alice and her dad had had to go into the water to get her out (Alice's mother is size 20—I would have thought it would have taken a couple of strong sailors with a winch and pulley to hoist her out, but never mind) and then how her mum then couldn't walk properly for the rest of the holiday 'cos she'd pulled a muscle in her leg.

Alice asked me what I'd been up to over the last week while she'd been away. I could hardly tell her that I'd spent just about every waking hour either with Hannah or thinking about her, so instead I just made up some rubbish about doing boring stuff at home and getting work ready for school next week.

Sunday 22 April

Mum asked me if I wanted to go to church with her again this morning. This is just 'cos I happened to go once with her, like, months ago! Now she thinks I wanna be a church-goer!

I said no, primarily 'cos I'd be in a holy place and all I'd do is have unholy thoughts of flinging Hannah over the font and kissing her face off.

I'm going to hell in a handcart.

Monday 23 April

Back to school! Groaaaaaaaan. Why do the holidays go so fast?

Alice kept us all entertained at lunchtime with tales of her mum in Scotland, which was just as funny as when she told me on Saturday. Was looking at Hannah and she looked straight back at me so I smiled weakly at her and she smiled back at me, which made me feel squishy inside. I hope I didn't look too stupid.

Tuesday 24 April

HRBH has become fixated with her look. She asked me tonight if her jeans made her bum look big and I told her no, and that her bum was big anyway. She threw a book at me and stomped out of the lounge. I thought honesty was supposed to be the best policy??

Wednesday 25 April

Was sitting in room 3b with Caroline and Matty at morning break when Hannah walked in with Marcie. My heart practically jumped into my mouth when I saw her! I can't believe how much I fancy her (Hannah I mean, not Marcie. Eww!) Hannah walks into the room and it's like all of a sudden I don't see or hear anyone else anymore; my whole attention instantly becomes focused on her, and it's like no one else matters. I try reaaally hard not to let my emotions show in front of her, but it's so darned difficult!

She's also quite touchy-feely, which I'm finding kinda difficult. If we're walking down the corridor together she'll link her arm in mine, and it makes me feel all funny inside. I do the same thing (link arms) with my other friends, but it doesn't make me feel funny like it does when I do it with Hannah. She also touches me quite a lot, like, when we're talking, she'll touch my arm and I like it, but it embarrasses me too.

She hugged me today and I got all flustered. I could feel the warmth of her body against mine and it made me go all silly. Part of me wishes she wouldn't do it—but I can hardly ask her not to 'cos it'll make her suspicious, right? The last thing I want to do is for her to find out I like her—*in that way*—'cos she'll run a mile and I'll lose her as a friend. Why is life so bloody complicated?

Thursday 26 April

HRBH has gone on a diet. She's joined the local Weight Watchers group. This is the funniest thing I've heard in ages. She's gone completely over the top as usual and is insisting on eating just Ryvitas and cottage cheese. Ryvitas are revolting! I told her it looked like a cork coaster so she told me, rather than criticising it, to taste it; so I did. It not only looks like a cork coaster, it tastes like one as well! Yuck yuck yuck! What IS the point? Have a burger, then run round the block, for God's sake!

Friday 27 April

HRBH was chewing on what I thought was Uncle Buck's bedding this morning, but she reliably informed me that it was muesli. I ate my toast, butter, and honey and pitied her. I think if I had to eat muesli every day I'd just pay someone to eat it for me—it would be worth every penny.

She's also taken up jogging (snigger) so I joined her on her run round the block tonight, 'cos I was sitting on the sofa having rude thoughts about Hannah and I thought it might take my mind off her. Never again! I got to the end of the road and got a stitch, so came home and watched the TV instead.

Saturday 28 April

Had a bit of a flirty MSN session with Hannah tonight. Maybe I'm reading too much into it, but there was some definite flirting going on between us, I'm sure of it. Is she sending me signals? Trouble is, I don't want to act on those signals in case I'm wrong and make a right tit of myself!

Sunday 29 April

More flirting on MSN again which I loved, but which also worried me ’cos I think maybe it’s just her way?? I’m sure it must just be her way of being friendly. Yes, that’s it. She’s just being friendly.

Good fun, though! I like the way it makes me feel.

Monday 30 April

Had a dentist’s appointment after school tonight. It wasn’t until 4:30 p.m., but I left school early anyway so I could get there in time to give my teeth a good scrub ’cos I’d been munching on Werther’s Originals all afternoon and half of them were still stuck on my teeth.

My usual dentist had broken his ankle backpacking across the Matterhorn and was currently being brought home from Austria in the back of an air ambulance or something. My emergency dentist greeted me at the door, thrust a latex glove-covered hand at me, and told me in a thick accent that she was called Anoushka and that she ‘vanted to hexamine tees’, which threw me a little. I smiled nervously at her and hopped into the chair, where she proceeded to stare down at me through heavily made-up Slavic eyes and told me to open ‘vide’.

Anyway, she seemed pleased enough with my teeth, muttering encouraging sounds from behind her mask and telling me ‘teess ees good’ every now and then, whilst poking at my gums with something rather too sharp for my liking. She told me that my ‘teess ees verrrry good, but gumss no so good’, and told me not to worry so much about cleaning my teeth, but to concentrate more on my gums when I clean my teeth. Brilliant! Fifteen years of cleaning routines and now Russian Rita tells me I’ve been doing it all wrong!

Pleased that my teeth are okay and that I didn't need any fillings, though. Had a Werther's Original on the way home to celebrate. There's no shame in it!

Tuesday 1 May

Hannah asked me at lunchtime today about Ben, which I thought was a bit strange, bearing in mind:

a. We broke up ages ago.
b. We only went out on four dates anyway!

I didn't think that Hannah even knew I'd gone out with him, so I don't really know why she wanted to know about him.

She asked me how long me and Ben had dated for, so I told her it wasn't very long, because, well, it wasn't very long! Just a couple of weeks, really. And weeks of hell on my part at that!! Then she asked how long exactly, so I told her, and she just nodded.

I was really vague, 'cos I felt uncomfortable talking to her about him, and if I'm honest I don't wanna be reminded of the little runt, but she just went on and on about him. She asked me why we split up, and was it me or him who did the dumping, so I told her it was him who dumped me and she went really quiet. I dunno why, though.

Then she asked me why he dumped me, and I thought, FFS!! Enough already! I kinda shrugged and said it was 'cos he'd said it wasn't working out, and she looked at me real strange. Then she asked me if I'd been upset about being dumped by him and I told her no, 'cos I really hadn't been! I dunno whether she believed me, though.

I couldn't stop thinking about our conversation all afternoon. Why did she wanna know about him? She was making it out to be a big deal, but nothing about Ben was a big deal, certainly not to me!!

Wednesday 2 May

OMG! I just had a thought! Maybe Hannah fancies Ben and that's why she wanted to know about him? It's just typical! Maybe she was only friendly with me 'cos she wanted to get close to Ben? Yeah, wouldn't that be just bloody typical?!

Thursday 3 May

That's ridiculous, Clem! You broke up with Ben weeks ago; Hannah would have been friendly with you then if she'd wanted to know about him. Not to mention that Ben is still with Matty, and Hannah doesn't seem the type to steal a girl's boyfriend. Stop panicking!

HRBH has been on her diet for a week! It seems to be going well; I haven't seen a scrap of chocolate pass her lips since…ooh… yesterday!

Friday 4 May

Had a vocabulary test in French today and I got 19 out of 20, which I'm really pleased about! Even Mrs. Howells seemed surprised. Maybe I'll become a translator when I get older.

Relieved that Hannah hasn't asked me any more questions about Ben since Tuesday. Guess I was just being paranoid (as usual)…

Saturday 5 May

Went into town with Hannah today. We went to Starbucks to see Matty (and get a free muffin with our coffee). Matty came and sat with us for ten minutes while she took her break, and all the time she was sitting there, I kept wishing she'd go away again and leave me and Hannah alone, which was a bit mean of me considering she'd sneaked us each a Double-Choc Delight.

Eventually she went back to serving customers and I had Hannah all to myself again. She really is as fit as a butcher's dog (Hannah, not Matty). I was watching her closely while she was talking to me, taking in every inch of her lovely face, and had to keep looking away 'cos I was sure she'd be able to read my mind, which was saying 'Fuck me, you are FIT!!!' over and over again, VERY loudly.

Oh bugger! What am I going to doooooooooo?

Sunday 6 May

HRBH's diet came to a shuddering halt today when for her lunch she had:

Roast beef
4 roast potatoes
2 Yorkshire puddings
Carrots in butter
Cabbage in butter
Peas in butter
Thick gravy.

Not content with that, she had two helpings of Mum's trifle for afters.

I hope she feels thoroughly ashamed of herself!

Hannah wasn't around on MSN tonight. Was a bit disappointed.

Monday 7 May

It was a bank holiday today, so we did what everyone else does on a bank holiday: we made the stupid decision to go out for the day, got stuck in traffic, couldn't get in anywhere to eat at lunchtime, so ended up buying sandwiches from Subway. Mum and Dad had an argument in the car coming home, and then we got stuck in more traffic trying to get back into town. Oh, and it rained as well.

I'll be glad to go back to school tomorrow. Missed talking to Hannah today.

Tuesday 8 May

Hannah asked me if I wanted to go over to hers tonight, but my sodding mother said I couldn't 'cos I had homework to do. She's such a bloody fascist at times.

Wednesday 9 May

Was busy chewing on my pen and looking out the window during our Psychology class this afternoon, trying to figure out the meaning of life and crap like that, and saw Hannah out playing netball on the courts just under my window. She had this damned sexy PE skirt on and legs to die for! Found myself thinking about those legs being wrapped round me, but my naughty thoughts were cruelly interrupted by Mr. Jones asking me a question about Freud, the answer to which, dear diary, I hadn't a flipping clue!

Thursday 10 May

Hannah asked me at break today if I wanted to go to the cinema with her tonight but I know Mum has strong views on me going out late during the week so I had to tell her no. It's so unfair! My parents are such disciplinarians at times! I bet Hannah's parents let her do anything—after all, they let her be a Goth—sorry, EMO—so they're sure as hell going to let her go to the cinema on a school night, aren't they?

Friday 11 May

We learned details of the coursework we need to do for our exams next year. Now I'm scared. I've put off thinking about the dreaded exams, but when you've got details in black and white in front of you, the cold realisation that they're actually going to happen slaps you in the face like a wet haddock.

We were given deadlines and how the coursework's got to be laid out—stuff like that. I was complaining about it to Dad when I got home, but then he went off and started banging on about how 'teenagers today' don't how know lucky they are, because at least we have the Internet and computers and stuff to help us. He said, 'in my day'—I hate it when he says that 'cos I know a lecture's coming up—'In my day, we had pen, paper, and book and we did all right. Everything had to be handwritten, not typed. We went to libraries and researched things from books. Are you familiar with books, Clem?' I smiled and laughed sarcastically, 'cos that's the only way to treat him when he's in one of his sanctimonious moods.

He has NO idea of the stresses we're under. Fair enough, we've got computers and all that now, but do you think he has ANY idea how numb my arse gets sitting in front of a screen hour after hour?

Saturday 12 May

Great Aunt May is coming to stay next week for four days!!!! It's not that I don't like Great Aunt May, it's just that she scares me a bit. She talks about 'the old days' all the time, and says phrases like 'when I was a lass,' a lot; she also hasn't yet grasped the fact that Britain went decimal in 1971 and presses pound coins into mine and HRBH's hands telling us 'here's a few bob to get yourself some sweeties,' which is very nice of her but:

1. I have *no* idea what a 'bob' is, and
2. Sixteen-year-olds don't eat 'sweeties'.

She also smells a bit; there's a dreadful pong of mothballs and dust whenever she walks past, which is pretty off-putting!

I sent Hannah a text tonight and told her my great aunt was coming to stay and I put a load of !!!s next to it. I told Hannah that Great Aunt May smelt of mothballs too, and she thought it was really funny.

Went to bed thinking about her again (Hannah, not Great Aunt May, of course!) and kinda pictured her in her bed, reading my text and laughing at what I'd written. Felt dead happy.

Sunday 13 May

I heard something which sounded like a cat being strangled in the bathroom this morning, but it was Mum standing on the weighing scales and realising she'd put on eight pounds. This is what happens when you eat like a woman possessed, convinced that you'll burn it all off, but then continue to eat like a woman possessed, and sit on your bum all evening rather than make the effort to burn it off.

So now she's decided to go on a diet as well. She took herself off to the supermarket tonight and came home armed with such delights as celery, cottage cheese, and crisp breads. Dad looked horrified until Mum waved a pie under his nose and told him not to be so melodramatic. I sneaked a piece of celery out to Uncle Buck, but even he looked at it like he wished it were a pie too.

Monday 14 May

Played tennis in PE today, which would have been good if I could have actually hit the sodding ball back once in a while. Now my back aches from picking the ball up at the back of the court every two seconds while Pippa Goldsmith fired down forehand after forehand at me like I was some bloody moving target, existing purely for her personal pleasure. Bloody Pippa Goldsmith! Now *there's* someone who should never wear a tennis dress.

Tuesday 15 May

Today that Lord Whatever-He-Was-Called bloke came and opened our new Art block. There was this sort of buzz of excitement round the school, even though most of us didn't have a clue why he was considered important. He turned up at the school in this huge ostentatious Mercedes, made a small speech, snipped a bit of ribbon, posed for some pictures, did a piece to the local evening news, then went again!

Me and Hannah managed to stand next to each other while he was doing his speech and I got a fit of the giggles when Hannah said she thought he was wearing a wig, then started looking closely at him to try and find the join on it. Mrs. Schofield glared at us both, but I didn't give a shit. I was just happy to have the chance to be with Hannah for five minutes!

Miss Michaels, the art teacher, was obviously bowled over by this

Lord bloke's presence, because, when she was presented to him by Mrs. Russell, the Head, she did this funny little curtsey like he was a proper member of royalty or something. When she was talking to him she kept fingering the hem of her cardigan with excitement and laughing a squeaky little laugh at all his jokes. A strange day all round, really.

Wednesday 16 May

Great Aunt May was at home when I got in from school. She was sitting in the garden with a newspaper on her head. She looks a lot older than the last time I saw her. Mum nudged me towards her and told me to give her a kiss, which she reciprocated with a wet kiss of her own, stabbing my cheek with her whiskers, and told Mum what a pretty daughter she had. Can't argue with that!

We had a strange tea tonight. We had fish with mashed potatoes, *and* mashed carrots, which I can only assume was because Great Aunt May could eat it okay with her few remaining teeth. HRBH muttered something about 'baby food' and earned an old-fashioned look from Dad.

Thursday 17 May

Great Aunt May was already up when I went to school today. She spotted me in my well-cool short school skirt and tutted loudly, saying to Mum, 'you're not letting her go to school in that are you, Margaret? In my day we had to wear our skirts down to our ankles or we'd get the cane.'

I looked at her and thought 'in your day, love, you probably rode to school on a penny farthing', but I kept shtum. I glanced at her wrinkled tights (at least I think she was wearing tights) and thanked the Lord for under-the-knee skirts; then I glanced down at my fine pair of teenage pins and thanked the Lord (again) for above-the-knee skirts, ha ha ha ha!!!

When I got to school I told Hannah what Great Aunt May had said about my short skirt and she said something really weird. She looked at me kinda strangely and said, 'Well I've got no complaints about it,' and it made me feel all funny inside. But then I felt dead self-conscious about my skirt for the rest of the day and kept pulling on it to make it look a bit longer.

Friday 18 May

Great Aunt May coughed then farted really loudly at the dinner table tonight!!!!!!! I swear it skidded off the chair and made Barbara's ears flutter! I thought HRBH was going to *die* laughing!!!!! I couldn't look her in the eye and nearly choked on my tea when Great Aunt May mumbled something about 'tablets giving me wind'. It was soooooooo embarrassing! Mum gave us both one of those looks that said, 'don't you *dare* laugh'.

Thank goodness she's going back to the home tomorrow (Great Aunt May, not Mum, obviously).

Saturday 19 May

Went with Mum and Dad after lunch to return Great Aunt May back to the Autumn Leaves Elderly Persons' Home. Felt a bit depressed seeing all these old dears sitting in chairs staring into space, apparently oblivious to everything around them. Made a decision to keep as active as possible for as long as possible so that I never end up in a home. Also made a decision to keep my brain sharp, so asked Dad to stop by the newsagent on the way home so I could buy a Sudoku book, even though I don't understand Sudoku.

While Dad was in the newsagents', I texted Hannah and told her about what Great Aunt May did at the table last night and she thought it was dead funny. I sat in the back of the car reading and rereading her text while Mum blathered on to me about nothing. I just like to look at Hannah's name 'cos it makes me feel good inside. I like to imagine her thinking about what she's gonna write to me, then I like to think about her actually writing it and sending it.

I also like to think she sits waiting for me to text her back, like I sit waiting for her to text me back, but I kinda think she probably doesn't.

Sunday 20 May

Went shopping with Mum and Dad for a sofa today. We went to one of those big out-of-town retail parks that always seem to have an ice cream van idling in the car park, no matter what the weather.

Mum is dithering over colours; she can't decide over cappuccino or oatmeal. Dad asked why we couldn't just have a brown sofa but Mum ignored him and wandered off among the two-seaters before an overeager salesman cornered her by the pouffes and started talking finance plans.

Monday 21 May

Got home from school to find Mum had spread out some colour charts the salesman gave her yesterday on the coffee table. She said she's gone off oatmeal and was now veering towards café crème but was worried it was too similar to cappuccino, and would I take a look? I dumped my school bag down and peered at the colours but couldn't tell what colour was what. I have to say I agree with Dad—why can't we just have plain brown? Mum did that funny clicking noise with her mouth that adults do and said, 'Just like your father, no imagination,' then gathered up the colour charts and went off in search of HRBH.

Hadn't really seen much of Hannah at school today so I felt a bit down tonight. Decided to log on to MSN on the off chance she might be there, and she was! We had, like, a really nice hour's chat just before bedtime, and by the time I'd logged off, I was much happier.

Went to bed thinking about her again. Sigh.

Tuesday 22 May

Walked to school with Alice today. She seemed in a bit of a bad mood, 'cos she kept saying she hasn't seen much of me lately and asked if I'd been busy, 'cos I haven't walked to school with her very much like we used to (well, certainly since the novelty of her dad taking us in his ridiculous 4x4 has worn off). She also said I don't text her much these days, and that when she texts me I either don't reply or I'm dead late in replying.

I didn't say much 'cos I was a bit annoyed with her, I suppose. I mean, FFS, it's like having a boyfriend nagging me about not being attentive enough. Not that I'd know, never having had a boyfriend before (Ben SO doesn't count), but it seems like that kinda thing. It's true, I guess, that I've not been as good a friend to her as I could be, but what am I supposed to do? My head's that full of Hannah that I don't have time to think about anything else!!! I just wish Alice'd give me a break.

Wednesday 23 May

Realised I hadn't even looked at the Sudoku book I bought on Saturday so had a quick flick through it while Mum was ensconced in front of the TV, but didn't have a flipping clue what I was supposed to do so promptly put it back down and read the first few pages of Harry Potter instead. Figured Harry Potter was slightly more intellectually demanding than Dr. Seuss, so didn't feel too bad about it, but made a mental note to have another crack at the old Sudoku one night when I'm not feeling so tired.

Thursday 24 May

Mum is very disappointed that she's only lost a pound since her diet started. I pointed out to her that she's been on her diet for less than a fortnight, but she looked at me sadly and said, 'But I've barely eaten a thing!' and looked longingly at a slice of white bread that was mocking her from the sideboard. This is true. When she's not looking sadly at things she knows she can't eat, her stomach is making noises like an old washing machine going round. I heard her telling Dad the other night that 'Inside me is a thin woman waiting to get out, Chris', and I had half a mind to tell her to give it a Mars Bar while it was waiting, 'cos it sounded bloody hungry.

Friday 25 May

Chatted to Hannah on MSN for most of this evening. She asked me if I wanted to go over tomorrow so of course I said yes. The weather's supposed to be great, so we're going to pack up a picnic and head off down to the reservoir. I might take my Sudoku book with me and ask her if she knows how to do it.

Oh, and the sofa saga rumbles on! Honestly, you'd never think it could cause so much such anxiety. When I've left home and got a place of my own, I'll be too busy having a life to worry about whether I should plump for Burnt Sienna or whether Sepia will clash with my rugs!

Saturday 26 May

Ohmigod, so much happened today, I don't think I have enough space to write it all!!! My hands are still shaking!!!

Went over to Hannah's house this morning, made up the picnic, and headed off for a walk down by the canal. It was, like, mega hot so we stopped under the trees, spread out our rug, and flopped down next to the water to watch the ducks paddling along and waggling their bottoms at us.

We ate our picnic and, as she passed stuff to me, our hands kept touching. I felt really embarrassed 'cos of it. She seemed…I dunno, *different*…and there were some awkward silences which made me feel even more uncomfortable, 'cos me and Hannah have never had any awkward silences, like, *ever*. We were sharing a bottle of Coke and I was watching her drinking from it and getting real hot. Hot, not like from the sun, but y'know—HOT!

Then we lay back on the rug with the sun was warming us through the trees, making us sleepy and happy. We just lay there chatting away and saying funnies and laughing and kidding with each other about stuff at school. We were talking about Mrs. Russell and her unfeasibly large bosoms and I was saying about what small feet she had, and that was probably 'cos they couldn't grow in the shade and then we were rolling around laughing and stuff, and we started pissing about with each other, trying to make each other roll off the rug.

And then…she kissed me!

It was AMAZING! I pulled the rug hard, and it made her roll over towards me, so that she was pressed up against me. She was still giggling a bit, but instead of moving away from me, she propped herself up on her elbow, and started stroking my hair, and then she kissed me! A bit hesitantly at first, but when she realised I was kissing her back, she carried on!!!

When she eventually pulled away and looked down at me, still propped up on one elbow, she just grinned and said, 'wow!' in a quiet voice. I said, 'wow indeed!' I reached up, put my arm round her and kissed her again, pleased at how enthusiastically she kissed me back. She stayed propped up, looking down at me, and I didn't know what to say to her, lying half underneath her, under a tree, down by the reservoir!

She grinned again, said, 'That felt good,' and flopped back down beside me. I asked, 'Did you mean to do that, or did it just happen?' and she said breezily, 'I've wanted to do that for ages,' leaning over to pick a piece of dry grass from my forehead. Then she started telling me that she'd fancied me from the first day she'd clapped eyes on me, and that she'd been trying to muster up the guts to ask me out, but was worried that I 'wasn't like that', and that's why she'd been quizzing me on boys and stuff, trying to figure out whether I was gay or straight.

Then she sat up and looked back down at me and asked me if I 'liked' her. What could I say? I told her that recently I'd been having strong feelings for her, and that I'd been thinking about her, like, a LOT. I wanted to tell her about J, but figured this was neither the time nor the place to be talking about J. Then she asked me if I wanted to go out with her, so I laughed and said, 'Like on a date?' and she said, 'Yeah, like a date. I want to go out with you, Clem.'

OMFG!!!

So I said, 'I'd love to go out with you,' and grinned at her. She said, 'Oh, thank God,' and puffed out her cheeks in relief (sooooo cute!).

So we're going out on a date! I, Clementine Atkins, am going on a DATE WITH HANNAH!

What a bolt from the blue!!

We're going to meet up tomorrow afternoon, and we're going for a pizza in town. I'm crapping myself already!!

I've just spent the whole evening in a daze, wondering if today really happened.

Thank God I forgot to take my Sudoku book with me!

Sunday 27 May

Hannah texted me late last night to say good night, and she put three xxx's after her message, which she's never done before. I liked that. A lot!

I spent the whole day in a panic, wondering if I was doing the right thing, whether it was wrong to be going out with a girl, and whether it was even more wrong to be soooooo looking forward to it! But then I figured I was so darned over the moon about everything, what was the point of spoiling such a lovely feeling by panicking?

Besides, how can something that makes you this ridiculously happy be wrong??

Anyway, I'm writing this up now (11 a.m.) so that I can hide you again, dear diary. Will tell you all tomorrow!

Monday 28 May

It's official. I'm going out with Hannah, and I'm the happiest girl in the world! We met up outside Pizza Hut at 1 p.m. yesterday. Hannah was already waiting for me, looking absolutely gorgeous.

We had a brilliant day. Hannah insisted on paying for everything, even though I wanted to pay for all my stuff. She said, 'You can pay next time,' and winked. I got butterflies.

It was like we'd never really spoken before, like everything we'd done and talked about in the past had never happened. I was seeing Hannah with new eyes, and I felt so damned happy just being with her there, in Pizza Hut, amongst all the students and little kids and stuffed crusts. There was an extra *frisson* to everything, knowing now what we both know, knowing that we both fancy each other and that we both know that we fancy each other! It felt a bit strange at first, but so completely natural after a while.

She also told me that she'd been dropping hints for ages that she liked me, but I hadn't cottoned on. She said, 'Haven't you ever noticed me looking at you at school?' and I felt a bit of a twit, 'cos I'd thought she was trying to suss me out when she did that. She told me she'd sent me a couple of anonymous e-mails, because it was the only way she'd felt able to let me know how she was feeling, but I hadn't replied. So Hannah was Loopy Lurve Puppy!!!

I had to go home at 8 p.m., 'cos that's the time I'd arranged for Dad to pick me up. Hannah rang her mum and arranged to meet her at the same place that Dad was meeting me, so we walked down through town together. She held my hand as we walked; she's held my hand loads of times before in school, walking down the corridor with the others, but it had never felt like it did when she held it last night. It was like there was this, I dunno, electricity running between us all of a sudden.

When we got to our meeting place, Dad was already there. Hannah said quietly, 'I s'pose I can't really kiss you, can I, with your dad sitting there?' and I giggled. Then her mum turned up, so I said, 'text you later,' gave her a quick hug, got into Dad's car, and watched as she got into her mum's car.

I'd felt so much older, so much more mature when I'd been out with her, like a proper grown-up on a date, but the minute I walked into the lounge at home, and saw Mum and HRBH sitting there, asking me if I'd had a nice day, I suddenly felt very young again, and it was like the day had never happened. I felt really deflated, and wondered how I was ever going to keep up this pretence!!

When I went to bed, I texted Hannah straight away to make sure she'd got home okay. She asked me if I'd had a good time. I said, 'the best time ever,' and she sent me a message full of grinning smilies back. So, that's it. That's official. We're dating, and it feels great!!!

Tuesday 29 May

Hannah texted me late last night to ask me if I still wanted to go out with her. Of course I do! She's the funniest, funkiest, most intelligent, and darned nicest person I think I've ever met. I texted her back and told her all this, and two minutes later she rang me, saying she wanted to hear my voice. I sat in bed, in the darkness of my room while we whispered things to each other. It was soooooooo romantic!

Then today at school we met up at break and had a hot chocolate together. I met her by the drinks machine and felt my tummy lurch with butterflies when I saw her again. I said 'hiya' and she said 'hiya' back, and it felt a bit awkward to start with, which was daft 'cos in the three months that I've known her, I've never felt particularly awkward in her company, so why would I now? We leant against the drinks machine, just looking and smiling at each other for a bit, then she looked round to make sure no one was around and quickly touched my hand, briefly linking her fingers in mine. All awkwardness instantly disappeared!

Hannah is my girlfriend. I have a girlfriend. I'm Hannah's girlfriend. Me, I'm her girlfriend. I still can't quite believe it!

Holy shit! [/giddy-as-a-kipper/].

Wednesday 30 May

Spent most of today wondering how all this happened. How marvellous that she fancies me! I don't think I've ever been fancied before! Ben never fancied me, I'm sure of it! She says I'm cute—no one's ever said that before either!

Soooooooo wanted to see Hannah again today but barely saw her all day, for one reason or another. She texted me mid-afternoon to say she was thinking about me, and that she was doing a good job of pretending to act normal, when inside she was churned up with butterflies over me. Wow!

Thursday 31 May

Hannah asked me today when I first realised I was gay, and I told her I'd thought I was bent for a while, but wasn't sure. She told me she'd known since she was about eleven and first started having feelings for girls in her class. I have to say I wasn't entirely comfortable talking about gayness, but she seemed really okay about it, really casual. That was a bit strange!

Was too wrapped up in loopy love-bunnyness to be bothered with cross-country running this afternoon (how can I concentrate on running across muddy fields when my head is so full of Han?) so I did that thing that Barbara does when she doesn't want to go out for a walk, and pretended that I'd hurt my leg so I was excused.

Friday 1 June

Was talking to Alice on MSN this evening and she asked me if I wanted to go to Cardiff shopping with her and her mum tomorrow. I was planning on having a whole day with Hannah, so I told her I had other plans. I think she was a bit pissed off, 'cos she logged off soon after that and didn't come back on. Never mind, 'cos Hannah logged on soon after that and we had a reeeeeeaally rude MSN convo.

Now I'm *really* worried: if she can talk like that in MSN-land, what on earth can she do in real life???? She's going to eat me alive! Ha ha ha!!

Saturday 2 June

Two days till my birthday! HRBH burst into my room this morning and told me, in no uncertain terms, that if I wanted anything from her for my birthday, I'd have to get my sorry arse out of bed and come into town with her this morning, 'cos she didn't have the *faintest* idea what to get me. So that told me!

We walked down into town and I considered telling her about me and Hannah, but then thought better of it. After all, it's still early days. And I'm a chicken!

After walking round town for, like, three hours negotiating all the tourists snapping away with their digitals, I finally plumped for this wicked black top with rips in it which clings to my top half and makes my hooters look pretty darned good. I thought Hannah would appreciate it. HRBH scoffed and said it wasn't the baggy crap I normally wear, but bought it nonetheless. She tried to give it to me there and then in town, but I insisted she wrap it up and give it to me on Monday. HRBH tutted in only the way she can, but I didn't care…I just thought about Hannah's face when she sees me in my new top.

Sunday 3 June

Mum and Dad have bought the sofa! Praise the Lord! They've plumped for a three-piece suite from We R Sofas, or somewhere like that, so there are sighs of relief all round. It's being delivered in eight weeks' time, which means it'll come just after we get back from France.

Monday 4 June

My seventeenth birthday!!!!! Switched my phone on first thing and lay in bed listening to it beep at me with all my birthday greetings.

Mum hugged me at breakfast and wished me 'many happy returns,' while Dad kissed the top of my head and said, 'Happy Birthday, Titch.' For my birthday I got:

- New jeans, some smelly soap and a Venus razor (!) (Mum)
- Take That (who???) CD and fountain pen (Dad)
- Sexy black top (sister)
- £20 Uncle Bob and Aunty Marie
- £20 Uncle David and Aunty Alison
- £10 Aunty Pam
- £5 Great Aunt May
- £5 gift voucher from Aunty Marge down the road, who's not my aunty but I call her aunty anyway
- Box of chocolates from next door

Kept checking my phone all the way to school, but no birthday greeting from Han. Met Alice on the way and she gave me a cute card with rabbits on (surprise, surprise) and a new pen drive for my PC, which I was *really* pleased with.

Didn't see Han till History at 10:45. Some of the other girls in class wished me a happy birthday and gave me cards just as Mr. Pritchard was coming in; Han stared hard at me and hissed, 'Why didn't you tell me it was your birthday today?' I said, 'I thought you knew!' but Han just frowned and looked away, putting her attention to what was Pritchard was writing on the whiteboard. Great! I thought, I've only been going out with Han for just over a week and I've managed to piss her off already.

After the lesson I said to her, 'I really thought you knew it was my birthday today! I thought I'd told you ages ago, before we got it together.' She just said 'Nuh-uh' and shook her head. She said, 'I feel really bad! I had *no* idea, and I feel crap that I didn't get you anything. I'm sorry.' I said, 'It doesn't matter, honest!' She said, 'I'll make it up to you, I promise,' and ran her hand up and down my arm, which made me go all goose-pimply!

I think I'm turning into a soft romantic!!!

Anyway, apart from worrying this morning that I'd blown things with Han before they'd even started, I had a fabulous birthday. All the gang bought me lunch in the canteen, and no one grumbled when I specifically asked for gravy AND cheese on my chips! Result!!!!

When I got home, Mum had baked me a chocolate cake and put candles on it. I made some feeble comment about being too old, at seventeen, to have a cake with candles but was secretly pleased that she'd made it. When I blew out the candles, I wished that it wouldn't be too long before me and Han got it together. I could have wished for health and happiness for my family, but noooooo. Felt a bit bad about that, so went out into the kitchen again later, lit the remaining candles that were clinging to the half-eaten cake, blew them out and wished for good things for Mum, Dad, and HRBH. Felt better!

Tuesday 5 June

Han came and found me at break and told me to meet her outside the science block at lunchtime so she could give me my birthday present. She said the science block was the best place for us to meet, 'cos it's quiet and secluded. Then I started fretting that she was going to pounce on me and kiss me, and I worried that the schoolyard wasn't the best place for that!

Anyway, I needn't have worried! Han gave me my card, which had a picture of a red squirrel up a tree throwing nuts down at someone's head; inside she'd written:

'To the fabulous, gorgeous birthday girl with lots of love and huggles from Han.' She'd put, like, a hundred kisses after it.

She gave me my present, which was wrapped up in red shiny paper. It was a small black jewellery box, and inside was the funkiest ring I'd ever seen (apart from Han's skull ring). It was quite big, silver, and had a sort of black swoosh around it, rather like waves. Han told me it's called a Bali ring. It looks very Goth, very funky, and also *very* expensive! I told Han it was gorgeous and that she shouldn't have, but she just grinned at me and shrugged. She said she'd gone down into town after school yesterday especially to get me a present, and knew the second she saw the ring that I'd like it. I have to agree with her; it's just the thing I'd *like* to buy myself but don't have the guts to do. Somehow having someone buy it for me makes it all the more special. It's too small for my middle finger, and I can hardly put it on my ring finger, so it's sitting pretty on my right-hand ring finger and it looks soooooo cool!

Wednesday 6 June

Everyone was admiring my ring at lunch today. I told them it was a birthday present and they were all, like, 'Wowwww, who from?' They all said it looked pretty expensive, and when I told them Han had bought it for me, I'm sure there were some raised eyebrows among them, but maybe I was just being paranoid??

Thursday 7 June

I got sent out of French today!!! I was in a foul mood (got my period—ugh!) and when Mrs. Howells (old bag) went to collect our homework (some crap about tourism in the Alps, which we were supposed to have completed over the Easter holidays, but which I couldn't be arsed to do), I told her I'd left mine on the bus (I walk to school—ha ha ha!!!!!!). Mrs. Howells said to me 'Do you think I was born yesterday, Clementine?' and I said, 'Not unless you age at the speed of light, Miss,' which made everyone giggle, but which got me sent out of the room for insubordination!!!!!!!!!

When class finished, she came out to where I was slouched against the corridor wall and put on one of her concerned faces and told me 'Not to let my work suffer just because I'd got myself a new best friend.' I have *no* idea what she was talking about, but can only assume she's jealous 'cos I'm hanging around with a damn sexy Goth—sorry, EMO—and she's just a dried-up old prune, ha ha ha ha!!!

Friday 8 June

Was thinking about what Mrs. Howells had said to me yesterday, then felt a bit bad about what I wrote about her, so I take that back x 100,000,000. I s'pose she's right in a way that I've not been concentrating so much in her class (or other classes for that matter) but that's only 'cos I'm in lovvvvvvvvvvvvvve!!! All I can think about is Han, not sodding schoolwork. I've made a mental note to myself to try a bit harder, though. Han's not going to want to go out with a thicko.

Saturday 9 June

Went round to Han's this morning and sat with her and Dan watching some channel that Han likes, called Kerrang! It's a music channel and plays all the stuff Han's into, like Goth, rock music type stuff. She knew *all* the groups that were on there, and I didn't know any! It's like a new world to me, and I can't believe I've missed it all! I never realised what a sheltered life I've led until I met Han; I know nothing about this Goth world she lives in, and I feel so naïve sometimes.

Anyway, we sat and watched Kerrang! till we got bored, then at about twelve o'clock, we went down into town just to get out. We went to this Italian place with the intention of having lunch (we could have re-enacted the Lady and the Tramp scene with the spaghetti!) but when we got in there, neither of us was particularly hungry.

Han sat opposite me, gazing into my eyes, and I felt this sort of... sexual tension. She fiddled nervously with her napkin, screwing it up in her hands, then flattening it out and screwing it up again. Finally she said, 'We're going to have to do something about this before I pop,' and I had to agree; I'd been sitting there looking at that lovely mouth of hers, just *dying* to kiss it. If I didn't get to do it soon, I'd have gone insane!

Then Han came up with the idea of going to the toilets and doing it. We both kept a close eye on the comings and goings in the Ladies', and when, finally, it seemed the coast was clear, we both went down to the back of the restaurant, into the Ladies', and flung ourselves into the nearest cubicle.

I leaned against the cubicle door and looked at Han. She grinned that lazy grin of hers, grabbed me, pulled me over to her, and kissed me, and it was just as brilliant as the last time!!!!!!! I had my arms round her waist and I felt secretly quite relieved that I could feel a pleasing amount of flesh poking out over her waistband. Thank bugger she's not a skinny wretch! We broke away and looked into each other eyes and grinned at each other. Just as we were about to go in for the kill one more time, someone came into the cubicle next to us. We both froze and listened intently as the person unzipped their trousers and sat down, then released a soft, breezy fart which echoed embarrassingly round her cubicle and punctuated the sound of her weeing.

Han got a fit of the giggles and I kept shushing her as best I could, but it was too late—Han had gone to pieces. With tears of laughter rolling down our faces, we made a hasty escape from the toilets, walked as fast as we could back down the restaurant and out onto the street where we ran, howling, down towards the river.

We sat on a wall, overlooking the water, and I felt so damned contented. Then I started to fret that I'm a crap kisser, so went a bit quiet. Han asked me if I was okay. When I said I was, she then started to worry that I'd regretted doing it again, or that I'd been disgusted by it. Nothing could be further from the truth! It felt perfect, so right, and not disgusting at all! Just perfect. I told her I was worried that I'd been no good at kissing; I looked down at my feet and said she was the first girl I'd ever kissed. She put her arm round my shoulders and said I wasn't to worry, 'cos I was the best girl she'd ever kissed! I was shocked. It had never occurred to me that she'd ever kissed someone before! I said (as casually as I could), 'So I'm not the first girl you've kissed?' and she said breezily, 'No, I've kissed others!' I'm gobsmacked! I suppose I should have guessed she wasn't as inexperienced as me (no one is!), but I never thought she'd had 'others'.

So I asked, 'How many others?' and she said, 'A couple. It's no big deal.' But it *is* a big deal for me! I didn't want it to ruin what had been a perfect day, though, so I told myself not to think about it too much. Inside, though, it gnawed away at me.

I went home and tried to act normal, even though my tummy was still all a-flutter at what I'd done this afternoon. Normality arrived, however, like a bite on the bum when Mum greeted me, wearing an apron and a grumpy look, and requested that I help her tackle the pots and pans.

What a day! I'm exhausted.

Sunday 10 June

Woke up to brilliant sunshine today. Han rang and asked if I wanted to go over to hers, 'cos she was babysitting Joe and she wanted some company.

We had such a laugh again on the trampoline! Poor Joe didn't really get a look-in 'cos me and Han were busy mucking about on it, so he went in and started shooting at aliens or something on his PlayStation. After about half an hour of flinging ourselves around like rag dolls, we sat on the grass and I asked Han how long she'd been an EMO. She said she'd started off being a Goth, 'cos she liked wearing black, but then she said everyone else became a Goth so she decided to become an EMO 'cos she thought she was a bit of a tortured soul and that no one understood her. She said that EMOs were misunderstood and that they walked on the dark side of life and were in tune with their souls, so I said, 'But are they allowed to bounce on trampolines?' and she flashed me this look of disapproval which made me laugh nervously.

We sat on the grass next to each other and I so wanted to touch her. She had a stray bit of hair that was driving me mad as well, but mainly I just wanted to touch her. I was just thinking how hard it was knowing that we can't do these things as freely as a boyfriend and girlfriend can, when Han put her hand right next to mine and stroked my hand kinda furtively with her fingers, just like she'd read my thoughts or something. It was real nice, just sitting there on the grass, our hands touching, Joe oblivious on his PlayStation inside.

Then my phone beeped and it was Mum telling me 'lnch rdy. Cm hm now.' Oh yes! My mother has finally got to grips with her mobile phone (only five months after we bought her the bloody thing) and keeps sending me random text messages which say things like: 'pork chops 4 tea,' and, 'Am in town. Do u want shoes?' and completely incomprehensible texts like: 'wd u pt chkn in oven 4t bk @ 6 Mum,' and 'Mrs. M frm chrch snds luv.' It's driving me potty! Is there anything worse than a parent who talks to you in text-speak?! And this from an English teacher! She should be ashamed of herself [/superiority/]. Anyway, I took that to mean that lunch was ready and that I was to come home, so I had to give Han a quick hug and set off back to Normal Land once again.

Monday 11 June

It was quite warm today so I decided to wear my short skirt to school. When I met up with the gang at lunchtime, I got some ribbing about it 'cos it's so short. Ems said, 'You trying to catch Troutt's eye, Clem?' and 'Don't let my Ryan see you in that,' which made everyone laugh. I caught Han's glance and she raised a brow at me, a mischievous glint in her eye, which made my tummy go to mush again.

As we returned into the school block, Han pulled me back and whispered, 'You trying to kill me, Clemmykins?' and the back of my legs went wobbly! I think I might continue to wear short skirts to school. I like the idea that it's driving Han mad and she can't say anything in front of the others! Does that make me some sort of pervert?

Tuesday 12 June

Went over to Han's house straight after school tonight, 'cos she said her mum and dad wouldn't be home till about 5:30 p.m. so we could have an hour's peace and quiet together. We went up to her room (Han's, not her mum's) and had, like, this marathon kissing session on her bed!!! I think maybe I'm okay at this kissing lark 'cos Han was making all the right noises. I feel a bit daft for fretting about it at the weekend now. Anyway, I was getting to the point where I felt like I was ready to perhaps do more, but then we heard a key in the front door, so had to tidy ourselves up and make out that we'd been sitting up there listening to music or something. I felt a bit guilty again—I'm sure I must have been Catholic in my last life!

Wednesday 13 June

Han's dyed her hair black with a red bit in it again 'cos she said she could see some of her natural mousey hair coming through. It looks dead cool! I think I might like to dye my hair black, but I'm worried about what Mum and Dad will say. It took them over a month to recover from the shock of HRBH buying herself a pair of thigh-high boots in 2004.

I've decided to grow my fringe a bit as well, so that it covers one of my eyes. Han's hair's a bit like that and it looks wicked. I need to do something different with my hair, anyway. It's the sort of hair that has a life of its own, and only the liberal use of gel and straighteners makes it look half-decent.

Thursday 14 June

Checked my e-mails before bed, but there was only one message in my in-box, telling me how I could increase the size of my cock, so I logged off and went to bed.

Han sent me a late-night text, which just said, 'Thinking about you.' I lay in the dark reading it over and over again and went off to sleep with a dopey grin on my face!

Friday 15 June

Woke up feeling in a naughty mood today so wore the short black skirt that I know Han likes so much. Caught her looking at my legs during French and it gave me a thrill. I think I'm turning into one of those exhibitionists that you read about in the papers. Han said I look 'as fit as fuck' in my short skirt, which made me giggle nervously. I've never been confident in my looks, so I love it when she tells me I look good (even if I don't particularly like her choice of vocabulary).

Saturday 16 June

Han came over at lunchtime today. This was the first time she'd been to our house, and it looked like she'd dressed for the occasion. She was dressed in what can only be described as rags, in black, with her *fuck-off* biker boots on and her hair looking like she'd just got out of bed (although I'm sure it had taken her ages to make it look so scruffy). My dad answered the door and stood there looking scared until Han greeted him with a breezy 'Hullo, Mr. Atkins' and flashed him her best smile. I appeared in the hallway and she poked her tongue out at me over Dad's shoulder.

We sat in the lounge and watched Kerrang! together until I heard Dad out in the kitchen muttering something about 'bloody racket coming from the lounge' to Mum. Not wanting them to embarrass me in front of Han, I suggested we went into town—anything had to be better than having to listen to Dad grumbling on like a miserable old fart.

Anyway, Han dragged me into the chemists in town and made me try some black makeup on. I put on black mascara and a bit of black eyeshadow, and turned and pouted at Han. I asked, 'What do you think?' and she whispered, 'I think I want to ravish you right here,' which made me go all giggly and girly.

Afterwards, we looked at the black hair dye, 'cos I'd told Han I was thinking about changing my hair colour. She picked out this dye called 'Midnight Seduction' (why can't it just be called 'Black'?!) and said she thought I'd look foxy with black hair, but then I thought of my poor parents' faces if I went home with black makeup AND black hair dye, so just plumped for the mascara instead. I think maybe I'll just wear it when I'm with Han, though, in case I get laughed at.

Sunday 17 June

It was Father's Day today and the sun was shining for a change, so we packed up a picnic and drove to a canal side pub that Mum and Dad like for a quick drink. The pub was packed! You'd think people had never seen sunshine before! The place was full of people high on beer and vitamin D! Dad got very grumpy 'cos there was nowhere to sit, so we walked on along the canal a little way and ate our picnic on the grass. It was very nice, but the pickle had squirted from our sandwiches, making everything taste of pickles, including the bananas.

Dad seemed to enjoy himself, though. Maybe a bit too much 'cos he insisted on stopping off at the pub again on the way home, then drank too much, so Mum had to drive us all home again. I don't think she was best pleased 'cos she got *that look* on her face which stayed there all the way home, right through the early evening news, and only lifted when she heard the opening credits of *ER* start up.

Monday 18 June

I wanted to ask Han about her previous girlfriends today, but:

1. I didn't want to get her annoyed, and
2. Do I really want to know??

Tuesday 19 June

Maybe I do want to know! Maybe I want to know exactly how experienced she is, whether she was ever in love with any of them, whether she's ever had her heart broken and, more importantly, whether she's actually *done it* with any of them.

Trouble is, I'm so square and I don't know what I'm doing. This is all so new and strange to me, and I know Han says she finds it cute, but how long is she going to find it cute for? I dunno, maybe I should just stop worrying about it and go with the cute thing? After all, I suppose it could be fun getting Han to teach me things!!

Wednesday 20 June

Wanted Han all to myself today so we had lunch on our own, much to everyone's puzzlement, I guess. I don't care. Sometimes I just want to be with my girlfriend on my own.

Han told me over lunch that she liked my button nose. I said, 'what button nose?' and she leant closer over the table and said in hushed tones, 'you have such a cute little nose,' which made me self-consciously touch it. She laughed and said she thought I was cute, and funny, and clever, and just about the nicest person she'd ever met! Me! I squirmed in my seat a bit, but I liked the compliments she was heaping on me.

When I got home from school, I looked at myself in the mirror. You see, she tells me these things, that I'm cute and all, but I can't see it. I've always thought I was a bit funny looking and had a lack of self-confidence. I know I'm not ugly, and yet I'm not pretty… just pretty ugly (ha ha). I'm too short for my liking, and I'm not fat—I know—but I always think my bum is too big. And my hair! Whatever I do to it, it still sticks up all over the place. I'm a scruffy little oik too; Mum says even a Versace suit would look like a sack of potatoes on me.

I stood and pulled some pouty faces in the mirror until HRBH walked past and sneered, 'if the wind changes you'll get stuck like that,' at me. Damn wind must have been blowing a gale for her to end up looking the way she does, then!!!

Thursday 21 June

Mrs. Russell is leaving! She gathered us all for assembly this morning, and told us in sombre tones that she was retiring at the end of term and that from September we would be having a new Head. I'm not sure what I think about this. She could be scary and annoying at times, but I think I might miss the sound of her six-inch stilletoes clip-clopping down the corridor at 80 miles an hour.

Realised today that I've been neglecting Alice again lately so asked her if she wanted to come to town with me on Saturday. Han's not going to be around so I'll be at a loose end anyway. It made sense to re-establish my best friend obligations whilst not missing out on being with Han!

Friday 22 June

Really hot day, so we all sat outside on the grass at lunchtime. Ems and Matty were quizzing Han on her love life and I thought she managed really well in keeping a straight face. They were asking her if she was seeing someone and she was really coy. I couldn't look at her, so just lay out on the grass with my eyes shut, listening to them all burbling on, and Han doing her best to fend off all the questions being fired at her.

Later she caught up with me behind the science block and we had a good laugh about it. She said, 'I wanted to tell them about us,' and I blurted, 'You're not going to, are you??' I stood there, panicked, until she laughed and said, 'Of course not! Do you really think they'd understand??' Then she said, 'I've been there and done that once, and I wouldn't do it again.' I wanted to ask her what she meant, but the bell went for afternoon lessons so she linked her fingers in mine, said she'd miss me this weekend, then turned and walked back into the building.

I wonder what she meant? Presumably she has, in the past, told people about being gay and got a bad reaction? I knew I couldn't tell my friends just yet, as close as we all are. I just don't think they'd understand.

Saturday 23 June

Our ferry tickets arrived for our holiday this morning; the ferry leaves at 8:30 a.m. from Portsmouth, which means we'll have to leave home at some ridiculous time in the morning to get down there. I don't do mornings! We got the brochure for the caravan site as well—it looks nice! It's in some pine forest in deepest darkest Brittany. What will the weather be like in Brittany in August, I wonder?

Met up with Alice in town and told her we'd gotten all the tickets for France. She looked dead happy and said she was really looking forward to coming with us, which is nice. I'm not sure how I'll manage without Han for two weeks, though. I haven't seen her since 2 p.m. yesterday, and I'm pining already.

Anyway, we went into town and I found myself looking at the black hair dye again. I really want to dye it now! I asked Alice what she thought I'd look like with black hair and she asked me if I wanted to dye it so I looked like Han, and stared at me kinda impatiently and a bit strangely. Longer than I felt comfortable with. I got a bit pissy with her and told her it had nothing to do with wanting to look like Han, but perhaps I do want to be like her really, or at least look a bit different from how I do now. My hair is a sort of mousey-boring-browny-pooey-yellowy colour and I want it to look funky. I've started to grow my fringe nice and long, so that looks good too, even if it drives me crackers pushing it out of my eyes every five minutes.

Plus, I don't want Han to think I'm boring, so I picked up this box that was called 'Midnight Hour' and paid the £6.99 for it. I hope it's worth it.

Sunday 24 June

Got a text from Han late last night telling me she was thinking about me and that she missed me. I texted her back and told her I was missing her too, and that I'd bought some black dye for my hair. She replied and said I was sexy enough now, but I'd drive her crazy with black hair. That comment made me feel really weird, in a good way, though.

Anyway, I plucked up the courage and dyed my hair this afternoon. I got black dye all over the sink, so tried to wipe it off with Mum's pink bath sponge and got black dye all over that as well, so then tried to wash the sponge clean and got black dye all in the sink again! I finally got most of the black out of the sink, and off the sponge, and off the floor, and off the hand-towel I used to wipe the black from the floor, and presented myself to Mum and Dad in the lounge. I got a better reaction than I was expecting! Dad just rolled his eyes at me and disappeared back behind his Sunday paper and

Mum said it looked 'nice'. Nice? I don't want it to look nice! I want it to look cool.

Got moaned at for making such a mess in the bathroom but I think, bearing in mind how funky my hair looks, it was worth the two hours of grumbling I got.

Took a picture of myself with my phone and sent it to Han. Got a reply an hour later, which just said, 'OMFG!!!' and lots of smilies, so sounds like it meets with her approval!

Monday 25 June

Everyone was admiring my new black hair at school today! Ems said it looked really cool. Han said, 'I think she looks really sexy now, don't you?' and I nearly spat my Coke out. I don't think anyone took what she said in the wrong way 'cos they all agreed with her! Matty said I looked 'hot' and that if I'd had black hair when I'd been seeing Ben, it would have driven him crazy, 'cos he loves girls with black hair. I noticed Han's jaw clench a little bit when she said that, but I just laughed at what Matty said, and took another slug of Coke.

Tuesday 26 June

Now I've got funky hair, I want to go even further, so I think I might get a tattoo done. I reckon Han will fancy me even more with a tattoo. I've got loads of design ideas in my head, but I'm a bit worried 'cos I've got a low pain threshold. If I prick my thumb with a pin, I feel sick. So how would I cope with a thousand needle pricks? Figured I'll think about a design first, then worry about the pain later.

Wednesday 27 June

Saw this really fit girl with a tattoo on her arm while I was walking to school this morning. It's gotta be fate! I decide one day to get a tattoo and then I see a fit girl with one the very next day? Fate. And it proves that all the fit girls have tattoos!!!

Thursday 28 June

I was told to 'buck up my ideas' in Spanish class today. I was staring out of the window and Mrs. Irwin told me to 'stop daydreaming about whatever boy was in my head and get on with my work.' I was, in actual fact, wondering what Han looked like naked, but that's neither here nor there.

Friday 29 June

Was supposed to be playing netball in PE today but the thought of standing under a net with my arms in the air while a bunch of muscle-bound schoolgirls bear down on me at speed left me cold, so I told Mr. Meadows, the PE teacher, that I had my period and couldn't possibly partake in the game. Mr. Meadows hates it when we girls tell him we have our periods; you can see him visibly shrinking before your very eyes, so we all use it as an excuse and it works every time!

The only downside was that he made me sort out piles of sweaty games shirts, including Pippa Goldsmith's, which could easily be fashioned into some sort of tent in the event of an emergency. Peeked out of the window and saw my classmates puffing and sweating up and down the court, though, and knew I'd definitely made the right decision.

Saturday 30 June

Went over to Han's for the day. Her dad had taken to his bed 'cos his spastic colon had flared up again during breakfast and her mum was crashing pans about or something in the kitchen, so we stayed in the lounge and watched *America's Next Top Model* from about three years ago. I told her I wanted a tattoo and she told me I was very brave, which I didn't really want to hear. Now I have to decide what I want done, and where I want it done. Han says something on the small of my back or on my shoulder would be cool (and it would mean Mum and Dad wouldn't see it). I think I want something Gothic, like a black cross, or some barbed wire, or a crow or something. Well, maybe not a crow, but something black, anyway.

Sunday 1 July

If I have a black tattoo it might just look like a dirty splodge. I don't want anyone to think I don't wash. Maybe I'll go for something bright instead, like a red rose or something.

Monday 2 July

Red roses aren't very Gothic, are they?

Tuesday 3 July

Thought about having my initials tattooed, rather than an actual item. I drew a design with my initials, CMA, in spiky italics but it's difficult to see what it says.

Re-designed my initials so that they're not so Gothic, but now, whichever way round you hold it, the design looks like a map of the

Birmingham Inner Ring Road. I give up! Thought about designing something with my initials mixed up with Han's initials. But that would probably weird her out.

Wednesday 4 July

Had another vocabulary test in French but spent most of the hour doing my design. Think maybe I've cracked it at long last. It's a design of some hands grasping a burning cross. Can't wait to show Hannah.

Got 13 out of 50 for the vocabulary test!

Thursday 5 July

Showed Hannah my design during lunch break. She giggled and asked, 'Why do you want a tattoo of a pair of dogs' paws holding the Olympic torch?' and then wondered why I was miffed.

Looked at the design again when I got home from school. I suppose, if you turn it round, it does look rather like the Olympic torch, but the hands do NOT look like dogs' paws.

Friday 6 July

Walked home with Alice from school today. She asked me over to her house tonight, but I turned her down. I suppose I could have gone 'cos Han said she was going to visit her Gran for the evening, but she also said she'd be back early enough to have a quick (and she added very naughty) MSN chat, and I didn't want to miss her. Once I get to Alice's house it's sometimes hard to get away without being rude, so I kinda thought it would be best not to go at all.

I thought Alice looked really disappointed, but I soon managed to stop feeling guilty about it when I logged on later and had THE most fabulous MSN sex chat with Han!!

Saturday 7 July

Went onto the Internet this evening to look up tattoo designs. Strayed into a website that talked about piercings and was intrigued to see I could have something called my labia pierced. I thought a labia was a type of car. Evidently, it's not. Ouch!!

Sunday 8 July

Decided to get the tattoo done during the summer holidays as:

a. It will give me more time to decide on a design, and
b. I won't be wearing my school uniform over the fresh tattoo. Acrylic can be merciless against raw skin.

Monday 9 July

Great Aunt May has come to stay until next Monday!! I heard her talking to Mum in the kitchen, telling her she needed something to 'help her along'. I was relieved later to see Mum pass her a bowl of prunes, and not a spliff.

HRBH looked like she'd been crying today. I wanted to ask her if she was okay, but I figured she was just hormonal 'cos she gets like that sometimes. Decided not to say anything to her. When she's like this, all I have to do is pass the time of day with her and she bites my head off.

Tuesday 10 July

Great Aunt May was at the breakfast table pushing prunes around her bowl and muttering something about being 'loose'. I didn't want to know what she was on about, so grabbed my toast and my school bag and left the house early before I had chance to find out.

Why do old people always talk about their bowels? They're obsessed! When they're not talking about not being able to go, they're talking about not being able to stop. Why is it okay for them to do this? If *I* did it, I'd get the thin-lipped treatment from Mum and an order to not be crude. Life's so unfair sometimes!

Wednesday 11 July

Han came round to our house after school 'cos we'd arranged to do some homework together. Great Aunt May was sitting in her usual chair in the lounge when Han stomped into the room (she was wearing her *fuck-off* biker boots, despite the fact it was 23 degrees outside. That's to say, Han was wearing the boots—not Great Aunt May). She flopped herself down on the sofa next to Great Aunt May's chair. I would wager that Great Aunt May doesn't see many Goths or EMOs at the Autumn Leaves Elderly Persons Home because she looked like she was about to be mugged, and instinctively grasped her handbag to her bosom.

Han smiled her best smile at her, but Great Aunt May just continued to look horrified until Han leant over and said gently, 'You must be Clem's Great Aunt May. I've heard all about you. It's really lovely to meet you at last,' and flashed her a winning smile. Great Aunt May smiled weakly back and said, 'likewise, dear,' but I noticed her whitened knuckles were still wrapped tightly round the handle of her handbag.

Thursday 12 July

One week left of school and I can't bloody wait! Han told me today that she's going to Portugal for ten days in August; it's not the same time that I'll be in France and I'm really pissed off! I was kinda hoping that we'd get loads of time together over the summer, but it looks like we're only going to have three weeks together. It's so unfair [/grumpy/]. She also told me today that her parents are going to a wedding the weekend after next and are going to be away for the whole two days 'cos the wedding's in Scotland, and would I like to go and stay with her for the weekend?!!!

I'd love to…but I'm already crapping myself 'cos without doubt we'll *do the deed* that weekend. Made a mental note to try and lose a bit of weight before then. And buy a sharp razor so I can shave my legs properly.

Friday 13 July

Me and Han share the same taste in music, which makes us even more perfect together! Well, I say we like the same music, but I think her taste is a bit more hard rock than mine. Hard rock verging on grunge, I would say. She is an EMO after all.

She told me that My Chemical Romance is playing in October and asked me if I wanted to go with her!! I've never been to a concert—sorry, gig—before! Han is opening me up to a whole world I never knew existed. I blame the parents.

Saturday 14 July

OMG, me and Han were lying on her bed this afternoon having a naughty shmoozle when she casually told me that her dad's a Theology lecturer down at the college!! Why didn't she think to tell me this before? As if I'm not eaten up with guilt already, I find out I'm (soon to be, hopefully) sleeping with the daughter of a religious man! Old Nick is waiting to spit-roast me even as I write this.

Sunday 15 July

Han came round for Sunday lunch today. Mum had a slight panic at around 11:30 when it suddenly occurred to her that Han might be vegetarian. I said, 'Mum, Han's a Goth! She eats raw budgies for tea.' I noticed the colour drain from Great Aunt May's face until I told her I was joking, and that, no, Han wasn't a vegetarian and that she would be happy to eat whatever Mum put in front of her. Mum looked relieved, but I noticed that her *Open Yourself Up to Vegetables* cookery book had been left open on the nut roast page. I was relieved too; God only knows what a nut roast would have done to Great Aunt May's bowels.

Anyway, Han turned up around 12:30 with a bunch of flowers each for Mum and Great Aunt May and proceeded to charm the pants off Great Aunt May, who now thinks she's the best thing since sliced bread!!

I asked Han after lunch about her dad being religious and all, 'cos it had been worrying me all night. She snorted and said, 'My dad? Religious? You gotta be kidding! He only teaches the stuff, he doesn't believe any of it.' So I asked, 'Doesn't that make him some sort of hypocrite?' to which she replied, 'Do you think old Mr. Jones believes all that psychology crap he spouts to us? All that psycho mumbo-jumbo? Course he doesn't! All Dad does is teach what others believe in, he just acts as the go-between.'

I can't quite get my head round that, so I made a mental note to have a good think about it later. I do feel a bit less guilty now she's told me, though. It would also explain why her dad swears like an old sailor when he thinks no one's listening.

Monday 16 July

Said good-bye to Great Aunt May before school and received a whiskery kiss for my troubles. She pressed TWO shiny pound coins into my hand and told me one of them was for my 'lovely friend Hannah'. Great! Han's known Great Aunt May for all of a week and already she's getting money off her AND she's getting the same as what I get! Where's the fairness in that? Thought about keeping the pound but worried that I might get run over on the way to school as punishment or something, so reluctantly handed it over to Han at lunchtime.

Tuesday 17 July

HRBH looked like she'd been crying again today. I figured she couldn't still be hormonal, so I bit the bullet and asked her if she was all right. She told me that she'd found out that Ade had been cheating on her with some girl behind the cheese counter down at the supermarket. I asked her how long he'd been seeing her and she told me, 'Around three months.' Three months?! I asked her if she'd had no idea what he was up to and she shook her head sadly, adding that now she understood why sometimes when she saw him, he had a whiff of Cheddar about him.

My poor sister! I hate to see her upset. She might be a right pain in the arse, and she might treat me like something she's trodden on in the garden, but she's still my sister, and anyone who messes with her messes with me. Made a mental note to go down to Aldi someday soon, order a large quantity of extra mature, extra smelly Stilton, then throw it at this scarlet woman who's taken Ade away from my poor sister. Don't think I'll mess with Ade, though, 'cos he plays rugby at weekends and is built like a brick shithouse.

Wednesday 18 July

It was SUCH a nice evening tonight so a whole gang of us decided to meet up over at the park and watch the hot-air balloons take off. Mum actually let me go, which means she's either mellowing in her old age, or she's figured there are only two days left of school, so what the hell? Personally I think it's the second. Mum is about as mellow as an electric storm!

Anyway, about ten of us went up there and it was mega! Some boys came too but I suppose you can't have everything. We all sat round on the grass chatting and laughing, and I kept noticing Han was looking at me all the time with this impish look in her eye, and I knew exactly what she was thinking, 'cos I was thinking the same thing—that we had this connection and *no one* else knew about it! I loved the fact we had this secret! It was so hot and so exciting! She kept catching my eye; she'd hold my gaze and smile this knowing smile, raising that damn sexy eyebrow of hers, knowing I was thinking the same thing as she was.

Then she started doing that thing of chewing her lip and smiling to herself, like she loved her secret. It got me so damned horny I stopped listening to what the others were saying. Suddenly, she hopped to her feet and said breezily, 'Hey, Clem, you said you wanted to show me the bonsais down in the gardens. Wanna go now?' and stood in front of me, holding out her hand. I grabbed her hand and hauled myself to my feet, and we managed to walk off down to the trees before anyone could think to follow us.

When we got down to the walled gardens, we collapsed on a bench and got a fit of the giggles. I said, 'Bonsais?? What made you say that?' She said, 'I dunno! It was the first thing that came into my head, silly. Got us away from them though, didn't it?' and she grinned at me. She said, 'I just wanted to be alone with you, you didn't mind, did you? Besides, I could see Charlie looking at you and I didn't like it so I thought I'd whisk you away from him before I thumped him one. You know I hate it when boys look at you.'

I'm always secretly pleased when I know Han's jealous, 'cos it makes me feel dead wanted and loved and I think it makes her dead sexy, but I didn't want her to know that so instead I just said, 'I wanted to be alone with you too. You were driving me mad up there,' and I tried my best to look seductive.

She knew what I meant 'cos then she grabbed my hand, said, 'C'mon, you,' and took me behind the Japanese gazebo where we had this fantastic kiss, enough to make my tummy flutter AND my legs go weak! She looked dead deep into my eyes and said, 'I love that we're so intense, don't you?' and I nodded at her, not really wanting to talk, just wanting to kiss her again.

She said, 'I feel such a connection to you, Clemmykins. It's like we're soul mates, like we were always meant to meet each other, don't you?' I just kinda went, 'Uh-huh,' because I've never been great with all that emotional shit. She leant against the gazebo and said, 'Sometimes I feel like we're so connected that I can hear your heart pounding in my head.' She took my hand and put it on her chest and said, 'Can you hear my heart pounding in your head, Clem?'

I have to say I couldn't actually hear her heart, but I could feel it beating fast against my hand, as well as the very pleasing feel of her bits cupped beneath my hand, but, not wanting to spoil the intensity of the moment, told her that I could hear her heart too. I would have been very happy to have left my hand resting on her chest all evening, but, worried about being seen, reluctantly removed it and instead carried on leaning against the side of the gazebo and secretly linked hands with her, both of us just lost in the feeling of being alone together.

We suddenly realised we'd been gone for over half an hour and so reluctantly went back and joined the others farther up the park, but it seemed no one had missed us, 'cos they were still talking about the same thing they were talking about when we left, and no one batted an eyelid when we came back and sat down.

Went home tonight feeling a very happy bunny indeed!

Thursday 19 July

We had a special assembly today so that Mrs. Russell could say her good-byes to us all. She stood up on the stage and blathered on about how much she'd enjoyed her years at St Bartholomew's, and that it had been her privilege and honour to know such lovely pupils over the last fifteen years, and how much she was going to miss all 'her girls'. Then Mrs. O'Keefe, the deputy head, came up on stage and presented her with a bouquet of roses and a gift voucher to spend down at some car accessory shop (Mrs. Russell likes cars and is often to be found at weekends, so it's said, under a car with a spanner in her hand tinkering with her big end), then got us all to stand and applaud her (Mrs. Russell, that is, not Mrs. O'Keefe—she's not going anywhere—worse luck!) Mrs. Russell started to get choked up which was embarrassing, but managed to gather herself in time to lead us all in a rousing rendition of 'All Things Bright and Beautiful', which she warbled through with her usual gusto. We also had a little presentation for some other teachers who were either leaving or retiring, including our Music teacher, Mr. King, who's moving to the seaside to start up a B&B with Tom Skirton, the Head Boy at King Edward's School.

Was supposed to be normal lessons this afternoon, but no one could be arsed, including Frauline Kretchzmar, our English teacher, who made a decision to send us all up to the library to do some 'private studying', so we all went down to McD's instead.

Friday 20 July

Last day of term! Thank the Lord. We didn't have to wear uniforms today, which was cool. I wore an oversized shirt with the cuffs all tattered and torn, jeans with the knees ripped, and my Airwalks, which I walk Barbara in. I'd also put gel in my hair to give it that just-got-out-of-bed look 'cos Mrs. Russell never, ever lets us have our hair anything other than 'conventional'.

Dad took one glance at me at the breakfast table and said, 'You're not going out of the house looking like THAT, are you??' with a look on his face that looked like he'd just seen aliens land in the garden or something. Mum said, 'Let her wear what she wants, Chris! She's not doing anyone any harm,' which I thought was a wicked thing for an old person to say.

I met up with Alice half way to school and she gave me a wolf-whistle and said, 'Good job it's old Russell's last day today! The old crone'll be in a good mood—just as well 'cos there's no way she'd let you get away with that otherwise!'

Han was looking wicked as usual and had gone completely over the top with her makeup, with loads of black eyeliner smudged right round her eyes and her hair all matted up and messy, 'cos she's trying to grow dreadlocks, but it still looked great! I could have taken her there and then, but a girl's got to show a little restraint!

Anyway, the day was a complete waste of time 'cos all we did was watch DVDs and hang around till around two o'clock when Russell graciously told us we could go home. What unparalleled joy! So that's it…six weeks of holiday and I can't wait!!

Saturday 21 July

Went round to Han's this morning. We sat in her room listening to music and I kept trying not to look at her bed, 'cos every time I did, I got a bit panicky about next weekend. I've lost loads of weight from all the worrying. I've hardly eaten a thing since last Saturday. I even waved away the offer of a Chinese takeaway last night, much to Mum and Dad's consternation, but just the thought of trying to force prawn balls down my throat made me queasy.

Sunday 22 July

Han has lent me loads of her CDs so I've been playing them all day today, despite it seemingly annoying Dad. I'm sure I heard him mutter something about 'bloody day of rest' on more than one occasion—but since he's not religious, he's got no right to want a day of rest!

I've always liked rock music, but the stuff Han's given me is wicked! I copied her Nirvana, Linkin Park, Slipknot, and My Chemical Romance and I've been playing them on my iPod on continuous reel so now my ears are buzzing and I can't hear anything properly!!

Monday 23 July

Had a major panic attack about this weekend at around two o'clock this afternoon. I suddenly realised I'm actually going to have to get naked in front of Han and I'm crapping myself about it. No one's ever seen me in the buff, except Mum—and that was about ten years ago. The second I hit puberty I started to wear sensible cardigans buttoned up to the neck, in case anyone should spot so much as one bump or curve.

Now I'm going to have to show all my bits and pieces to another person and hope she doesn't laugh. Made a mental note to have a bath before I go to Han's on Saturday and make sure I shave, scrub, pumice, polish, and buff so that I'm shining like a sixpence on a sweep's bum (as Great Aunt May says) by the time I'm stripped down to me undies!

Tuesday 24 July

Oh flip, what if Han's into kinky underwear? I hadn't thought of that! What if I get there and she's wearing naughty knickers and the like? Or if she's wearing lacy stuff? I'm not used to lace; my hands would shake so much I'd probably rip it, then she'd be pissed off with me!

What if she's into kinky shit too? What if I get there and she's got contraptions rigged up in her room 'cos she knows her parents aren't going to be around? She might be into bondage and all that, 'cos Goths—sorry, EMOs—are into pain and punishment and all that malarkey, aren't they? She might decide to tie me to the bed and leave me there. Or worse, put me in a leather collar and walk me round the house on all fours, like judges and politicians do at weekends. Leather chafes so; I can't wear leather shoes without Dad softening them up for me first—I can hardly ask him to soften up a studded leather sex collar and matching nipple clamps (or whatever it is they use), can I?

Wednesday 25 July

I'm panicking, aren't I? I've been in Han's bedroom loads of times and never seen any evidence of whips or thongs or anything remotely leathery. I'm being ridiculous. Calm down.

10:30 p.m,

Made a mental note to take a quick look under Han's bed before I strip down to just my socks, though.

Thursday 26 July

Chucked all my underwear out onto my bed this morning. Took one look at my knickers with no elastic and my bandage-grey bra and realised, in a panic, that I have NO nice underwear to wear this weekend so dashed down to the lingerie shop in town to buy some new stuff. I bought a six-pack of bikini briefs and a new sports bra. Bought them, then had a crisis of confidence outside the store, so went back to see if there was anything else more flattering, and dare I say it, sexy? Found a nice bra and knicker set for £20 and stood there dithering about the price until one of the sales ladies with a T-shirt saying, 'Can I Help You?' stretched right across her ample bosom sidled up to me and said I could go and have a bra fitting with one of their experts. She pointed towards the changing rooms where one of her colleagues was leaning on a counter chewing gum and looking bored. I'm sure I saw her crack her knuckles, so I smiled at the sales lady and told her I was okay. I put the bra-and-knicker set in my basket and hurried over to the till where I reluctantly handed over my £20.

It better be worth all this hassle, I'm telling you!

Friday 27 July

Packed my rucksack for going to Han's tomorrow. Figured I'd wear my new undies so just packed a spare pair of knickers and some jeans and a couple of tops. Packed my Winnie the Pooh pyjamas but thought Han might think me a baby for wearing Winnie the Pooh pyjamas so took them out again. Packed my toiletry bag and bath sponge. Packed Nurofen in case I get a headache. Packed my straighteners. Packed some plasters (thinking about the nipple clamps again).

Went back downstairs and sat with Mum and Dad trying to act

normal. Suddenly thought Han might think me a bit forward if she realises I don't have pyjamas so went back upstairs and packed the Winnie the Pooh ones again.

I never thought dating could be so bloody complicated!

Saturday 28 July

Going to Han's now. Am hiding you away, dear diary, in case you get found. Will tell all tomorrow! Am crapping myself!

Sunday 29 July

What a weekend! Was so nervous, but really no need 'cos everything was sweet and lovely and Han is just the best person in the whole world and I'm soooooooo in love with her!

Her parents had already left when I got there. Dan had gone off to some festival for the weekend already, and Joe was still there but he was soon picked up by his friend's mum, so me and Han had the place to ourselves. She seemed as nervous as me, 'cos we both had the same thoughts in our head. Anyway, we sat on the sofa and watched TV for a bit, kinda snuggled up to each other, she was stroking my hair and I was trying not to nod off on the sofa. Then we had this, like, mega kissing session and I felt dead horny and wished we could go upstairs but felt nervous at the thought of going upstairs. She broke away and looked long and hard at me and said, 'Shall we go to my room? Do you want to?' and I just nodded.

So we went upstairs and lay down on her bed and kissed a bit more. I tried to lean over the bed and look under it for anything dodgy but she kept pulling me back and then she started tugging at my T-shirt! She said, 'Take it off,' in a way that made me go all silly inside, so I took it off, but the static made my hair go fuzzy and stick up so I was trying desperately to flatten it down with one hand, while trying to kiss Han.

We were just getting to the nitty gritty when I realised my bladder was full to bursting (the nerves) and I needed to have a wee!!! I said to Han, ‘I’m really sorry about this but I need to go pee,’ and she laughed and said, ‘Really??’ which made me keep apologising so she laughed again and said, ‘Don’t be sorry, you silly sausage! I think it’s cute,’ which flummoxed me a bit.

I tell you, it’s never like that on the TV!

Anyway, it was great (the sex, not my wee). Han was as nervous as me, I think, but it was all so natural and wonderful that I wondered why I’d been worrying myself silly about how to do it and whether I’d make a tit of myself!

We lay there afterwards in each other’s arms and I honestly thought I’d never felt so happy in all my life. We realised we were really hungry, so Han ordered us takeaway pizza which we ate in bed and I felt really grown-up for the first time in my life.

We kinda did it (sex, not eat pizza) like, another five times after that until I was so tired I couldn’t muster up any more energy so we slept through till about eleven today (Sunday) when we realised we hadn’t actually been out of Han’s bedroom since about one o’clock the previous day, apart from to pee and collect pizzas at the door.

What a weekend! Am back home now but can’t take the smile off my face!

Monday 30 July

Met up with the gang in town this morning. Felt like everyone knew what me and Han had been up to at the weekend and found

I couldn't look anyone in the eye. It was like me and Han had this secret knowledge between us and we kept looking at each other and getting the giggles. Ems said at one point, 'You two look thick as thieves—what you been up to?' and Han made a very good job of brushing the question off. She'd be great as a politician!

Tuesday 31 July

Han's still trying to get her hair into dreadlocks so she hasn't washed it for three weeks now. It looks dead greasy and it's driving her nuts, but she said she read somewhere that hair only stays greasy for so long, then the hair's natural oils make it all sleek again. She asked me if it looked awful so I just told her not to go swimming in the sea 'cos she'd kill all the sea birds with her own personal oil slick, which I don't think amused her much!

Wednesday 1 August

HRBH told me she's taken up Buddhism. I'd laugh my socks off at this if it weren't for the fact she's still raw over all the business with Ade. Apparently she's still feeling anger towards him and it's messing with her mojo, so she needs something to channel her anger through and thinks Buddhism is the answer. I thought mojos were sweets, but I don't think they can be, 'cos I don't see how anger could affect sweets, unless of course her anger makes her clench her fists and she squashes them.

Instead I told her I thought Buddhism was a great idea, especially considering the fact she already has a belly like Buddha, but she didn't find that in the least bit funny. She told me that she meditates every day and it's helping her to rid herself of pent-up anger and negative thoughts against 'that snivelling little fuckwit who ran off with the fat tart from the cheese counter'. I noticed how screwed up and red her face was when she was saying this, and wondered if maybe she needed to concentrate on that meditation just a bit more.

Thursday 2 August

Went over to Han's this afternoon. Her dad had taken Joe to football, then her mum said she was going to the garden centre and invited us along. We declined, and managed to have a quick fumble in Han's room while she was out. Felt guilty about being so naughty.

Friday 3 August

It was Chairman Meow's birthday so Mum gave him a tin of tuna as a treat. We also sang Happy Birthday to him but he just gave us that withering look that cats have and stalked out of the room with his tail up like a lightning conductor. I also saw him sicking up his tuna in Dad's dahlias this afternoon. Decided not to tell Dad about it. I figure he'll find it soon enough next time he's weeding out there!

Saturday 4 August

Han's mum is working tonight so she was there all day, hence, no shagging. Instead, we sat up in Han's room and re-did my tattoo design. I decided against the hands clasped round the burning cross, bearing in mind Han's jibes about it, and I've plumped for my initials, CMA, in Chinese letters. I figured it would be less hassle than the burning cross, and not so much inking either! I made absolutely sure that what I'd copied from the Internet were actually my initials, and not some code for takeaway crispy noodles and wonton soup. We're going to go later this week and get it done.

Sunday 5 August

Han's mum and dad at work so went round for the day. Han was babysitting Joe so we couldn't be naughty. We were both wracked with horns so took Joe to the park to take our minds off it. Was still horny when I got there, but the sight of all the sunburnt, dowdy mothers trying to squeeze their fat arses into the kiddies' swings soon put paid to that.

Monday 6 August

Oh God, I'm turning into a sex maniac! It's, like, ALL I think about! I think about when I can do it, how I can do it, why I *should* do it!! I'm sure there are some pills I could take.

Tuesday 7 August

Looked up 'sex maniac' on Google but it directed me to a load of dodgy porn sites with offers of all manner of unsuitable things from characters with names such as Busty Brenda and Lusty Lucy.

I remembered something we'd done in History about how during the war (first or second, I can't remember) they used to put something called Bromide in the tea of soldiers who were horny. Went down to the health food shop in town and asked the spotty youth (you'd think she'd have marvellous skin working in a health store) behind the counter if they sold it. She looked perplexed and asked me what Bromide was for. I leant closer and said, 'Erm, for brewer's droop,' and nodded knowingly at her. She smiled and pointed to the yeast in aisle two.

I give up! Maybe I can buy some in France? They're weird like that over there.

Wednesday 8 August

Han's hair is driving her potty! I have to say, I wonder if it's worth it, but she insists it'll look great when it's all knotted and matted! She wears it all up a lot so doesn't look *too* bad, but when it's down it looks awful. I daren't say anything to her, though, 'cos she's already gone and bought some beads and leather strips to thread through the dreadlocks…

Thursday 9 August

Han's mum and dad took Joe into town to buy him some new trainers or something, so Han and me made the most of it and went up to her room. Felt guilty as hell for *doing it* while her parents were out in town doing good, normal things like buying trainers.

Han's mum rang her on her mobile to tell her they were having lunch in town so wouldn't be back till around two p.m. Managed to *do it* two more times before they got back—result!

Friday 10 August

Han and I went into town today to get my tattoo done. We found this place just off the High Street called 'Holey Smoke' which did tattoos and body piercings and stuff like that. I had my design with me and was feeling pretty confident until I clocked one look at the girl at the counter inside who was built like a brick shithouse and didn't look like she had a qualification in Metal Welding, let alone whatever it is they need in Body Art. I hissed to Han, 'I'm not going in THERE—have you seen the size of her? I'll look like a pin cushion by the time she's done with me.' Han looked suitably worried but said, 'She'll be the assistant, thassall. The person who'll do you'll be out the back probably.' I noticed a distinct wobble in her voice when she said it, though…

I thought about this for a while but then decided that she looked like she'd be more at home on the meat counter down the market and told Han I'd changed my mind. Han said I might as well have it done considering we were here anyway, and if I gritted my teeth I'd be okay, so I said to her, 'Why don't you get one done as well, then?' which made her visibly pale. I said, 'You're an EMO! You're supposed to enjoy pain. In fact, you're supposed to positively *encourage* anything that causes you pain and torture,' to which she replied 'So I'm an EMO! That DOESN'T mean I like pain and torture. It's not written in the rules, y'know.'

She got one of her looks on her face then, so I thought it best not to bother replying to that. Instead I decided there and then that I didn't want the girl in the tattoo shop anywhere near my fresh, young, unblemished teenage skin after all. Maybe when I'm older, say 21, I can get some tattoos done then? It won't matter 'cos I'll have loads of wrinkles by then anyway.

Saturday 11 August

Went into town to buy my euros for France today. I'm still really pissed off that our holidays don't coincide, but Han keeps telling me that we'll only be apart for a few weeks and we'll still have some time left at the end of the summer holidays together.

Sunday 12 August

Got a text from Han this morning saying she was going to wash her hair 'cos it was driving her potty. Rang her later and she told me it took her and her mum over an hour to wash it and disentangle it. She said it took a further 20 minutes to fish all the hairs out of the sink afterwards! Poor Han!

I can't say I'm sorry, though. It *was* getting a bit smelly, and her constantly scratching her head was beginning to make me itch too!

Monday 13 August

Going to France tomorrow! We're catching the early ferry across and have to leave at some ridiculous time in the morning, so Alice came and stayed the night. I managed to get over to Han's this afternoon for about an hour so I could say good-bye to her. She started crying! You have no idea how strange it is to see a Goth (EMO) cry; her eyeliner ran down her cheeks and made her look like Alice Cooper.

I said, 'You're a Goth—you're supposed to be black to the core!' and she said, 'Shut your face,' (which was charming) and then 'I'm an EMO as well, you know! We're emotional. We're allowed to blub, especially when we're not going to see our girlfriends for sodding ages,' and forced a half-smile. I was touched.

We exchanged rings so we can have something to remind ourselves of each other, so I have her well funky skull ring, while she's got my Bali ring that she gave me for my birthday. I promised her I'd look at the skull every night and think of her.

It's now 10 p.m. (I'm writing this up while Alice cleans her teeth) and I miss her dreadfully already (Han, not Alice). How on earth am I going to manage for the next few weeks?

Was a bit disappointed we didn't manage to *do it*, but perhaps it's for the best, bearing in mind I'll be going without it for bloody ages anyway!

Tuesday 14 August

In France.

Didn't get off to sleep till gone 1 a.m., 'cos Alice was chattering away half the flipping night. You'd have thought she would have taken the hint when I stopped replying to her but noooooo! She blabbed on and on about nothing in particular until her words got few and far between and I figured she'd dropped off at long bloody last.

Dad banged on the door at 4 a.m. to tell us to get up, so I've had three hours of sodding sleep and my eyes look like two piss-holes in the snow!

Very grumpy, very tired, so will write up more tomorrow.

Wednesday 15 August

Well, the campsite we're staying in is very nice! We're staying in this mobile home thing that's got everything we need in it. It's got a really nice wooden veranda type thing attached to it, which Dad said would be nice to eat our meals out on. Poor Mum! I think she was hoping to be taken out every night.

Me and Alice had an explore round the site; we went into the toilet block and I was pleased to see it wasn't just a hole in the ground (well, you read about such gross things). The only thing that's off-putting is that the shower blocks are unisex, so I'm very glad we have a shower in our mobile home 'cos I don't relish the idea of having to do my beauty regime (ha ha) pressed up next to some hairy man standing there tugging at his bits and pieces. I pity those poor people who are camping here.

Am dismayed to discover that texts to England cost 50p each (!!!!!) so have only been able to text Han five times today. I hope France sells top-up cards!

Thursday 16 August

Went to the site shop and bought Han a postcard this morning. Don't actually have anything to write on it yet, so will keep it safe until I do.

We went to the beach today 'cos it was, like, 100 degrees! The sea was bloody cold, though. I thought it would be the Mediterranean, but Dad says it's the Atlantic Ocean!! An ocean??!! I don't want to swim in an ocean! I want to swim in a nice, calm, warm SEA. Dipped a toe and thought I'd get cramp if I went in further, so came back to my towel, lay down, closed my eyes, and thought of Han.

Later when we were back at the campsite, Alice told me how much she was enjoying her holiday in France, which was nice, I suppose. She said something about how happy she was to be with me, which I thought was kinda sweet. I was busy flicking croissant crumbs off my T-shirt at the time so I just smiled back at her and nodded. I hope she didn't think me rude!

Bought a top-up card at the campsite shop. It cost me 30 sodding euros!

Friday 17 August

Me and Alice hired a couple of bikes today, which was a hoot! We cycled around the lanes by the campsite; I didn't know cyclists had to cycle on the right (I thought it only applied to cars) and couldn't understand why we kept getting honked at! We cycled for what seemed like miles and I got really outta breath, so we stopped off at a café at the side of the road. Alice ordered two Cokes while I sat there looking very English, smiling and nodding like a donkey at the man who was serving us. I was glad that Alice has been paying attention in our French lessons!

Wrote Han's card out and sent it off. Wrote really boring stuff on it, like 'weather hot, beach great' when all I wanted to write was, 'Miss you like crazy. Can't concentrate for thinking about you.' That and, 'Dying for a shag.'

Tonight we had a barbeque outside the mobile home. Dad took it upon himself to cook the food, and suddenly he's an expert at cooking! This is despite him barely ever stepping foot in the kitchen at home. Hand him a large fork and stand him in front of an open fire and suddenly he's Gordon Ramsay [/sarcasm/]. Alice looked like she was struggling with the burnt offerings that were plonked on her plate, but I thought once all the burnt bits had been picked off the beef burgers they tasted okay.

Dad asked me later if I enjoyed the barbecued pork! Oops!!

Saturday 18 August

We went to another beach today. We walked through these lovely pine forests to get to it, climbed up and over a sand dune, and saw this beautiful expanse of beach and sea laid out below us. Shame the waves were crashing down like in a force ten gale, but you can't have everything!

Boiling hot just sitting there, so me and Alice went for a long walk along the shore until Mum and Dad disappeared from view. We found a beach café and Alice ordered us two Cokes (I wanted a lemonade but we couldn't remember the French for 'lemonade,' so I had a Coke instead). I was texting Han and I think it was annoying Alice 'cos she kept asking me who I was texting so furiously (I think she was pissed off 'cos I was ignoring her). I told her (casually, like) that I was texting Han, and she said, 'Why're you texting her, like, ALL the time? You were texting her all morning, and yesterday all day as well.' She looked a bit grumpy. I shrugged and said I was just keeping in touch with friends. Then she said, 'You're not keeping in touch with Ems or Matty, 'cos they texted me and asked me if we were having a good time.' Sheesh! It's like having my bloody mother checking up on me sometimes, so I reluctantly put my phone down and decided to pay more attention to Alice. I didn't want her to have a strop.

When we got back to Mum and Dad they hadn't moved in the two hours we'd been gone. Mum had this angry red mark on her face and I thought she'd been stung by a jellyfish or something, but she told me she'd fallen asleep on the blowhole of her inflatable pillow, that was all.

Sunday 19 August

I'm going to tell Alice about Han, I've decided. I'm going to tell her just before we come home, so that if she freaks out on me, I don't have to put up with it for very long before we go home!

Tonight Dad let me and Alice have some wine with our tea. It went straight to my legs and Alice got all giggly and started finding the smallest things hugely funny. Dad was looking at her strangely; I can't see him letting us have it again!

Monday 20 August

Went to a market in the next town this morning, which was an education in itself! Never have I seen so many French people in one place—why do they have to shout at each other? Even when they're only standing a foot away from each other? Are all French people deaf?

Had a bit of an argument with Alice 'cos she was grumbling at me again for texting Han. I just wanted to tell Han how much I was missing her and it pissed me off that Alice seemed to be watching my every move, so I snapped at her and she didn't speak to me till after lunch. I texted Han and told her that Alice was peeing me off a bit; Han texted me back and said, 'My poor baby. I think it's time you came home to me,' and that made me miss her even more.

I really do want to tell Alice about Han now, but I'm worried what she'll say. I hate keeping this to myself and I resent the fact I have to sometimes. Han makes me so happy, so why don't I feel like I can share that happiness with someone? If I was seeing a boy, I'd be able to shout it from the rooftops, but because Han's a girl, I can't. It seems so unfair sometimes.

Tuesday 21 August

OMG, what a straaaaaaange day! So, me and Alice went for a walk down along the beach and ended up sitting up on one of the sand dunes. I was texting Han again and Alice made yet another comment about it, so I decided to bite the bullet and say something to her (Alice, not Han). I said I missed Han and that's why I was texting her so much. Alice said, 'You miss her that much? So much that you're happy to use up all your credit on her? You've done nothing but text her since we got here.' I grunted some sort of reply and she went on. 'Your phone's always beeping! You're either busy texting away, or reading replies—what on earth can you find to talk about all the time?'

I said, 'We just talk about stuff. Tell each other what we're doing, about the weather, stuff like that. Nothing much.' My heart was beating faster than it normally does. She said, 'You're spending, like, 50p a text talking about the weather? You're mad!' and she laughed. I said, 'We talk about other stuff too. How we're feeling and things.' She said, 'How you're feeling?' I said, 'Yeah, like how much we miss each other and can't wait to see each other again.' She raised her eyebrows and said, 'Well, I don't miss ANYONE from home, that's for sure!' Then as an afterthought, 'Hmm, maybe Mum and Dad...but certainly no one from school!' and she snorted.

I said, 'No, but I REALLY miss her, and she REALLY misses me,' and looked long and hard at her, trying to make her understand. It was a bit like pulling teeth really! She didn't reply so I said, 'Alice, I gotta tell you something but I don't know what you're going to say.' She smiled and said, 'Try me,' so I said, 'Well, it's kinda, it's like, um, it's like me and Han, we're um...' and she said, 'You're what?' so I said, 'Ah fuck it, we're going out with each other,' and then looked intently down at my scuffed-up trainers. She said, 'What, like boyfriend and girlfriend?' and I laughed and said, 'Well, no—like girlfriend and girlfriend,' and, OMFG, she started crying! I asked, 'Uhhh Alice, you okay?' and she looked away. I thought I'd get either disgust or excitement, but I never expected tears! Alice snuffled and wiped her nose on the back of her hand and said, 'I wanted it to be me you went out with.' I said, 'Eh?' and picked at my shoelaces. She said, 'I really like you, Clem. Been thinking about you lots and, well, I really like you.' I didn't know what to say, so just said, 'Oh,' so Alice got up and started walking back to our mobile home. I got up and followed her and walked back with her in silence.

Sweet Jesus, Alice fancies me! Has the whole world gone mad?

What am I going to say to her? The trouble is, I've only ever seen Alice as a friend—anything else would be just toooooo weird!! Even if I wasn't so wrapped up in Han, I wouldn't see Alice in *that way.* I mean, she's okay looking and all, but she's...well, she's *Alice!*

What am I going to do?? [/stressed/].

Wednesday 22 August

Back home! And I've never been so glad in all my life to go home! Me and Alice barely said another word to each other for the rest of yesterday, or today, mainly 'cos I didn't know what the hell to say to her. In hindsight, I should have talked to her about it but instead I just kept shtum. Mum and Dad thought we'd had a tiff, 'cos I heard Mum say something to Dad about 'teenage angst'. If only they knew!

We got the night ferry over last night, dropped Alice off at her house around midday and came on home. Instead of ringing Han first, which is what I wanted to do, I thought I ought to text Alice so I wrote, 'We need to talk.' I sat on my bed waiting for her to reply but she didn't, so I rang Han and told her I was home. After she'd finished squealing with delight, she asked if she could come over, so she came over and had Chinese takeaway with us.

I was pleased at the admiring looks Han gave me when she saw me, which must have meant she approved of my tan. When we were up in my room after tea, she ran her hands over my brown, brown legs and told me I was looking 'as fit as fuck', which made me go a bit giggly, but pleased me greatly. She whispered in my ear, 'I don't know how I kept my hands off you downstairs, Clemmykins,' and I felt my tummy lurch.

Then she said, 'You look so hot, I wouldn't be surprised if you didn't have half the male population of France after you. You didn't, um, you didn't *do* anything with anyone when you were away, did you? You know I'd die if you ever cheated on me, don't you?' She was trying to sound bright, but it's difficult not to sense threatening undertones when a Goth—sorry, EMO—is standing in front of you dressed head to foot in black, with chains and studs and smudged lipstick talking about death and stuff, so I just stepped over to her, held her tightly in my arms, and told her I spent the whole two weeks thinking about her, which is true. (If you don't count the sodding awful 48 hours when Alice randomly declared her lust for me.)

Anyway, as if on cue, we were busy having just the best kiss ever

(I made sure my door was locked) when Alice texted me back, just saying 'Sorry 'bout yesterday. Nothing to talk about. A xxx.' When Han asked who'd texted, I told her no one, then immediately felt like a rat.

Why is my life so fucking complicated??

Thursday 23 August

Figured I'd make the most of my last day with Han for over a week rather than trying to sort this shit out with Alice, so didn't contact Alice all day. Instead, I went over to Han's where her hallway looked like the baggage reclaim at Heathrow Airport. I swear to God, four of us going to France for two weeks had a third of the luggage the Harrison family had for ten bloody days in Portugal!

Han's mum was having a panic, 'cos she suddenly realised she hadn't packed a first aid kit and was rifling through the bathroom talking about bandages in a loud voice until I heard Han's dad shout from the hallway 'For Christ's sake, Jeanette, we're going to Portugal, not white-water rafting up the sodding Zambezi. Just throw a roll of Elastoplasts in the wash bag and calm down, will you?'

For a man who teaches religion for a living, he's not very tolerant!!!

Me and Han took Toffee for a walk down by the railway and had a quick kiss behind a tree which felt very naughty, but VERY exciting. We said our good-byes, and I felt awful knowing I wouldn't see her again for a whole ten days, but she said, 'Don't be upset, baby boo…think of how much fun we can have when I get back. And if you're really good while I'm away, I'll show you my all-over tan,' and she kissed my forehead, which made me go all silly inside. When we got back to hers, she showed me her bikini (but where's she gonna hang her chains??) that she'd bought. I got a small pang of jealousy at the thought of Portuguese men ogling her in it, but I didn't say anything. Even if Han's prone to the odd bout of jealousy, I sure as hell don't want her thinking I'm one of those nutty bunny boilers like you see on *Jerry Springer*.

Just got home now and am missing her like crazy! On top of all this, I still gotta sort out all this shit with Alice [/joy/]. I bet even Romeo and Juliet never had hassles like this.

Friday 24 August

Took a deep breath and rang Alice's house today. I figured if I rang her mobile then she wouldn't answer it, but she'd have to speak to me on the landline. I told her I wanted to come over and she said, 'If you want,' so I went over just before lunch.

She looked awful! She looked like she'd been crying, and I felt an absolute rat for not trying harder to speak to her before now. I didn't know what to say, but the embarrassing silence on the doorstep was solved by Alice's mum calling from the kitchen, asking me if I wanted some coffee and cake. Alice snapped at her that we were going upstairs. When we got into Alice's room, I worried for a nanosecond that she might try and kiss me but then told myself I was being ridiculous.

She sat on her bed and I said, 'I'm sorry I didn't ring or text you. I didn't know what to say to you,' and she shrugged and said, 'S'ok.' Then she said, 'I'm sorry I ever told you how I felt—it was stupid of me,' and I didn't know what to say, so I didn't say anything. She said, 'I'm sorry I ruined your holiday and all,' so I said, 'Don't be daft. You didn't ruin anything.' Too many sorrys.

I asked, 'How long?' and she asked, 'How long what?' so I added,

'How long have you felt like this?' and she shrugged and mumbled something I didn't catch. Then she said, 'A while,' and all I could do was nod, 'cos I didn't know what to say. She said, 'I've felt like I wanted you to be more than just a friend for a while, but when school ended for summer, I didn't see you for ages and the feelings started to go away, but then being with you, on our own, in France for all that time made the feelings come back again. Now I'm as confused as hell.' She bit her lip.

I didn't want her to start crying again, so I tried to explain about how I liked her, but not like that, and that I had a girlfriend already, and that having another one would be waaaay confusing, and she giggled and said she didn't want to be a scarlet woman. I was mightily relieved that she was smiling again, and it made me relax. I said I thought she was great, and that she was my best friend in all the world, always had been, always would be, but that I just didn't fancy her. It felt weird talking to Alice about girlfriends and fancying girls—all these thoughts I'd kept to myself for ages—and here I was talking to Alice about them. Too strange!

She asked me how long me and Han had been going out with each other so I told her about how I'd liked Han for ages and how I'd been dead confused about my feelings, just like Alice was confused now. I told her about the day Han asked me out, down by the reservoir, and how happy I was. Alice looked a bit sad, but just said, 'Han seems lovely. You'll make a nice couple,' which I thought was sweet of her.

I decided not to tell Alice about J, 'cos it all seems so insignificant now. That, plus the fact I don't want it getting back to J that I used to fancy her like rotten (and cry myself to sleep over her some nights). I asked Alice not to tell the others about me and Han, so I hope she doesn't.

Anyway, I was glad that we'd sort of cleared the air, and I went home feeling happier than when I'd left it. I walked home looking at Han's skull ring, which I kept for while she's in Portugal, and got an aching feeling inside, wishing she was with me.

Saturday 25 August

A note! From Alice! It was pushed through our letterbox last night and it said:

> *Clem*
>
> *I found it way too difficult to say half the stuff I wanted to say yesterday so thought I'd be better writing them down instead. I'm sorry I fucked up what we had left of our holiday. I just hope that u enjoyed the time that we had before Friday as much as I did.*
>
> *I'm also sorry I told u what I told u. I think it would of been better just to keep stuff to myself and hope that it went away, but when u told me about u and Hannah it just hit me like a thunderbolt. I suppose I kinda hoped that one day u'd see me the same way as I see u so when u told me u were going out with Hannah it ruined any hopes I might have had.*
>
> *I'm really confused at the moment, I don't even know if the feelings I have for u r more than just the normal feelings friends have between each other, or whether they're something more. All I know is that I miss u when ur not around, I think about u all the time, and right now I'm as jealous as hell of Hannah. Sounds like I'm pretty confused doesn't it?*
>
> *I think it's best I don't see u for the rest of the summer, so I can figure out what's going on in my head. I can't figure*

out what's what when ur around, but that's not ur fault, it's mine.

See you soon
Alice
xxx

I have to say, I agree with her about not seeing each other for a while.

Sunday 26 August

Our new sofa was delivered today! The colour is called 'Café Society', which could mean anything, really. It's kinda coffee coloured and it's very squishy and comfortable. The delivery drivers plonked it in the lounge and Mum immediately put a dark-brown throw on it! All those months of agonising over the colour and she throws a blanket on it! I saw Dad look at her in exasperation but he knew better than to question her.

Monday 27 August

Thought my tan was fading a bit so stayed out in the garden all day today, topping it up. Lay on the sun bed thinking about Han in Portugal and pictured her wearing her bikini, then got all horny, so went inside and helped Mum chop up some lettuces for tea to take my mind off it.

Tuesday 28 August

Got a postcard from Han today! She had the sense to put it in an envelope so our nosy postman wouldn't read it. It said:

My lovely,

Weather flipping hot! Spending most days down at the beach, swimming and lying in the sun thinking of you. Mum keeps telling me not to wear black 'cos it attracts the heat but I'd rather boil than wear white. It's against my beliefs.

Miss you like crazy and can't wait to see you again. Love you loads. Han xxx

Now I'm worried in case she overheats in all her Goth gear. I hope she didn't take her *fuck-off* biker boots with her as well.

She loves me! How cool is that?!!

Wednesday 29 August

Maybe she just said she loved me for something to write at the end of her postcard? People say it to each other all the time, don't they? Without really meaning it? Probably best not to go declaring my love for her in case she runs a mile!

Thursday 30 August

The fair is in town! Well, it's been here a week but today was the first day I had a chance to get over there and see it for myself! I went over with Matty, Ems, and Caroline and we had a blast!

We went on the Dodgems, Freak Out, Roller Ghosta, Afterburner, and then the Wall of Death. I was okay until I looked down and saw the spotty youth with the shaved head and no teeth who was in charge of the on/off button, and who looked like he shouldn't be in charge of a pair of scissors, let alone a 30-foot ride with 20 people on it. Felt a bit sick from being thrown around on all the rides, but had a blob of candyfloss and the sugar seemed to perk me up again.

Ems asked if me and Alice had a good time in France, then asked me if I'd seen her since I'd been back, 'cos she'd seen her on Sunday and she'd seemed a bit down. I got a bit flustered and said that I hadn't seen her, and that she'd probably been down 'cos we're going back to school soon. Then I felt bad 'cos I knew Alice was feeling down and it's all because of me. Thought about ringing her, but couldn't bring myself to do it, then felt even worse!

Friday 31 August

Got dragged into town by Mum today who remembered in a panic that I'm back at school on Monday. How could she forget this? She's a teacher, for God's sake!

She's got it into her head that the clothes I wore perfectly well all last term aren't good enough for this term, so hauled me off to the shops to buy new shirts and jumpers. Managed to persuade her to buy me some more shoes AND I managed to make her buy me Doc Martens shoes on the basis that the soles are thicker and will therefore last longer. Ha ha ha!

They rub like buggery, mind, but it'll be worth it in the long run!

Han's home tomorrow!

Saturday 1 September

Woke up at nine to a text, which read: 'I'm back in Blighty! Got up with the sparrow's fart 'cos flight was at 5:30 a.m. Just landed at Heathrow. Home sooooooon xxx'.

How marvellous! I wonder if she'll be too tired for sex?

11 p.m.: Just got back from Han's house. Didn't get a chance to see her all-over tan 'cos her mum and dad were hanging round the house all day. Han brought me back this wicked wristband that's kinda like tapestry material and has lots of Mediterranean-type designs on it. Am still pretty tanned from France so it looks well cool on my wrist!

Sunday 2 September

Realised with a jolt that I've made no effort to contact Alice since she pushed her note through our door over a week ago. She did say she thought it best we didn't contact each other, so I suppose I'm doing the right thing, but I still feel guilty not texting, e-mailing, or calling her.

Mum and Dad went out for the day to go walk round some boring, dusty old stately home somewhere, HRBH went to town to meet up with some friends, so I seized the moment and ushered Han over for what could be our last chance to *do it* before school starts!

While we were *doing it*, Han told me she loved me but I kinda wondered if that was just the sex talking and she didn't really mean it, so I didn't reply. Maybe I should have, but I didn't want to scare her off so I just stayed shtum and concentrated on what I was doing.

Monday 3 September

Teacher training today so at least I had one more day of lie-ins! Heard Mum grumbling out on the landing about having to go 'back to the workhouse', but her persistent grizzling was soon muffled when I turned over and pulled the duvet up over my head…

Tuesday 4 September

School! Ugh! Whoever invented school was a sadist.

It was really good to see everyone again, though. I'd barely seen anyone except Han and Alice, 'cos we'd all been busy, away, or working. I was dead nervous about seeing Alice after what had happened in France, and I was fretting about how she would react to seeing Han, but I needn't have worried 'cos I hardly saw her all day. Don't know if that was something planned by Alice 'cos she just didn't want to see me, or whether it was because, despite it being our first day back, the school took it upon itself to bombard us with orders and useless bloody information about the year ahead. Sheesh!

To top a pretty crap day all round, our new form tutor Mr. Harman has been banging on all day about how important this year's going to be, 'cos it's our GCSE year, and how we have to work hard and concentrate and hand all our work in on time and blah, blah, blah. By the end of the day, my head was thumping, and I've only been back a day. How am I gonna last until June??

Wednesday 5 September

We got our new timetable today. I was shocked and dismayed to see I have double Maths first thing on Mondays this year. Who decides these things? The Gestapo?

We had a whole school assembly this morning so the new Head could address us all. Her name's Mrs. Unwin and she looks like Judge Judy, but I'm not holding that against her. She seems okay actually; she was wearing an argyle cardigan and a string of pearls and looked dead nervous but I think she'll fit in well. I think she must have a sweet tooth, though, because every time you pass her, there's a terrible whiff of Mint Imperials.

Nabbed Alice during afternoon break and asked her if she was okay. She looked at me like she didn't want me to talk to her but I didn't care. I'm fed up with her avoiding me and making me feel like I've done something wrong when I haven't. She wouldn't look at me and kept biting her bottom lip but she did at least tell me that she was all right, and that she was 'working on some personal issues', whatever the fuck that means. She said, 'I kinda need to stay away from you for a bit, Clem, 'cos when I'm around you I can't think properly. I'm hoping that if I don't see you or talk to you, then I'll be able to forget you and move on. You can understand that, surely?'

I nodded meekly but still tried to have a conversation with her about school, just so I could talk to her, but she just told me she was busy and walked off down the corridor, leaving me standing there feeling like a right prat.

I'm not sure if I feel better for having spoken to her or not. On reflection, I think I feel worse!

Thursday 6 September

We've got some student teacher person teaching us French until Christmas. He's called Henri and he's proper, genuine French with an accent and everything! He's very excitable and prone to talking louder than what I consider acceptable. He's also got shocking halitosis, so we all try and avoid doing anything that requires him to stand any closer than a foot away from us.

Friday 7 September

Was thinking about my all-too-brief conversation with Alice on Wednesday, and now I'm wondering if I should try and talk to her again or do as she asked and just leave her alone. I want to talk to Han about it but the realist in me tells me it ain't such a good idea, bearing in mind what a hothead Han can be. If she gets so much as a whiff of someone else fancying me, she's just as likely to rip their head off, and as much as I secretly like the idea of someone being jealous over me, my conscience won't let me allow Han loose on Alice. Besides, Mrs. Unwin would have us drawn and quartered in the school yard if even so much as a drop of blood got spilt in her shiny corridors!

Saturday 8 September

Mum and Dad had their friend Celina over for dinner tonight. I can't stand Celina. Her biggest claim to fame is that she once hiked across the Andes wearing nothing but a bikini to highlight the plight of cashmere farmers in Peru or something, and she never fails to manage to drop it into the conversation. Big, fat, hairy deal! I could slip a leotard on and tap dance through the Grand Canyon in my flip-flops if I wanted to, but I've got far better things to do with my time.

Couldn't face listening to her telling Mum about how the local press were amazed she was 47, and how everyone in Primrose Avenue bought a paper the week she was in it, even the ones who normally hated the local rag and only considered the national papers worth spending their money on. So I invited myself over to Han's for tea. We went down to the chip shop 'cos her mum was at her tae kwon do class until seven. That's the second bad meal I've had in as many days (I had baked beans for tea last night), so have vowed to eat just greens until next weekend!

Sunday 9 September

Tried to find something green in the fridge but the only green thing I could find was a piece of Gorgonzola with mould on. Was buggered if I was going to eat that so had fish and chips, apple crumble and ice cream for lunch, and baked beans on toast and three Oreos for tea.

Well, you can't say I didn't try!

Monday 10 September

A new girl has started today and *I* have to sit next to her in English 'cos my name's the nearest to hers on the register. Her name's Susan Divine. If there was a prize for the most inappropriate surname, it would go to her 'cos she's anything *but* divine! She's about six foot tall in her socks and nearly as wide, and she looks like she's been chasing parked cars. Even Mr. Pritchard looked scared of her.

Caroline found out at lunchtime that she used to go to All Saints School but was expelled for 'misdemeanours'. I'm not sure what classifies as 'misdemeanours' but you can bet your life it had something to do with violence. Great! Not only does she *look* like a psycho, *she is one!!*

Tuesday 11 September

Went up to the library with Han during our so-called private study time with the intention of doing some research for our coursework, but ended up holding hands at the back of the linguistics section instead.

Refused to feel guilty for not doing any studying. I'm in love, and that feels way too brilliant to be wasting precious time on bloody reading!

Wednesday 12 September

Han says it's really hard to get booted out of school these days, so she reckons this Susan Divine girl must be as hard as nails. This isn't really what I want to hear, bearing in mind she sits within touching distance of me in class. I made a mental note to steer clear of her, and to avoid eye contact with her at all times, in case I antagonise her and get stabbed with a pen or something.

Han caught up with me in the corridor this afternoon and told me how much she loved being up in the library with me yesterday. She said, 'It was dead clandestine, don't you think? I liked that, made me feel real hot.'

I wasn't sure what 'clandestine' meant, so I just nodded and linked my fingers in hers when no one was looking. Made a note to make an effort to see what clandestine means later, to kind of educate myself, so that it doesn't feel like our secret liaison at the library was all for nothing.

Thursday 13 September

Really hot day again, so me and Han ate lunch outside on our own. We found a quiet corner over by the tennis courts and if it wasn't for the fact we were at school, we could just as well have been on a date! There was no one else near us, and Han leant over to me and told me she loved me!! How cool is that? I mean, she's said it in passing, like in texts, and when we're *doing it* and things, but never actually face-to-face with me. She said, 'I love you, Clemmykins—you do know that, don't you? You make my life complete,' and my legs went funny, even though I was sitting down. I didn't really know what to say so I just kinda smiled and grunted something back at her and she looked down and started to tug at the grass. She asked, 'Do you love me?' which gobsmacked me! Of course I love her! I adore her! Why would she think otherwise? So I told her that—that I adored her and that she was the best thing that ever happened to me, and she seemed to cheer up a bit. She said, 'I've told you, like, three or four times that I love you, but you never say it back. Just makes a girl wonder.' So I told her that I'd been scared to tell her in case she ran a mile from me, and she laughed and said, 'Quite the opposite, you silly sausage.' I felt a bit daft.

Women! I think this gay dating lark could be more complicated than I imagined!

Friday 14 September

Another really hot day. Sat outside the Art block at lunchtime and saw that Susan Divine girl sunbathing over by the toilets. It wasn't a pretty sight. Caroline leaned over to me and whispered in my ear, 'I didn't know they did teenagers in that size,' and I got a fit of the giggles. She looked like she was on a slow cook in the sunshine; every time she moved, I half expected to get a whiff of roasting pork crackling…

Saturday 15 September

Han rang me up first thing this morning and asked me if I wanted to go 'scrumping' (???!) I thought scrumping was a sort of dance or something, so I was a bit disappointed when she told me it's taking apples from someone's garden but it's not classed as stealing. Not sure how that works, but never mind.

Han has this old lady next door who lets Han pick apples from her tree. Han says it's ever so handy having an old lady living next door, 'cos they can take her down to the DIY store with them and buy hammer drills and shelves and CD racks and the like with her 10 percent off pensioners' card (that is, 10 percent off purchases, not 10 percent off pensioners). Anyway, in return for using her discount card, this old lady asks Han to go round every autumn and collect apples from her tree 'cos she can't do it. So Han was exaggerating when she said it was scrumping, 'cos it's nothing more exciting than doing an old dear a favour, really. I didn't think EMOs did that sort of thing!

We took Joe with us 'cos we could hang him by his arms from the branches, pull on his legs, and make all the apples fall down. Result! We managed to pick over 20 lbs. of apples in the end, so we shared them out amongst ourselves, but when I took my 8 lbs. home and triumphantly presented them to Mum, all I got was a sour look from her and a grumpy 'Do I look like I've got time to peel all those?' for my efforts. This is typical! The government's always telling us to eat more fruit, and all I get is grief for trying improve my family's dietary habits.

Next time I'll just throw the market's finest apple pies at her and hope she feels a stab of guilt when I'm struck down with rickets by the time I'm 21.

Sunday 16 September

Had an emergency text off Matty telling me that Ben had dumped her. She wrote, 'You understood him' (did I??) and 'Maybe you can tell me why he broke my heart.' Was tempted to text back and say, 'You're well off out of it, love, I thought he was a prat,' but instead I sent her my sympathies and agreed to meet her in town so she could cry over me.

When I met her she looked like she'd already been crying. She told me he'd finished with her 'cos he thought he was too young to be tied down to one person, and that he wanted to 'play the field' a bit. She kept banging on about what a fabulous kisser he was (must have missed that one) and what an even more fabulous shag he was (*definitely* missed that one—thank God!). Then she said, 'You must know what I'm going through 'cos he broke your heart too, didn't he?' I didn't have the guts to tell her that the only person capable of breaking my heart was Han, and that the memory of kissing Ben was so bloody awful that it still makes me shudder just to think of it. Instead I put on my caring face, nodded in all the right places, and thanked God for my Hannah!

I think she felt a little bit better by the time she left me, 'cos she'd replaced tear-soaked eyes with a determined stare, and had started talking about binning everything 'that measly little bastard' had ever given her. I assumed she meant Ben. Hell hath no fury and all that…

Monday 17 September

Caroline told me today that she'd had something called a Brazilian wax done at the weekend. I had no idea what this was, so asked Han at lunchtime. Apparently it's when you have all your *lady hair* waxed off, except for a neat little vertical line, rather like a goatee beard. I'm not surprised I didn't know this; I was fourteen before I found out what a scrotum was…

Brazilians sound like too much hard work to me! I mean, Caroline had to go to a beauty parlour place to get it done! Can you imagine the shame? I go to the hairdressers to have a trim and feel my scalp reddening with the hairdresser's every touch. No, it would be far easier, less embarrassing and, most importantly, far cheaper, just to shave everything off with your Venus and draw a neat line with a Berol marker. Granted, it wouldn't be permanent, but it would save a few pennies. Maybe I should approach some entrepreneurs with the idea?

Tuesday 18 September

Had a dream last night about Brazilians and Susan Divine. It wasn't pretty! She handed me a pair of garden shears and told me she wanted some *Lady Topiary* then hopped up on a snooker table and started knitting scarves. She wasn't wearing anything either. It was one of those dreams that stays with you all day; every time you shut your eyes, you get images of it, like it's burned into the back of your eyelids or something. I couldn't look at her during History today, and I shall *never* think of hedge-trimming in the same way ever again!!

Wednesday 19 September

Am trying to really knuckle down in school at the moment. It's less than nine months until our exams start and they're really pushing us in classes. Tonight I had three lots of homework to do, plus stuff for my English coursework, AND we're having a mock test in Spanish next week so I gotta study for that. It's not fair. I bet even Einstein wasn't pushed as much at school as we are!

Thursday 20 September

Susan Divine asked to borrow my ruler today. After getting over the initial fear that she was going to try and garrotte me with it or something, I tried to drum up a conversation with her. I noticed she had the name 'Benji' tattooed on the fingers of her left hand, each letter on a finger and her thumb, so I asked her if Benji was her boyfriend. She glared at me and said, 'No. He's my dog. He died,' so I asked her what he died of and she glared at me again and said, 'electrocuted'.

I told Han, Matty, Caroline, and Ems about it at lunchtime and we nearly coughed up a lung laughing. Ems said she didn't know what was funnier—that she had her dog's name tattooed on her fingers, or that Benji'd gotten electrocuted. Han said it was just as well it had a short name like Benji so it could fit on her fingers, and not a long name 'cos she'd have to have it tattooed somewhere bigger. I said she could have it tattooed round her belly 'cos that's sure as hell big enough, and everyone fell about laughing again.

I don't think I'll bother having my dog's name tattooed on me. I think if I walked around with the name Barbara on me it would cause a few raised eyebrows!

Friday 21 September

Thank God it's Friday! I'm knackered! We're only two weeks into term and I'm fed up with it all already. At this rate, I'll be booking myself into some health spa by Christmas and demanding that comely maidens feed me grapes by the pool. Instead of that, I had to content myself with sitting in my bedroom till 9:30 tonight doing History coursework and answering texts from Ems asking me if Hitler was Austrian or German, and was his moustache real or had someone drawn it on in the book she was reading? If she doesn't know something as important as this by now, how the hell is she ever going to pass her exams?

Saturday 22 September

Had a brilliant day with Han today. Weather was great, so we took a picnic and headed off to the woods at the back of the house and hid ourselves away deep in the copse so we could have some privacy. The sun was shining down through the trees and we spread a rug down and lay out on it and I felt so darned contented, I think I could have cried.

Han was stroking my hair and telling me how much she loved me, and I felt so wanted and protected by her. I love her confidence and the security she gives me, and I love the fact she loves me and I love her. It feels so real, so grown-up! Han's like the final piece of the jigsaw. I feel happy. Free, like a weight has been lifted off my shoulders 'cos I now know exactly who I am. It's like all that worry over J, over Ben and, I suppose, over Alice has all been for nothing 'cos at last I'm deeply, madly, in love with someone who loves me just as deeply and madly back!!

Went to bed feeling VERY loved up!

Sunday 23 September

Went bowling at the Multi-Plex with Han, Ems, Ryan, Marcie, Charlie, and Caroline this afternoon. Alice came too but did her best to ignore me all afternoon, I noticed. I can't say I cared too much, 'cos I was too busy looking at Han, who has recently rediscovered her EMO roots and so came dressed looking like she was the living dead, decked out from head to foot in black, with a studded choke chain round her neck and matching wristbands, joined together by a long chain. Charlie looked dead scared of her, like she was going to bite his head off or torture him slowly or something, the wimp! I think maybe Goth gear isn't the best thing to go bowling in, though, 'cos I noticed Han getting narked 'cos her accessories were getting in her way. She finally conceded defeat and removed her ankle-length black leather coat, oversized jumper, and the wrist chains, which she said were interfering with her swing.

Han's like, still tanned from Portugal and she was wearing this dead tight T-shirt which made her look sexy as hell. I noticed Ryan giving her admiring looks (all this while Ems' eyes bored into his back like some kind of laser beam) and I felt this flood of smug satisfaction that she was mine and not his!

Came back from bowling early 'cos had, like, three hours' worth of homework to get done for next week. It's so unfair to work us like this; if school kids had a union I'd be a fully paid-up member, I'm telling you!

Monday 24 September

Henri asked us in French today whether any of us had been to France during the summer. Bethany Jones meekly put her hand up and Henri flung his arms around in that tiresomely exaggerated Gallic manner of his and shouted, 'Merveilleux, merveilleux' at the top of his voice. He asked her where in France she'd gone and she said, 'Calais, for a day.' Henri seemed to deflate in front of our very eyes, poor man. So I put my hand up and told him I'd been to Brittany for two weeks, to which Henri replied, 'en français,' to which I replied, 'Oui, en France.' Fancy a Frenchman not knowing that Brittany is in France! I bet he comes from Paris.

Tuesday 25 September

Han asked me if I wanted to go over to her house after school tonight. She said we hadn't had much 'quality time together alone' lately. Which meant she was probably horny and wanted to have a session in her room before her parents got home from work.

I sent Mum a text and asked her if I could go to Han's and she just sent one back saying, 'No', so I had to make up some story to Han about how Mum wanted me to help her with something tonight.

I don't want Han thinking my mother is some trussed-up fascist. I have standards.

Wednesday 26 September

Had a mock listening test in Spanish today. It was okay. It helped that the narrator spoke in a really slow voice, and in a really obvious English accent, so I was able to ascertain that:

- Yes, the weather *will* be nice tomorrow. We will go to the beach.
- Ah, thank you! The train will leave in ten minutes from platform one.
- Pablo wanted an orange juice, please.
- Maria-Theresa's father is a teacher of Mathematics, and
- Rafael lives in Madrid with his mother, father, sister, and a dog called José (at least that's what it sounded like—although José doesn't sound much of a fun name for a dog. I wonder what the Spanish for Barbara is?)

Thursday 27 September

Went into town after school tonight to buy a present for Han's birthday. There's this clothes shop that she likes to go to called Goths and Cloths, so I went there in the hope of finding something suitably black and scary. The guy behind the counter looked at me suspiciously 'cos I was still wearing my school uniform, but I would have thought he was well used to seeing people in school uniforms (even the 30-somethings). I saw a T-shirt that said, 'Dip Me in Chocolate and Throw Me to the Lesbians', which made me giggle. I was sorely tempted to buy it, but then thought it wasn't really the sort of thing I could wear to do the weekly supermarket shop with Mum!

Anyway, for Han, I plumped for a black bandana, a new pair of black sweatbands with a skull and crossbones on it 'cos I know that her brother Joe nicked her other ones and she hasn't had the heart to take them back off him. I also got her a leather necklace with big black, green, and white beads on it. Had a crisis on the way back down through town that my presents were crap, so went into the Virgin Megastore and got her a Green Day CD with my last tenner.

Spent a flipping fortune on her, but I figure she's worth it.

When I got home, Mum was in the kitchen and asked me what I'd bought her. When I showed her all the Goth gear that I'd bought, she just sighed and said, 'Y'know, Han's such a *pretty* girl. Why does she live in black all the time? A nice bright jumper would show off those lovely eyes of hers.' I sighed impatiently and said, 'Mum, she's a *Goth.* Goths don't do colours! Don't you know *anything*?'

She clearly doesn't [/exasperated/].

Friday 28 September

Han's seventeenth birthday! How I would have loved to have woken up next to her on her birthday, but I had to content myself with sending her a 'Nappy Birfday' text first thing. Went over to her house before school to give her her presents. When I got there, she was beaming with excitement, 'cos her mum's told her she can get her eyebrow pierced! She's soooo lucky! Mum and Dad would, like, *never* agree to me ever doing anything like that! The only concession is that Han's mum said she's got to get it done during half-term so it can have a chance to heal, 'cos she's not allowed to wear it in school. Chance would be a fine thing! Old Mother Unwin would have a fit if she saw it anyway!

Anyway, I gave her the presents and she seemed suitably pleased. She wore her sweatband but made sure she hid it up her sleeve so she wouldn't be told to take it off by the KGB (Unwin and her henchmen). We bought Han a birthday cake at lunchtime and sang Happy Birthday to her, and she got a bit flustered, which was well cute!

She's going out for a meal with her mum, dad, and brothers tonight, but I've promised her a slap-up meal at Burger King tomorrow night.

Saturday 29 September

Went over and picked up Han from her house at around 6 tonight. Her mum was in the lounge doing her yoga (I heard straining sounds behind the door so I assume that's what she was doing), so me and Han went to her room for a bit before going out. Her parents gave her a wicked iPod for her birthday, as well as the eyebrow piercing, so we spent some time downloading some new music onto it, then went down to town to find somewhere to eat. I thought Burger King was a bit of a naff place to go for a birthday, so we ended up at Nice Noodles, the Chinese place next door to the Unemployment Benefit office, and had a very grown-up time asking for a table, perusing the menu, and ordering our food and drinks. It descended into childishness when the chopsticks arrived, but on the whole I think we acquitted ourselves quite well over the course of the evening!

Sunday 30 September

Had a weird dream about noodles and chopsticks last night. I dreamt me and Han were in Nice Noodles and the chopsticks on our plate were dancing over the noodles, kicking their 'legs' like they were a Tiller Girl or something. Then the noodles slithered off the plate like worms and Cliff Richard came in wearing a matador's outfit and singing 'O Sole Mio' while a group of pensioners did the conga behind him. The dream was teetering on the edge of insanity when I woke up needing a pee, so thank goodness for my weak bladder 'cos bugger only knows how the dream might have ended!

I don't know why I keep getting these weird dreams. Apparently eating cheese before bedtime can give you vivid dreams, but I only had a handful of jam cookies before I went to bed so I can't understand it.

Monday 1 October

Henri gave us a vocabulary and grammar test in French today. He kept telling us to write our answers down on a 'piss of pepper' and got very cross when we kept giggling. Such are the puerile minds of a bunch of seventeen-year-olds!

Tuesday 2 October

Spotted Alice in the corridor today and called after her. She stopped and turned to look at who had called her, but when she saw it was me, she just carried on walking!

Bloody great! I'm really trying with her but it seems she doesn't want anything more to do with me. I feel a bit sad about it. She WAS my friend, after all, before all that stuff in France happened, and now it seems like I've lost her.

Wednesday 3 October

We did something about German philanthropists today in History but I got philanthropy mixed up with philately and spent the whole lesson wondering why we needed to know about German stamp collectors! I'm never gonna to pass my exams at this rate.

Thursday 4 October

Have spent the last coupla days thinking about Alice and wondering how she is. It's been, like, nearly two months since France and she still won't talk to me properly! She never speaks to me anymore when we're all at school together, but doesn't make it obvious enough so that the others will notice. But I notice. I really wish I could talk to someone—ANYONE—about it, but if I do, then everything's going to come out, isn't it? And I don't feel ready for everything to come out.

It's such a bloody mess.

Friday 5 October

Dad's thinking about buying a new car 'cos his is too small. He's been round some showrooms and picked up some brochures but can't decide what he wants. He knows he wants something bigger than the one we've currently got, but he doesn't want something too big, and he doesn't want it to be a 4x4 because 'they guzzle fuel and only wankers drive them'. Mum said to me, 'I thought Alice's dad drove one?' Enough said.

Saturday 6 October

England played Australia tonight in the Rugby World Cup. We got ourselves a takeaway curry in, draped the flag of St George over Barbara, and sat glued to every minute. We won! Mine and Dad's voices are hoarse from shouting at the TV. Mum kept telling us that the players couldn't hear us, so why shout at the telly? She has no idea what it's like to be a full-throttle sports fan.

Sunday 7 October

Han came over today. We took Barbara out for a walk up in the woods and held hands when we knew we were out of sight of my house. Han told me she loved me again today and I loved it! Thought for a minute about telling her about how worried I was over Alice, but I couldn't be arsed having to explain everything, and if I'm honest, I didn't want to spoil what was a perfect afternoon talking about bloody Alice!

Monday 8 October

Got given loads of work to do by Mr. Harman today so went to the library at lunchtime with Han, Matty, and Caroline with the intention of starting some of it, but ended up having a paper-throwing contest behind the geography books instead!!!

I figured study can wait. I'll only be young once!

Tuesday 9 October

Dad tried to get Mum interested in the car-buying malarkey. He showed her some from his well-thumbed brochures and she pointed at one costing £24, 000 and said she liked it. When he asked her why she liked it, she said it was because it was Pomegranate Red and she liked the idea of driving a car with pomegranate in its name. Dad just picked up the brochures and walked out of the room without another word. Poor Dad! She'd probably put a brown throw over it anyway, Pa!

Wednesday 10 October

Went up to the library in between lessons this morning to try and find a book I'll need for some pointless essay Mrs. Schofield's asked us to do for next Monday. Alice was sitting up there doing some work so I bit the bullet and sat next to her. She didn't show any emotion when I sat down next to her, just kinda looked up at me then back down at her book.

I said, 'Hiya, how're you?' and she said, 'Fine.' We sat in silence for a bit, I picked at my nails while I thought of what the hell I could say to her. In the end I just started waffling on about this essay we had to get done, and had she done any work for it, and she kinda tapped her pen irritably onto her book and said, 'Trying to do it now, Clem,' so

I took the hint and left her again.

I stood outside the library door and wondered if I could have done anything differently, or maybe said anything differently rather than prattling on about essays, but it's dead obvious now that no matter what I do or what I say, Alice just doesn't want to have anything to do with me anymore, and that makes me sad.

Thursday 11 October

Had a rude MSN convo with Han tonight when I should have been doing some work on the computer. Dad came into the room just as I was licking my way down Han's heavenly body in cyber-space and asked me how I was coming on. How I didn't choke on my Dr Pepper is anyone's guess!!!

Friday 12 October

Tried to talk to Caroline about Alice today. I asked her if she thought she was okay, 'cos she seemed a bit down to me. Caroline said she hadn't noticed, but thought maybe it was because we're in our so-called 'important' year and maybe her parents were giving her grief about studying hard and stuff like that. Caroline said she was meeting Alice in town tomorrow so she'd ask her what was up. Felt a bit better.

Saturday 13 October

Woke up in a cold sweat in the middle of the night thinking about what Caroline had said to me yesterday. If she meets Alice today, asks what's the matter, and tells her that I was worried about her, maybe Alice will open up and tell Caroline everything that's happened! I don't want that. I don't want Alice telling Caroline anything about me, about Han, about me and Han, about me and Alice. I don't want her to tell Caroline anything!

I was too worried about Caroline and Alice to enjoy my tea properly tonight. I kept looking at my phone, expecting Caroline to text me, wanting to know what had been going on, but then I told myself I was being ridiculous and to stop worrying. Sometimes I think I could turn worrying into an Olympic sport. I'd sure as hell get the gold!!

Sunday 14 October

Sent Caroline a text late last night asking her how she got on with Alice, 'cos I knew if I didn't I'd just end up spending the whole night worrying about what Alice had told her. She sent me a text back about an hour later saying that she forgot all about it, and Alice was on dead good form anyway so the thought never even came into her head to ask her!!

Bloody great! So I sacrificed a plate of Korma because I was worrying so much and after everything, Caroline forgot to even sodding-well ask her!

Monday 15 October

Caroline caught up with me at lunchtime today and said sorry she hadn't spoken to Alice. She said she rang her last night and asked 'cos she knew I was worried about her. My blood ran cold when she said that, and kinda braced myself for what Caroline was gonna say next, but she just said that Alice had said I had no need to worry about her 'cos she was fine but if I honestly wanted to know the truth, she was a bit pissed off with me 'cos I seem to spend all my time with Han now and never have any time for her.

Caroline took my hand and said she hadn't noticed that I was spending a lot of time with Han (to my relief) and that Alice was sensitive to these things and that I shouldn't worry so much about her.

Relief flooded through me that Alice hadn't said anything about things and made up my mind there and then to try and talk to her again about stuff.

Tuesday 16 October

Matty is having a party in two weeks' time for her seventeenth birthday! This is great news! The last party I went to I ended up crying after seeing J kissing Gareth (HOW long ago was that??!!), so it'll be good to go to a party and actually enjoy myself. The fact I have a gorgeous girlfriend to take with me will just make it even better!!

Wednesday 17 October

Remembered in a blind panic that it's Mum's birthday tomorrow, so shot off down to town after school to buy her a present. Realised I only had a fiver left until Dad gives me my allowance, so I bought her some aromatherapy oil and a funny little contraption with wooden balls on it that she can run up and down her back to massage it. Not very exciting, I know, but it was either that or buy her a set of coasters with grinning cats on it, which was the only other thing that was £5 in the shop!!

Thursday 18 October

Mum's birthday! I gave her her present at breakfast and she seemed pleased with it. She looked at Dad in a funny way and said he could test it out on her in the bath later, which made him drop a saucer on the floor. I don't care for such talk at the breakfast table, regardless of whether it's her birthday or not! It's not nice to think that your parents are still *intimate* with each other, and I'm very surprised they bother with all that stuff now, especially at their age (Mum is 43 today).

Anyway, we're going to go out for a meal to celebrate tomorrow night 'cos Mum hates going out on a school night (!!!)

Friday 19 October

We went out for Mum's birthday meal. I wanted to bring Han, but I thought it would invite too many questions 'cos I've never asked if other 'friends' can come out with us before, so I stayed shtum.

We went to a pub near our house but got seated next to a large group of people talking louder than I personally thought was acceptable, one of whom sounded a bit like a buffalo down a mine shaft. It put me off my dinner a bit so we decided to come home via the supermarket and picked up a dessert to eat at home, which secretly pleased Dad, 'cos it meant the pub meal was cheaper than he was expecting it to be!!

Texted Han when I got in and asked her what she'd been up to. She took ages to reply, finally texting me at eleven to say she'd been to the cinema with Ems and Matty, which gave me a brief stab of jealousy, but then I told myself I was being ridiculous. I don't want to turn into one of them bunny boilers that you read about on the Internet, but I still went off to sleep kinda wishing that I'd gone out with them rather than out in a pub listening to some boorish bloke hollering over his chicken in a basket.

Saturday 20 October

Me and Han went into town to buy a present for Matty this morning. I had NO idea what to get her. Han told me to just get her something I'd like myself, but me and Matty are like chalk and cheese. She likes makeup, pink stuff, fluffy kittens, girly things—I don't! I wouldn't have a clue about makeup (unless it was black eyeliner) and any shop with pink fluffy things just makes me feel really self-conscious, so I chose a set of pens from the stationers. Han bought her a *High School Musical* picture frame (yuk!) and some body cream and scoffed that I was clueless about women. I told her that EVERYONE needed nice pens but she just rolled her eyes at me and disappeared into the Hallmark shop to buy a card. Matty just LOVES *High School Musical* (Zac Efron in particular—ew!!), so I very reluctantly bought her an HSM card. Personally, High School Musical leaves me cold; I've never seen the attraction in a bunch of hyped-up brats over-acting and dancing about like squirrels on speed, but there y'go.

I asked Han (casually like) if she'd had a good time at the cinema. I added (casually like, again) that she hadn't mentioned that she was going out with Ems and Matty, and she said breezily, 'Oh, it was a last-minute thing. You weren't around to play with me, so I thought I'd go out and play with someone else,' and poked her tongue out at me. She said they went to see *The Bourne Ultimatum*, and it was just as well I wasn't there 'cos she'd have had to have explained the complicated plot to me. She linked her hand with mine briefly when she said this, and smiled, but she has a point. I've watched both *The Bourne Identity* and *The Bourne Supremacy* at least three times each, and I still don't have a flipping clue what's going on. Anything more complicated than the plot of *Bambi* and I'm lost. *The Matrix*? Don't even go there! Not-a-bloody-clue.

Sunday 21 October

Great Aunt May has come to stay with us for a week. *A week!* She's having her room at Autumn Leaves redecorated, so Mum's told her to move in with us while it's being done. If this isn't bad enough, she's brought Bertie her budgie with her. Gerald from the next room normally looks after him if she ever goes away, but the staff at the home thought all the men with ladders, noise, and paint fumes might distress him (Bertie, not Gerald) so he's come with her. I loathe Bertie with a passion. If he's not pooing everywhere, he's twittering on the hour, every hour, which not only drives me mad, but drives Chairman Meow mad too 'cos he knows he can't get to him. Bloody bird.

Monday 22 October

Ems had a tattoo done over the weekend!! I don't know whether I'm jealous that she had the guts to go through with it when I didn't, or pleased that I decided not to abuse my body [/superior/].

She showed it to us at lunchtime and I have to say it's quite nice. She's had a butterfly tattooed onto the back of her neck but it's a bit difficult to tell what it actually is 'cos she told us she took the plaster off too early and woke up yesterday morning with her skin stuck to her pillow so her neck looks a bit angry at the moment.

I got a bit queasy looking at it but stuffed an emergency Werther's Original into my mouth and felt better.

Tuesday 23 October

What an embarrassing evening! Great Aunt May started asking that perennial question about boyfriends again! She asked me at the dinner table tonight if I had a 'young man' (WTF??) and when I didn't answer, Mum took it upon herself to answer for me and said that she and Dad were sure I was seeing someone 'cos I'm always checking my phone, I sometimes get flustered and leave the room when my phone rings, and I always get very coy whenever I'm on the Internet talking.

I sat there and squirmed as they all looked at me and smiled, not wanting to tell them that the only reason I go coy when I'm on the Internet is because I'm either Googling new sex positions to try out with Han, or I'm having a marathon sex chat with her, and I don't want anyone to bloody-well see!!

Then they started going on about how 'sweet' young love was so I just got up and left the table. Why do they always do it? It's soooo bloody embarrassing!

Wednesday 24 October

Han came over to ours after school tonight. Great Aunt May has only ever seen Han in her Goth clothes, so I think she was a bit more relaxed seeing her in her school uniform 'cos I heard them having a conversation in the lounge about the pros and cons of flannelette sheets, which was surreal.

Suddenly remembered the conversation they all had about boyfriends last night and couldn't wait to get Han out of the room in case Great Aunt May started pestering her about boyfriends as well!

Thursday 25 October

School was, like, so boring today I can't even begin to describe it! We got the dates for our French and Spanish oral exams and it threw me into a complete panic. Me and Han decided to speak only French to each other on the way home so we could practise, but got as far as the school gates and ran out of things to say to each other so reverted to English. This isn't good. If I can't even muster up a casual conversation with my girlfriend, how the hell am I going to be able to talk to a complete stranger under exam conditions??

Friday 26 October

No school for a week after today! As if that wasn't fabulous enough, HRBH is going to Italy for a week with the school tomorrow, so I get seven days without her!!

I went to see a medium tonight with Mum and Great Aunt May. It was a hoot! It was one of those shows where some charlatan stands on stage and tells people that their long-ago deceased loved one has a message for them. We went along with Great Aunt May's friend Sheila, who lives across town. She said she wanted to get in contact with her late husband, Bernard, 'cos she'd broken the remote control and she was hoping he'd be able to tell her where he'd put the spare one.

I didn't believe a word that the medium was saying, but others there seemed to get some comfort from what she was saying. A woman across the aisle from us had to be led from the conference hall in hysterics though when the medium told her that her late sister was refusing to tell her why she left all her money to the Tiddlywinks Rest Home for Elderly Cats rather than to her, so that was a bit sad.

Great Aunt May seemed to lap it all up, and thinned her lips and tut-tutted along with Sheila when the medium told her she couldn't raise Bernard to ask him about the remote control. I heard her telling Mum in the car going home that she wasn't surprised Bernard didn't appear, 'cos Sheila 'never managed to raise him when he was alive, so she sure as hell wouldn't be able to do it now he was six feet under'.

Texted Han when I got in and told her all about it. She sent me one back saying she wished she'd been there 'cos it sounded dead funny, but I was kinda glad she wasn't there. The way Han dresses for a night out, the poor medium would have thought she'd personally managed to drag her direct back from the grave, and that would have given all the old dears there the right willies!

Saturday 27 October

The search for a new car is over! Dad has plumped for the Vauxhall! HRBH thinks it's because he didn't want to incur her wrath if he bought a Kia, but he told me in the kitchen it was because the guy at the showroom offered him £1000 more for his car than the guy at the Kia showroom, adding 'But don't tell your sister that', with a wink. He's picking it up on Thursday and he's like a kid looking forward to Christmas!

HRBH went to Italy this afternoon so a week of peace and quiet awaits us all!!

Sunday 28 October

Went to Matty's birthday party last night and had a ball! Matty's parents had reluctantly gone out to visit friends for the evening, leaving her with strict instructions 'not to let anything get out of hand'. I thought her dad had the look of a man condemned as he was led down the driveway and shuffled into the car by her mum, but they drove off without a backward glance, which was brave of them, I suppose.

Anyway, the party was sick! Me and Han drank too much Slovakian beer and threw caution to the wind, slow dancing with each other on the lounge floor and not caring a damn who saw us. I think I got a thrill from that, but better still, later we sneaked away to the garden and kissed under the pergola, nearly getting caught when Caroline staggered out and threw up over Matty's dad's geraniums. She looked at us cross-eyed and asked us what we were doing, before going visibly green and throwing up again and sitting down hard on the patio giggling to herself.

I was panicked—a bit like a rabbit caught in headlights—but Han said Caroline was so drunk she wouldn't notice if we stripped off and shagged right there under her nose (so to speak). Sure enough, Han slung a casual arm over my shoulders, nuzzled her face in my neck and kissed my neck loudly and all Caroline did was hiccup and try to focus on her feet. I felt a bit better then, and, I'm almost ashamed to say, slightly titillated at the thought we nearly got found out…

I think given the opportunity, I could turn into one of those exhibitionists that are always on the front cover of the Sunday papers waggling their bits and pieces about.

Monday 29 October

A whole week off starts today!

Took Great Aunt May back to Autumn Leaves. Her room looks very nice, I have to say, but it still pongs of cheap paint a bit. All her knick-knacks and photos had been taken down, so she got a bit upset, cradling her photo of herself and Great Uncle Ralph on their motorbike and sidecar until it was covered in greasy thumb marks. She cheered up considerably when he was hammered back up on the wall, and so we all went down to the dinner room then to have a celebratory slice of cake to mark her return home.

Tuesday 30 October

Han decided to go and get her eyebrow pierced today. Her mum, true to her word, didn't renege on their agreement, and handed over the money for it without so much as a whimper! I just know that if that had been my mum and dad (not that they'd let me have my eyebrow done in a million years), they would have conveniently 'forgotten' about the agreement, then refused to talk about it.

The guy in the shop looked like he'd be happier sitting astride the back of an oily Harley-Davison rather than piercing body parts, but he had clean fingernails and nice teeth, and seemed to make a good job of it, and I was pleased that Han only squeaked a little bit when he actually did it!

It looks really cool, but she jerked her head when she was being pierced and it bled a bit, and now she's got dried blood in her eyebrow hair and it's a bit off-putting. She said it hurts like buggery and she can't raise her eyebrow, but she seems pleased with it, 'cos I keep catching her looking at herself in the mirror.

Wednesday 31 October

Mum and Dad went out tonight and left me to the mercy of all the Halloween trick-or-treaters knocking on our door, threatening to firebomb our house. I put some red devil's horns on Barbara and sat her in the lounge window to frighten everyone away; it must have worked 'cos we only had three callers, one of whom was Jamie from down the road who came round with his mum (who was dressed in a damn sexy Dracula outfit!!)

I wanted to put a pumpkin in the window too, but of course Mum had forgotten to buy one, so I hollowed out an apple and put a birthday candle in it, but it fizzled and died within about five minutes. Then

I got moaned at later on by Dad for wasting an apple. He's such a dictator sometimes!

Thursday 1 November

Picked up the new car today, and it's wicked! It's an MPV and there's, like, soooo much room inside. He took us for a spin out into the countryside and it felt like we were sitting in a minibus! So high up! He seems really pleased with it 'cos when we got it home, he started washing it. I asked Mum why he'd want to wash it already 'cos it would have been valeted at the showroom, but Mum just looked pityingly at Dad and told me to leave him be 'cos he was happy.

I must say, he looked extremely happy—the simplest things, hey?

Friday 2 November

HRBH came back from Italy tonight, worse luck! At least she didn't come home with some Italian in tow.

She dumped her luggage in the hall and went out to cast her expert eye over the new car, then came back in and declared herself pleased with it 'cos she said she'd be able to get all her friends in it. Dad laughed a hollow laugh at that one.

Saturday 3 November

OMG! Me and Han have had our first lovers' tiff!! Not bad for a couple who've been going out with each other for five months and seven days! We were up at the park, sitting out on the grass and I just got to this point where I wanted to kiss her soooooo badly but knew

I couldn't, so I harrumphed and made some flippant comment about wishing I was straight so I could enjoy being in a relationship, and she went into a right bad mood! Okay, maybe I could have chosen my words better and it came out wrong, but I knew what I meant and she took it the wrong way. She went all dead sulky and said something like, 'Do you wish you weren't gay, then?' and I said, 'Sometimes,' which is a bit of a lie, really, 'cos I've never really given it a huge amount of thought (like most things—ha ha ha).

Anyway, she just went, 'Fine,' and got up and walked off!! I jumped up after her and asked her what was the matter, but she went into silent mode and got this look on her face which I knew meant she wasn't to be messed with! So we walked home in silence, with me not knowing what to do. When we got nearer her house, she sat down on a wall and started picking at her fingers. She said to me, 'Do you still want to go out with me?' What a question! I said, 'Of course I do! I adore you,' and she cheered up a bit. She asked me why I'd said I wish I was straight and I told her I just thought life was easier for straight people, because they could be affectionate with each other in public. It didn't matter what people thought of them, and they just had it a hell of a lot easier. That's my opinion anyway.

She said to me that she'd never given it a thought, never questioned her gayness 'cos she was completely comfortable with it, and so hadn't ever wished she was something else. I said I was comfortable with who I was as well (at long last), but I just thought my life might be easier if I wasn't who I was. But that wasn't to say that I wanted to be different 'cos I was very, very happy in my life. This was all very profound for me, so I was kinda relieved when she ran her hand up my leg and told me she was sorry for stomping off at the park, but that she'd been worried that I was having second thoughts about going out with her. I told her the day me and her got together was the happiest day of my life, and that every day I loved her more. That cheered her up no end!

So lovers' tiff over as quickly as it started, thank God! Do you know, for a Goth—sorry, EMO—she's a bit of a sensitive pansy sometimes.

Sunday 4 November

Han came over today and brought me a bunch of flowers!! She thrust them in my hand and said, 'For you. To say sorry for being such an arse yesterday,' then looked down at her booted feet. I think being sheepish and apologetic doesn't sit easily with Han 'cos I noticed she was blushing when she said it. I took the flowers and told her no one had ever bought me flowers before and she grinned at me and said, 'Well, I won't be making a habit of it. I got a reputation to keep, y'know,' and winked that damned sexy wink of hers at me.

We had, like, this marathon kissing session in my room whilst Mum was making lunch, and I thought the fight with Han was worth it if only for the making-up afterwards!!!

Monday 5 November

It's Bonfire Night so me and Han went to the fireworks display at the university. It was wicked! They'd set up a fair there with rides and stalls and stuff, so we went on the big wheel and held hands as it went round. I was slightly scared when we got to the top in case she was still mad at me over our tiff and tried to push me out of the car, but told myself I was being ridiculous (but clung on tight to the side of the car nevertheless).

We lit sparklers and wrote our names in the sky until an officious student in DayGlo tabard came over and told us to extinguish it 'cos it was a fire hazard. Han drawled sarcastically, 'Oh yes, because of course fireworks aren't a fire hazard, are they?' to which the student replied, 'Just put it out and belt up, will you?' How eloquent! And these people are our future doctors and lawyers?

Tuesday 6 November

Caroline is having a sleepover at her house next weekend 'cos her parents have gone to Wales on a bird-watching weekend. Whatever turns them on, I suppose. I have to say, two days sitting in a draughty shed in the rain watching for the merest hint of feathers isn't my idea of fun, but it's good news for all of us 'cos it means we get to have a fun weekend at Caroline's.

Wednesday 7 November

HRBH has gone back on a diet!! Actually, she's calling it a Health Drive rather than diet 'cos she says the word 'diet' has such negative connotations and she only has to think about being on a diet and it makes her want to reach for a packet of Pringles. We were watching an article on the news tonight about how it's important to have a varied diet, and how it's best to have a variety of coloured foods every day, but when I pointed out that Smarties have a variety of colours, she shot me a look that told me not to mess with her!

Why does everything that's supposedly good for you have to be so yucky? I don't get vegetables. I figure if God (or Charles Darwin—depends on who you believe in) had wanted us to eat lots of vegetables he'd have given us teeth like the were-rabbit in Wallace and Gromit. He wants us to eat M&Ms—that's why he gave us little diddy blunt teeth. End of.

Thursday 8 November

Han got hauled into Mrs. Unwin's office today 'cos she forgot to take her eyebrow ring out!!! Apparently Mrs. Unwin told her that *she* 'might like looking like some Hell's Angel, but the school certainly doesn't', and 'what on earth would members of the public think if they saw a girl in a St Bartholomew's uniform wearing an eyebrow ring?' Han said it was on the tip of her tongue to say they'd probably think it was a cool school to go to, but she said the look on Unwin's face was enough to make her think twice.

Han removed her ring but I noticed she had it back in when we walked home tonight, with a defiant look on her face that even old Mrs. Russell in her heyday wouldn't have wanted to mess with.

Friday 9 November

Caroline told me today that she's posted a message on her Facebook page about the party tomorrow. I had NO idea what Facebook was, so asked Han about it when we were on our own later 'cos I didn't want Caroline to think I was a complete prat!!

Han laughed and said, 'Oh, everyone who's anyone's on Facebook these days—didn't you know that?' to which I replied (kinda indignantly), 'Err, no. Are you on it, then?' and she said (a bit too breezily for my liking), 'Of course! I've got loads of friends on there. I thought I told you about Facebook ages ago?'

Friends? Facebook?? I told her she might as well have been talking Swahili for all I could understand but she got one of those looks on her face again and just said, 'God, you're, like, *so* naïve sometimes, aren't you?' which made me bristle a bit, before adding, 'But that's what I love about you,' and pushing a strand of my hair from my eyes when she knew no one was looking. I felt my tummy flutter and forgot about her unfair words, but still made a mental note to check out this Friends/Facebook thing when I got home from school, whatever it might be.

Saturday 10/Sunday 11 November

Weekend at Caroline's
Han came over first thing this morning and told me she'd got a treat for me for later. I looked quizzically at her, and she leant over to reveal the skimpiest, blackest, sexiest bra I've ever seen!!! After my heart had returned to its normal beat, I said to her 'You can't wear that! You'll drive all the hormone-infested boys there tonight wild.' Han said, '*They're* not going to see it, silly! This is for your eyes only.'

OMFG!! Can you imagine how hot it'll be knowing she's wearing it, and it's all for me? I laughed and said, 'You're lucky I've got a strong heart, y'know,' and she said, 'And YOU'RE lucky you have such a *hot* girlfriend,' and grinned at me. Can't argue with that!

Anyway, we went over to Caroline's around sixish and the whole gang was there. Ems had had a tiff with Ryan, so he wasn't there, thank God, but it meant she spent the whole evening snivelling and pouring her heart out to Matty, who looked like she just wanted to seek out the vodka in the kitchen and get drunk!

Alice turned up too and smiled weakly when she spotted me in the corner with Han, then headed out into the garden to talk to Caroline. I wondered if I ought to follow her and talk to her, ask her if she was okay seeing me and Han together, 'cos this was the first time she'd seen us together since all that shit in France happened, but then I remembered Han's black bra and didn't want to do anything that might upset Han and prevent me from seeing her in it later. I'm so shallow sometimes.

Anyway, later we watched this really crap horror movie about a bunch of teenagers who get lost in a wood and then get stalked through the wood by some crazed axe murderer called Kevin. Personally I would have thought they could have thought of a more menacing name for an axe murderer, but there you go. Whenever he caught anyone, Kevin would skin his victims, accompanied by blood-curdling screams. Han leant over to me and whispered, 'I'm all for seeing movies with girls' bare skins, but it'd be better if the girls actually had their skins still on their bodies.' We turned all the lights off to add to the atmosphere, which made Caroline whinge a little bit. Han held my hand in the dark, linking her fingers in mine and stroking the inside of my palm with her thumb, making me very sleepy.

I peered in the dark over to where Alice was sitting and suddenly noticed she was getting it on with some boy called Vince who'd come with Charlie. It felt weird watching Alice kissing him so I stopped and carried on watching the movie but I couldn't help wondering why she was doing it if she was only telling me not long ago that she fancied me? Maybe she was drunk? Maybe she's still pissed off at me and this is her way of trying to show me she's moved on. *But with a boy???* [/queasy/].

I tried to concentrate on the movie, but it had started to descend into farce a bit, with bodies being axed left, right, and centre, so we all sat and threw popcorn at the telly and booed and hissed every time Kevin came on screen wielding his bloody axe. Then we told ghost stories for a bit to freak each other out, but then we got bored and decided to go to bed. I couldn't see Alice anywhere but figured I didn't want to sleep too near to her anyway, just in case she tried to get into my sleeping bag in the night or something (if she was that drunk she was willing to kiss Vince, she might do anything), so I put my sleeping bag next to Han's over in the corner and put some cushions round us, kinda blocking us off from the others.

Matty sidled up to me and said she didn't want to sleep next to Ems, 'cos she'd be banging on all night about Ryan, and Matty wouldn't get a wink of sleep. So she asked me if she could sleep next to me. Han slung a lazy arm round my shoulders and said to Matty that I snored a lot, and did I really want to be kept awake all night with that instead? I smiled and shrugged my shoulders. Matty thought about this for a minute before gathering her *High School Musical* pyjamas and bedding, and slinking off into the corner of the room to sleep alone.

Me and Han found a perfect little spot between the sofa and IKEA footstool-cum-CD rack. I was disappointed that it was pitch black in the room so I didn't get a good look at her skimpy bra, but she let me have a good feel of the lace in the dark. I must have drifted off into one of those light sleeps pretty much straight away 'cos the next thing I was aware of was the sound of heavy breathing coming from underneath Caroline's mum's faux oak coffee table at the other end of the room. I lay there for a while in the dark, listening to this breathing getting heavier and heavier, when it was suddenly punctuated by a low groan!! I hissed at Han to wake up and she stirred and whispered 'What??' at me, rather grumpily I thought. I said, 'I can hear something! Listen!' and we lay there looking at each other, listening to this breathing getting faster and faster. I said, 'Do you think they're okay?' and Han sighed and said, 'They will be in a minute.' I said, 'You what?' and she sighed (again) and said, 'They're having sex, dopey!' My eyes widened in the dark and I stifled a giggle. I said to Han, 'Who do you think it is?' and peeked out over my sleeping bag, trying to get a glimpse. Han yawned and said, 'Well, judging by the irritating little squeak she just made when she came, I'd say it was Alice. Now go back to sleep.'

Alice! *Doing it!* With Vince (presumably)! Right there in the corner of the room! Has she no shame? I spent the next 20 minutes listening to Han wriggle and sigh next to me, until finally she rolled over and whispered, 'Can't sleep. Got the horn,' in my ear. I told her to forget it. Alice, whom I'd always thought of as being such an innocent girl, might have the morals of an alley cat, but I sure as hell don't! Besides, I'd have been too worried someone would hear to concentrate on the—er—matter in hand!!

Monday 12 November

Thought about Alice doing it with Vince over and over again (that is, I thought about it over and over again, not Alice and Vince doing it over and over again—shudder) and wondered why she'd done it. Thought about texting her but, bearing in mind we've barely spoken to each other in nearly four months, I thought I could hardly text her out of the blue and ask her why she was shagging him, could I?

I wish there was someone I could talk to about it, but there isn't. If it was a case of a boy fancying me and me not fancying him back, or something like that, then I could talk to Matty, or Ems, or Caroline about it. We'd have a good laugh about it, think it funny that he chose to get over me by shagging someone right under my nose (so to speak) then forget about it. I can't do that. I can't talk to anyone about it, and I can't seem to forget about it either.

Uncle Buck stayed too long out in the rain today so his fur's gone all matted! Han texted me tonight to ask me what I was doing, so I sent her a reply saying, 'I'm brushing my bunny.' She sent me one back saying, 'Is that a euphemism?'

Uncle Buck is now shining like a conker once more. I think he was pleased to have been brushed. I definitely detected a spring in his step tonight when I gave him his bedtime carrot.

Tuesday 13 November

HRBH has taken up jogging again. Apparently she's not losing as much weight as she'd like to on this Health Drive of hers. She says she put on half a stone in a week in Italy but it's taken her six days to lose just one pound of that. I declined the offer to go jogging with her, bearing in mind I didn't even make it to the end of the road last time without doubling over with a stitch. I've come to the conclusion that me and exercise don't mix. I just don't get it; it's supposed to release endolphins or something, and make you feel great, but all it does for me is make me feel tired and out of breath. Besides, if God really wanted us to be serious about exercise, he'd have made Lycra more forgiving.

Suddenly realised tonight that I didn't find out anything about Facebook the other day so Googled it when I got in from school today. What a revelation! It's like this networking thing where you can add friends and leave them messages, post pictures, videos and stuff like that. You can even take quizzes to find out what your name would be if you were a porn star. (I didn't bother with that, but the point is it's there, so I could if I wanted to!)

I found Han on there and sent her a request to be my friend, and then did the same for Ems and Matty. Didn't really want to add Alice, or see her profile, or anything like that—I don't know why.

But I'll have three friends on Facebook. How cool is that?!

Wednesday 14 November

Found Caroline on Facebook and added her. So now I have four friends!! Wrote on my profile that I was fed up with all the schoolwork I gotta do at the moment but when I checked just before bed, no one had replied to it.

Thursday 15 November

HRBH has bought herself one of those dance DVDs that bimbos who were in some lousy soap opera, like, five years ago, are always bringing out. Anyway, this one is called *Boogie Your Way to a Better Belly* and is by some bird who came fourth in *I'm a Celebrity, Get*

Me Out of Here in 2005. She, of course, is built like an ironing board, so she has this air of superiority as she's jogging on the spot, grinning like a buffoon and telling her unseen audience to 'squeeze them buttocks.' Personally, I think it would take an industrial car crusher for HRBH to get her buttocks anywhere near something resembling clenched, but that's neither here nor there.

Sat and watched HRBH bouncing and do-si-doing up and down the lounge until the sight of all her jiggling, and the nasally northern tones of the Ironing Board on the screen were finally too much for me, and I went to seek sanctuary with Chairman Meow up in my room.

Friday 16 November

Invited Han over after school to have a play on *Boogie Your Way to a Better Belly*, 'cos everyone was out so we could piss about in peace. We dressed up in jogging bottoms and Han put her school tie round her head so she looked a bit like Rambo, and we danced and wiggled along with the bimbette on the screen in front of us. This dance exercise stuff is harder than I realised. I couldn't keep up with her, and every time she told me to go left, my brain (and legs) sent me right so I kept crashing into Han, who had the dancing down to a fine art and was boogie-ing and side-stepping as if she was the spawn of Jane Fonda or something. I kept tripping over my feet as well, but that was probably because I still had my Snoopy fluffy slippers on.

Started to get a bit grumpy with the whole thing, so flopped down on the sofa and contented myself with watching Han's jiggling arse from behind, but my viewing pleasure was rudely interrupted when HRBH came home, stomped into the lounge, and turned the bloody DVD off. Somehow I think all the fun left that girl when she hit adolescence.

Saturday 17 November

Me and Han went into town this morning to buy some gear for the My Chemical Romance concert—sorry, gig—tonight!! I went to the pet shop and got myself a wicked studded dog collar, then to the chemist to get some black nail varnish and some black ribbons to tie in my hair. Han's got some black lipstick and eyeliner at home, and some other bits and pieces that I can wear to complete the look. I also bought a false eyebrow bar 'cos I think they look great, but unlike Han I'm way too squeamish to ever get my brow pierced.

We went back to Han's afterwards and started putting ourselves together. I have to say, we looked sick! My eyebrow bar looked well cool; I'd smudged black eyeliner round my eyes and put loads of mascara on so my eyes looked wicked as well. Han wore a full-length black leather coat which she said she would be boiled in, but it would be worth it 'cos it looked wicked. She had these black and red striped tights on and her *fuck-off* biker boots, a black mini-skirt and ripped shirt and she looked hot as hell! I wore some skinny jeans and a T-shirt I'd borrowed off Matty which said 'Bitch Ass' on it.

Anyway, we came downstairs and presented ourselves to Han's parents, who were sitting in the lounge watching *Oprah* on the telly. They both looked totally unbothered by our gear, but then I figured Han's mum's a nurse so she's probably seen it all before! Toffee did look a little bit worried but cheered up a bit when Han tickled her ears and coochy-cooed at her.

Han's dad dropped us off at the venue, with strict instructions 'not to talk to anyone who looks like they might knife you', before driving off again. The concert—sorry, gig—was sicker than sick! It was dead hot and dead dark inside and Han did well to keep her leather coat on for a full hour before admitting defeat and taking it off. We bought T-shirts and mugs and posters while the support act was on (we watched them for 10 minutes before deciding they were crap) and then wondered how we managed to spend, like, 50 quid in the space of 2 minutes.

Then it was the concert—sorry, gig! Oh My Actual God! It…was… mental!! I'm not a seasoned gig-goer so I didn't know what to expect. But there were these kids, no older than ten or eleven, I reckon, dressed from head to foot in black, with various bits of themselves covered in fake tattoos. They wore My Chemical Romance T-shirts, held up banners, and, like, threw themselves down into the mosh-pit five minutes before the band came on and then refused to move for the next hour and a half.

These kids were scary, I'm telling you! When Han's dad told us not to look at anyone who looked like they'd knife us, I doubt he meant ten-year-olds dressed in studs and leather. The parents of these kids looked so…respectable! They hung around in groups, by the bar area, looking like they'd rather be at home reading their *Reader's Digest* than squashed up against some sweaty Goth reeking of beer. There were small groups of mothers, who would break off their conversations about how 'Harrods have struck gold in their knicker department at last', to occasionally wave and 'yoo-hoo' to their little dears who were busy moshing as if their lives depended on it.

Then there were the other types of parents. OMG! They were sooooo old (like, in their 30s) and trying sooooo hard to keep up with their kids. Some had squeezed themselves into tiny jeans and even tinier 'I was at Glastonbury '96' T-shirts, while others had gone for the grunge look and looked like bag ladies (but with posh accents). Trying desperately to keep up with their kids. This lot of parents grunted and squirmed at the sides of the crowds (obviously the mosh-pit was a step too far) while sweating profusely and occasionally saying about how they were only here 'cos 'Toby so loves this genre of music', but that next time 'they'd really rather prefer to see *Phantom of the Opera*'.

Me and Han had a great time! We got ourselves down in the pit so we had a really good view and were jumping up and down and screaming and singing along with everyone else. My Chemical Romance played the whole range, and Han videoed 'Mama' on her phone for Matty, 'cos that's one of her favourite songs. Everything was wicked until some little brat next to us jumped up and bashed me in the face with his studded wristband, and it was only when I felt something trickle down my face that I realised the little shit had smacked the fake metal bar out of my eyebrow and cut me to ribbons in the process! Great! So not only had I lost my eye bar, but now I had blood all down my face and my T-shirt. Han got me into the loos and cleaned me up, but I looked like I'd done ten rounds with some heavyweight boxer!!

Of course, the only non-black thing I was wearing *had* to be my T-shirt, and that now had blood all down the front of it. My eye had swollen up, I was sweating so my hair was wet and sticking up, and I had dried blood in it. Needless to say when Dad met us outside the venue, he took one look at me and paled. Great! The first concert—sorry, gig—I ever go to and I look like I've been scrapping with bloody ten-year-olds!

Sunday 18 November

Woke up and tried to open my right eye but couldn't. It's swollen right up and beginning to bruise magnificently!! I think it looks revolting but Han keeps telling me she thinks it's sexy and is making a meal of looking after me in the privacy of my bedroom (not that I mind, of course). She says I need a steak to help the swelling go down, but I'm not sure if I need to eat it or put it on my eye?

I took my swollen eye over to show her mum this morning after getting no sympathy off my own mother when I staggered downstairs looking like a prize-fighter. The fact I hadn't taken last night's black eye makeup off probably made me look 100 times worse as well, but I have to admit I was expecting a bit more sympathy than, 'Dear God, what DO you look like?'

I think Han should follow in her mum's footsteps and become a nurse because she has a *very* good bedside manner, and keeps planting kisses on my swollen, hot eye (not that I expect your average nurse to do that). I kinda enjoy being looked after by her, but now I'm a bit worried that I might have that funny old Munchkins Disease, or whatever it's called?

Monday 19 November

Got, like, a MEGA reaction from people at school today 'cos of my eye!! Everyone crowded round me and kept trying to touch it, asking me if it hurt very much. It's still swollen practically shut, and I can't see very well out of my other eye anyway, so I'm hoping Mrs. Unwin will take pity on me and send me home. Han had her arm slung casually round my shoulders while everyone was fussing round me and took great pleasure in telling them how she'd looked after me all day yesterday, because she thought it her duty, bearing in mind she'd been with me when it happened. She said something about nursing me, adding that she'd 'Drawn the line at giving her a bed-bath, though', and everyone laughed. I noticed Alice went bright red, though.

Didn't get sent home from school, worse luck!

Realised tonight that I STILL have hardly any friends on Facebook so added Susan Divine (yes, I know, dear diary, desperate measures!) 'cos I don't want to look like a right old Billy No-Mates. I just hope I don't ever write anything on there to upset her 'cos she'll probably put a fatwa on my head or something.

Tuesday 20 November

Ohhh the best news! It's Mum and Dad's twentieth wedding anniversary in December and they've booked up to go to Paris for the weekend. It means I'll have to put up with HRBH for the weekend, but if I annoy her enough she'll bugger off to a mate's, hopefully, leaving me to install Han in our house for 48 glorious hours! I can't wait! I'll just have to work on HRBH, make absolutely sure she stays away, then I can have my lovely girlfriend to myself aaaaaall weekend. Can't wait!

Eye still kinda gummed shut. Han says I look cute, HRBH says I look like a nutcase and asked me to 'stop leering at her with that wizened old hen's eye'. This is all the sympathy I get off her! She'll make a great stepmother one day.

Wednesday 21 November

Watched England getting a thorough spanking by Croatia in the football tonight so looks like we're not going to the European Championships next year. HRBH said she was pleased 'cos at least she won't have to put up with the sight of overweight men squeezing themselves into England strips and singing 'Olé Olé Olé' down the High Street whilst slurping from cans of high-strength lager and waggling their flags in her face. She has NO sense of patriotism!

Thursday 22 November

Woke up with a head that felt like I'd been smacked with a baseball bat this morning, and a throat that felt like I'd been moonlighting as a fire-eater, so stayed off school. Texted Han to tell her I wasn't well and she replied with 'My poor baby. I'll mix you up some special medicine in the Chemistry lab later xxx.'

It's now 7:30 p.m. and my head's pounding, my nose is streaming, and my throat's still on fire, so I think it's safe to say I have a common cold.

Friday 23 November

Why is it called a common cold? Why *common*? Does it live on a council estate? Does it steal cigarettes from the newsagents? Does it wear cheap gold jewellery? Has it taken lie detector tests on *The Jerry Springer Show*?

I think I'm delirious. Maybe I overdosed on Lemsip??

Saturday 24 November

HRBH is going out with some bloke called Joe who's a drummer in a band. She's on a diet again, no doubt spurred by the fact she's actually going out with someone for the first time since all that business with Ade. I hate it when she does this dieting lark; she eats, like, *nothing*, then sits and looks at my dinner like some hungry spaniel, irritating the hell out of me!

I got up for the first time since Wednesday and managed a little scrambled egg on toast in front of *American Idol*. Han wanted to come over and see me but I look like shit. My nose is bright red and my good eye is competing with my bruised eye in the puffiness stakes, which is streaming as though someone's squirted onion juice in it. Needless to say I declined her kind offer to come over and rub Vicks on my chest!!

Sunday 25 November

Sat downstairs this afternoon wrapped in a fleece blanket and watched *The Great Escape* from beginning to end on Channel Five. It's one of those movies that you never see all of—like *Gone with the Wind* or *The Sound of Music*—just kinda dipping in and out of them, so it was good to see the whole lot. Decided at around 8 p.m. that I was still too unwell for school so told Mum I would be staying off tomorrow as well. When she said she thought I was sounding better, I blew my nose and showed the tissue to her, then sat back and smugly listened to her cooing at the state of the brown/green mess within. I nodded wisely when she told me I was to stay off school until my snot was clear again.

Monday 26 November

Got up around midday and drank a bit of the chicken soup Mum had left for me in the kitchen. Actually feel a lot better but decided to stay off until tomorrow just to be sure. Besides, we had a Maths test today and I've done zippo work for it. Well, I've been ill, haven't I?

HRBH told me about this Joe fellow she's seeing. Apparently he's 20 and a student (studying Music Technology at uni) and he lives with two other boys in some rented pit across the other side of town. This is all the information I can get out of HRBH. She's notoriously cagey about her boyfriends, but particularly cagey about this one, which means she probably really, really likes him.

Tuesday 27 November

Went back to school today and was disappointed that no one said I still looked ill.

Alice did at least ask me how I was, which was nice of her; I seized the opportunity of talking to her, and managed to finally ask her about *that night at Caroline's.*

I tried to act all casual, like, and asked her if she was still seeing Vince. She did have the grace to blush, I noticed, at the mention of his name but told me she hadn't seen him since Caroline's party. I was shocked but I thought I hid it well, instead I just asked her why, trying really hard not to add: 'bearing in mind you *did* sleep with him that night' and trying *even harder* not to add 'trollop'. She was dead vague about it all, just saying that she was drunk the night of the party and hadn't really known what she was doing, but that the next morning reality had hit her like a hammer when she woke up and found Vince snoring next to her with all his dangly bits hanging out.

She went on to say that she realised she'd made a huge mistake and she had no idea why she'd done it but she sure as hell wouldn't be doing it again, she wouldn't touch Vince with a barge pole ever again and she said she'd more or less told Vince that when he'd texted her later in the week. I don't know Vince from Adam, but I have to say I do kinda feel sorry for the guy; it must be dead confusing to think you've scored only to be told it was a mistake and not to go near the girl you scored with ever again or she'll punch your lights out!

Anyway, I was pleased that Alice did at least speak to me, bearing in mind we've hardly said two words to each other since the summer. I don't know what I feel about her and Vince, though. Perhaps part of me wants her to get herself a boyfriend, especially if it means it takes her mind off me (if it's still on me, that is) but at the same time, I feel a right cow thinking that she probably only slept with Vince because I was there at the party that night and maybe it was her way of getting over me. Or getting back at me??

Either way, it's way too confusing for me to think about too much right now!

Wednesday 28 November

HRBH was telling me some more stuff about Joe today. She met him when she went over to the uni bar with her friends a couple of weeks ago and he was playing in his band. Their eyes met across his drum kit apparently. She told me she really liked him (I KNEW it!) and that she'd already slept with him, and that the sex was—and I quote—*'amazing'*. Yuk, yuk, yuk! This is toooooo much information!

She also told me that she was trying to get Joe interested in Buddhism too, but he told her he was 'too rock 'n roll for all that mellow shit'. She said she'd work on him and chant mantras at him or something.

Thursday 29 November

HRBH came into my room tonight and told me she was planning to spend the weekend that Mum and Dad are away over at Joe's. She hissed at me, 'So you better make sure you get one of your cronies to come over and baby-sit you, 'cos I won't be here and if Mum and Dad find out you spent the weekend alone I'm for the high-jump. So sort it.' What a result! I sooooo wanted to say to her, 'Like I give a shit where you'll be? My girlfriend's coming over anyway and we're gonna spend the whole weekend in bed,' but I just smiled sweetly at her and said, 'Whatever.'

Friday 30 November

What a shit day!! I think me and Han are finished, and it's all bloody Alice's fault. Me and Han were having our lunch together and I started to tell Han about my conversation with Alice about Vince the other day, because what she did has been eating me up a bit and I'm fed up with having to carry the guilt and worry around with me.

I told Han that Alice had said she regretted sleeping with Vince and then blurted out that I wondered if she'd done it for my benefit. I laughed as I said it, to try and make light of it, like, but…OMFG! She went right off on one, demanding to know what I'd meant. So I mentioned (as casually and as vaguely as I could) about what had happened between me and Alice in France last summer, about how I thought it had been a flash in the pan and had tried to forget all about it, but then had begun to wonder if the business at Caroline's party had been Alice's way of either getting over me or getting back at me. I don't remember my exact words, but I told Han (quite flippantly, I thought) that Alice had had a crush on me and that although I'd been horrified about it at the time, now I thought it was quite funny.

Oh boy, what a mistake! She went mental, asking me why I hadn't told her at the time. I said it was because she was just about to go to Portugal when it happened, and that I'd tried to sort it all out myself and that I'd thought it was irrelevant since me and Alice hadn't seen each other since she told me, and anyway, Alice had then slept with Vince. Han made out that I'd kept it from her because something had actually happened between me and Alice, and I told her not to be ridiculous. She got up and without another word, walked off back into the school building, just like when she'd walked off in the park that time before. This time I didn't go after her 'cos I was so gobsmacked at her reaction and, if I'm honest, a bit pissed off at her.

I didn't see her for the rest of the afternoon 'cos we didn't have any lessons together, and I've heard nothing from her all evening. I don't want to ring her because, if I'm honest again, I'm shit scared about what she'll say to me. So now I'm lying in bed, willing my phone to light up with a text from her but so far, nothing.

Saturday 1 December

Still haven't heard anything from Han. I don't know what to do! I don't see why I should have to be the one to contact her, 'cos as far as I can see I haven't done anything wrong. But then I know she's as stubborn as hell, and she'll probably be thinking the same thing. I sent Alice a text 'cos there's no one else I can talk to about it, and told her that me and Han had had 'words'. Alice replied and asked me if I wanted her to contact Han, but I thought that was probably just about the worst thing she could do.

I'm miserable. I love her so much that sometimes it hurts. I thought love was supposed to be fun. If I'd known it would cause me this much pain, I would have just stayed ~~celli~~, ~~sellybat~~, ~~cellibut~~, well, I would just have stayed single.

I just love her. Why can't she see that? How could she possibly think I'd have eyes for anyone else when all I think about is her? She's with me all the time, she's in my head day and night, I miss her when she's not around, I get butterflies in my tummy every time I see her, every time she texts me, every time I hear her voice and yet she still thinks I could be after someone else!

Seems I'm not so hot at this relationship stuff after all! What the fuck am I supposed to do??!

Sunday 2 December

I'm tying myself up in knots over all this and I don't know what to do for the best. I know I should contact Han and try to explain, but there's some stubborn voice inside my head telling me I've got nothing to explain to her 'cos I haven't done anything wrong. How can we be finished when it feels like I'm only just getting to know her? How can she just cut me out like this and not care? Maybe I didn't mean as much to her as I thought I did? But she's everything to me and I'm so sodding miserable it's unreal. I was talking to Alice about it today and Alice said she thought Han was overreacting and I have to say I agree. I tried to make some joke to Alice about never getting involved with another woman but I don't think she found it very funny.

I've just spent probably the most miserable weekend of my life, looking at my phone every five minutes, willing her to text me, not knowing what to do. Mum asked me if I was okay today 'cos I've been so quiet so I just told her I had a headache. I'm going to try and grab Han tomorrow at school, I've decided.

Monday 3 December

Managed to catch up with Han in morning break. She looked as miserable as I felt. I said, 'We need to talk,' and she said, 'There's nothing to talk about,' which wasn't a great start! I asked, 'Why haven't you contacted me all weekend?' and she just shrugged. 'I needed time to think.' (!!!) She looked sad and said, 'I gotta go. I'll catch up with you later,' and walked off to her next lesson.

I didn't see her for the rest of the day 'cos she disappeared somewhere at lunchtime. Matty and Caroline asked me if me and Han had had an argument, 'cos they were detecting 'an atmosphere' between us, but I just smiled my best smile and brushed off their questions. Alice asked me later if we'd sorted stuff out, and I shook my head miserably. I wanted to shout at Alice that it was all her fault me and Han were having this hassle, but there wasn't much point. I finally took the plunge and rang Han tonight but her phone was off, so here I am again, lying in the dark, willing my phone to ring, and wondering what the hell I can do to get us out of this mess.

Tuesday 4 December

I went into school early today so I could wait for Han before registration. I'm fed up with feeling like shit over something so trivial, and I wanted to get it sorted. So I pulled myself up to my full height of 5-foot-4 and told her I needed to see her at lunchtime, and I wouldn't take no for an answer. She agreed to meet me round the back of the Science block at 12:30.

While I was waiting for her at 12:30, I ran through all the things I'd thought I'd say to her, but when she turned up she just stood in front of me and said, 'What did you want to say?' and I was shocked by her coldness. I said, 'I just wanted to sort all this mess out, thassall,' and she just grunted something back at me. I said, 'I would never have told you about Alice if I thought you'd react like this,' and she said, 'How did you expect me to react when my girlfriend tells me someone else is after her?' I told her she was being ridiculous, and that Alice wasn't after me. It had all been something and nothing, and Alice had slept with sodding Vince since then anyway, and would she sleep with sodding Vince if she was still interested in me?! Han didn't like being told she was being ridiculous, and did the whole 'Oh, forget it' malarkey and turned to go.

That's when I surprised myself and bellowed, 'Not until we've got this sorted,' not caring if anyone heard us. She came back and I said, 'You do want to sort it, don't you?' and she mumbled something back at me, which annoyed me so I said, 'So do you want us to finish over this?' and she looked horrified (which pleased me) and said no. She said, 'Every time I fall for someone, someone else comes along and takes them away from me.' I thought it was neither the time nor the place to ask her if she'd fallen for lots of people, so I just said, 'No one's taking me anywhere. Not without a helluva struggle anyway,' and I saw the tiniest hint of a smile from her (thank God). I said, 'If you could just hear how daft all this is! Alice just had a blip when she thought—*thought*—that she might fancy me, but she obviously still doesn't like me 'cos she wouldn't have hopped into bed with Vince if she did, would she?' I said that there wasn't a single ounce of me that thought Alice remotely attractive, adding for good measure that sometimes she drives me nuts (which is true), and I couldn't think of anyone more unlikely as a girlfriend (which is also true).

Then I hit Han with a double whammy, telling her she was everything I'd ever wanted, that it felt like I'd waited my whole life for her and that there was no room in my heart for anyone else, 'cos my heart was so full of her! I tell you, I could write romance novels! She said, 'I'm nuts about you, Clemmykins, I don't think you realise quite how much,' and my legs went weak. 'I think about you 24/7. Sometimes I love you so much I feel like I can't breathe, that's what you do to me. The thought of someone else fancying you just tears me up and makes me go a bit barmy, I think,' she admitted. I told her that I was nuts about her too, that she'd made me the happiest girl in the world and that there was no way I was about to give all that up for someone else (and *certainly* not Alice!!!). I also told her I'd never even so much as looked at anyone else since she'd come on the scene, which is true.

I haven't looked at or thought about J since me and Han got together. My head's so full of Han that I don't have room for anyone else, and that's exactly how I like it. There's no comparison between Han and J, and sometimes I can't believe I wasted so much of my life chasing after someone who didn't even know I existed half the time.

I think Han was feeling a bit sheepish by now, 'cos she said she was sorry for not contacting me all weekend, and was sorry for being such a cow, and was sorry for making mountains out of molehills and for overreacting. She asked me if I was going to dump her and looked hard down at her shoes, as if she didn't want to face me. I told her of course I wasn't going to dump her, quite the opposite—I thought she was going to dump me, at which point she grabbed my hands and said she'd die without me (which I thought was a bit melodramatic but kept shtum—she is an EMO after all, and they're always banging on about death and the like). Then she said she wanted to kiss me! I said we couldn't do it at school, but secretly wished we could. Han grabbed my hand and told me to come with her, and I got a little shiver of excitement at her forcefulness, which was a bit perverted I guess, but I followed her anyway. She took me round the back of the Science block, where there's a sort of blind spot where you can't be seen from any angle from the school. It's where all the little Year 7s go to have a smoke 'cos they haven't yet discovered that they can hop over the wall down by the tennis courts and go into the cemetery next door. After kicking all the bum ends out the way, Han looked round furtively to make sure no one was coming, and gave me possibly the best kiss I've ever had. I felt lost in her, oblivious to anything else, and I dare say if it wasn't for the fact we heard some little shits coming, giggling in anticipation of a crafty fag, then I could have stayed there all afternoon kissing the face off Hannah Harrison!!

So, dear diary, all's well that ends well. I'm lying in bed and my phone has lit up with dozens of texts from my lovely girlfriend telling me I'm the best thing since sliced bread and how much she adores me. At least I'll sleep better tonight!

Wednesday 5 December

Had a crap night's sleep 'cos kept waking up and wondering what the best thing used to be before sliced bread was invented.

Texted Alice first thing and told her that me and Han had sorted things out. She replied with a text that just said, 'great'. I was talking to her about it during Biology this morning as well and I told her me and Han were back to being all loved up, and that it had all been a storm in a teacup. I didn't tell her that I'd barely eaten during the four days me and Han didn't speak.

I thought Alice looked a bit pissed off when I was telling her all this, which annoyed me a bit, I have to say. I would have thought that, bearing in mind it was all her stupid declarations towards me, and her acting like a prat at Caroline's party that caused all of this, she would have at least had the grace to be pleased for me. Sometimes

I'm so unforgiving, but I nearly lost my girlfriend over all of this, so I think I'm entitled to be just a bit unforgiving!

Anyway, I've got my appetite back now, thank goodness, so caught up with four days' worth of advent calendar chocolates.

Thursday 6 December

Today went in a blur. Lessons have been packed with things to do and things to learn, almost like the teachers have suddenly realised we'll be doing our final year exams soon and have run out of time to teach us everything we need to know! Have been given yet another pile of homework to do for next week as well but I keep putting it off and going online to talk to people and check out if anyone's left me a message on Facebook, rather than learning about Nazi Germany or Statistics or *Othello*, or whatever crap they want us to learn.

Mum and Dad are off for their romantic weekend tomorrow. Mum has packed enough to survive a month in the rain forest, while Dad has sensibly opted for a small overnight bag. She's packed insect repellent, even though she's going to France in December! I noticed Dad take it out of the wash bag but hastily put it back in when Mum came into the room.

Anyway, they're flying over there at two o'clock tomorrow afternoon, so that means they won't be here when I get in from school, which will be a bit weird 'cos one or the other of them always makes sure they're here when me or HRBH come home from school/college. Mum has left us enough food in the fridge to feed an army, and Dad has left us a small pamphlet, it would seem, full of instructions and phone numbers and what to do if we have a power cut, or a plague of locusts infest the house, or if we find an unexploded WW2 bomb in the garden or some such.

Friday 7 December

HRBH caught up with me as I was walking to school and told me she was going straight over to Joe's after college and wouldn't be back all weekend, and that if I blabbed to anyone I'd be dead meat. She asked, 'Now, you're sorted out for the weekend, aren't you? 'cos I won't be back till Sunday. I don't want you ringing me tonight telling me you're on your own.' I said, 'I'm sorted! I've got people round all weekend,' and she seemed satisfied with that. She said, 'Right, have a good one,' and walked on (heaven forbid she should be seen out walking to school with me!) Good to see the Buddhism's mellowed her [/sarcasm/].

Caught up with Han before morning register and as I walked past her I whispered to her, 'The dragon has flown'—by that I meant HRBH, not Mum—'you're all mine till Sunday,' and grinned as I turned back to look at her. She called out 'Tease!' and I noticed she'd gone red, which pleased me greatly.

Today dragged on and on and on. Why is it when you're soooooo looking forward to something, time moves like a tortoise with a heart condition? And when you don't want time to go by, it races off like a hare on steroids? Got ticked off by Mr. Spencer in Science for knocking over my Bunsen burner, but it wasn't my fault! I was distracted by Han leaning over to me and whispering 'Wanna feed me strawberries in bed tomorrow morning?' in my ear. What's a girl to do?!

We stopped by Han's house on the way home so she could pick up her stuff. She put in a few things of each, saying that she wasn't expecting to wear many clothes all weekend anyway, then fished out the skimpiest, laciest, blackest set of underwear I'd ever seen and held them up to me, asking 'You like these?' I spluttered and nodded like some demented idiot, and she grinned lazily and put them in her bag. As we were leaving the house, her mum called out to her and asked her if she had everything she needed. Han called back 'Yup. Underwear and a toothbrush—that's all I'll need.' Her mum's a nurse. She'd understand.

2:40 a.m.

The black underwear was *much* appreciated by me! Han is downstairs getting drinks (replacing lost fluids). Am shattered and utterly, utterly in love!!!

Saturday 8 December

Had a really lazy Saturday morning wrapped in each other's arms. We went downstairs, Han wearing my nightshirt, which turned me on something chronic, and I saw that Mum had bought croissants for me and HRBH as a treat. Felt awful and hideously guilty. We made coffees and heated up the croissants and took them back up to bed, Han licking the crumbs off my tummy, which made me giggle.

Mum sent me a text just as me and Han were *doing it* for the second time this morning (the licking of the crumbs got out of hand), and made me jump like a rabbit. It said, 'Arr'd ok. PaRis gr-8. Lv M.' No, she *still* hasn't got the hang of texting. Reluctantly got up around 3 p.m. and took Barbara out for a walk 'cos she was looking miserable and had all four legs crossed. We walked hand in hand up in the woods (me and Han, not me and Barbara) and didn't care who saw us!

Then Han cooked us some food tonight. She was standing frying up bits and pieces in just her bra and knickers (and an apron—lest the hot fat should spit). She has a figure to die for, and legs up to her armpits and as I watched her, I felt a million butterflies fluttering in my tummy (and not 'cos I was hungry). She turned and saw me leaning against the sideboard looking at her and said, 'What?' with a grin. I just said, 'Nothing. You're gorgeous, thassall. And I'm very lucky to have you,' and she poked her tongue out at me and said, 'Yeah, you are,' then flicked a piece of hot mushroom at me.

What a girl!

Sunday 9 December

Spent another lazy morning in bed wrapped round each other. *Did the deed* another three times. Feel a bit like some randy rabbit. Am slightly worried I'll be walking like John Wayne soon.

We got up around twelve and took a bath together. I spotted Mum's floral shower cap on the side and felt horribly guilty again. I hate feeling bad about something I should be feeling so happy about. I mean, I AM happy when I'm with Han, but there's always this feeling that I'm doing something wrong, and there shouldn't be. I don't like lying about stuff, and creeping round trying to cover my tracks. It feels so…I dunno…sordid, and it isn't!

Anyway, we spent our last afternoon of freedom just lost in each other—walking, talking, laughing, hugging, kissing…

Peace was shattered when HRBH arrived home around 4 p.m. looking like she'd been dragged through a hedge backwards. I think she must have spent the weekend living the rock 'n roll life with Joe, 'cos she stank of stale cigarettes and beer and her voice was hoarse. She looked a bit like one of the Rolling Stones the morning after a particularly fruitful bender. She fell in through the door, looked cross-eyed at me and Han, flung her bags on the floor, and muttered something about taking a shower.

When she came back down, me and Han were still sitting on the sofa. She sniffed, looked us both up and down in disdain, and said, 'You two look like you just got up. I s'pose you've spent, like, the whole weekend in bed?' After Han had finished choking on her tea, she added, 'Y'lazy buggers,' and Han's face returned to its normal colour once more…

Mum and Dad returned from their sojourn in Paris at around 7 p.m. looking (and acting) like a pair of loved-up teenagers. Yuk, yuk, yuk!

Monday 10 December

Had a real sweet text from Han thanking me for 'the best weekend of her life'. Wow! What an amazing text for a girl to get first thing in the morning! My tummy kinda went to mush when I read it! I'm not sure that was from remembering everything we'd *done* over the last few days, or the fact that Han was actually thanking me for it! Anyway, it made me feel dead special.

Tuesday 11 December

Started thinking about what to buy Han for Christmas but I honestly have NO idea what to get her. I figure I'll go take a wander in town one day next week and hope something jumps out at me! Luckily she's not fussy, so anything suitably black, depressing, and Gothic will be appreciated!

I made a list of what to get other people and came up with:

- Mum—something for the kitchen
- Dad—something for the garden
- Sister—something for that miserable face of hers (cream or face pack or paper bag or some such)
- Alice—something rabbity
- Ems—something Ryan can't nick off her
- Caroline—something. Just something (I have NO idea yet)

- Matty—something with Zac Efron on it.

I think I'll get Han to go and buy that last one. I bought enough of that crap already this year for her birthday, and I don't want that fit girl who works in the Hallmark shop to think I'm some sort of loser.

Wednesday 12 December

I think Han's predictive texting is up the crapper because she sent me a text today saying 'Hi pewsou, hows trials?'

I had NO idea what she meant so just sent her one back saying, 'Eh?' but she didn't reply so maybe she was a bit embarrassed that she seems to have lost the art of texting!

Thursday 13 December

We had our school Christmas concert this afternoon. It was crap. The school orchestra played a piece that sounded like it had only been rehearsed for the first time yesterday (it probably had, knowing our school). Me and Han sat at the back of the school assembly hall making derogatory remarks about the size of the oboist's chest, and stifling giggles at the sight of Miss Barker's attempts to conduct (note to Miss Barker: flinging your arms around as if you're being attacked by an angry wasp and pulling funny faces at the orchestra doesn't constitute conducting). Some girls from Year 7 came up onto the stage and murdered a few Christmas carols; I definitely saw Mrs. Unwin wince as though she'd just eaten a lemon when the entire choir failed to hit the top A during their rendition of 'O Come All Ye Faithful,' but I thought she did well not to let her emotions show when Rosie Butler from 9CS sang flat throughout her solo of 'Once in Royal David's City'. It struck me as I was walking home that Mrs. Unwin would make a fine poker player.

Friday 14 December

I asked Han about her weird text to me the other day but she just said, 'Oh, I sent that to you by mistake. Soz.'

So I asked her what she meant to say and she was, like, really vague, just saying, 'Blimey, I dunno, it was two days ago, Clemmykins! Do you expect me to remember?' I was a bit pissed off, to be honest, 'cos she seemed a bit short with me, so I said, 'So if you sent it to me by mistake, who did you really mean to send it to?' and she nearly bit my bloody head off! She said, 'Jeez, Clem! What's with all the questions all of a sudden?' which took me aback so I just laughed nervously and shut up. I've no idea why she was so sodding moody about it all. Maybe she's got her period. That tends to turn her into Frankincense's Monster at the drop of a hat.

Saturday 15 December

Han sent me a text late last night saying sorry for being a bit snappy yesterday but said she'd had a headache all day. That would explain it then (!)

Sunday 16 December

Went into town with HRBH this afternoon to buy some presents. I bought Mum a new casserole dish 'cos she smashed her other one, and Dad a new spade. Not very exciting, I know, but useful, so they should be grateful. Me and HRBH clubbed together, as we always do, and between us bought Dad a new MP3 player 'cos his was looking old and decrepit, and Mum a slow cooker. Felt a bit bad 'cos I've bought Mum two kitchen things, but as she spends half her life in the kitchen so at least she'll get some use out of them, unlike, say, a gift voucher which she'll probably just leave in a drawer somewhere and forget about.

HRBH went off to buy my present, and one for Joe, so I slipped into the chemist to try and find something for her, and started looking at the makeup. I have NO idea when it comes to makeup. I think the dolly-bird behind the counter felt sorry for me 'cos she offered me a free makeup advice session with free samples. Bearing in mind she looked like she'd trowelled on her foundation from a wheelbarrow behind the counter, I thought she might offer me a free gardening session with it and a bag of compost. I politely declined.

I decided to buy some shower gel and massage cream for HRBH, then went up to Sole Trader and bought Han some black Vans that she'd dropped major hints about wanting when we were last in town together. They cost a flipping fortune, and as I shakily handed over my money, I kept thinking about how they'd probably be £10 cheaper come the sales. I also got her some more leather wristbands 'cos I know she likes to have a choice to wear, and some obscure CD which I found in the bargain bucket at the Virgin Megastore for 3 quid.

So that's it! Christmas shopping done and dusted by December 17. Sometimes I'm so perfect it scares me!!

Monday 17 December

I've just noticed (how did I not see this before?!?!?) that Han has 88 friends on Facebook!!!!! Why would one person need so many friends?? I've now got 12, and that's only 'cos Ryan added me after Matty told him I didn't have many friends, and he felt sorry for me.

I asked Han why she had so many friends and she shrugged and said, 'People keep adding me. So I'm popular, what can I do?' and winked at me, which made me go a bit silly, like it always does. I asked her who her friends were 'cos I'd looked at them and only recognised some people from school. She laughed drily and said,

'Checking up on me, Clem?' but linked her fingers with mine when she said it, so I knew she wasn't pissed off or anything.

I said, 'No, just curious,' and made sure I kept my voice light so she wouldn't get pissed off with me. She just said breezily, 'Oh well, you know, there's friends from where I was before, people I knew, people I used to hang out with.'

I wanted to know if there were any ex-girlfriends on there, but I was too scared to ask. I kept thinking about it for the rest of the day, though, right through school, right through tea, and for the rest of the evening. I kept thinking about the text she sent me as well, but which she reckoned was for someone else, and then of course my mind started going into overdrive, so just before I went to bed I sent her a text and asked her if any of her exes were on there but she hasn't replied yet.

Am I being paranoid? Am I being stupid? Or am I just being like those clingy, whingy women you see in soaps?

God, maybe I'm being all three??

Tuesday 18 December

Spent most of the night thinking about bloody Facebook and why Han's got so many people on there, and why she's never thought to tell me about it. I mean, it's like, we tell each other EVERYTHING, so why wouldn't she tell me she's, like, Miss Popular in the world of Facial Networking?

Then at school today I wanted to ask Han about it all again, because it was all doing my head in thinking about it, but I didn't 'cos I was too scared to ask her, although I'm not sure exactly what it is I'm scared about. We didn't see each other much today anyway.

So I sent her a text asking her about it instead, but she hasn't replied yet.

Feeling a bit down.

Wednesday 19 December

The school canteen was offering Christmas dinners at £3.50 a go today, so me, Han, Alice, Ems, and Matty all met up and dined in style at lunchtime. Caroline decided not to join us 'cos she's vegetarian and the only vegetarian thing on the menu was nut loaf, which Caroline said looked like a piece of house brick. Our lunch was okay, surprisingly enough.

Han didn't really say much to me over lunch, so I wondered if she really was pissed off with me for asking about Facebook the other day. I dunno. I kept looking at her and smiling, but I got the feeling that I wasn't getting much back from her.

Came home tonight and discovered Mum had made us roast chicken for tea. She said, 'Why didn't you tell me you were having a roast at lunchtime?' and I said, 'I had a wee at 3 p.m. this afternoon. Should I have told you about that as well?' then got shouted at for being cheeky!

I can't stop thinking about stupid Facebook. It's eating me up. I dunno whether it's just curiosity or paranoia, but I just kinda want to know who some of Han's friends on there are. Maybe part of me needs to know who Han was before I knew her, 'cos she doesn't really talk about it much. Or maybe I'm just being nosy? Nosy and paranoid at the same time. Jeez. I mean, she's a good-looking girl; anyone with two eyes in their head can see that, and she could, like, have anyone she wants. If she knows that many people, someone's bound to come along and catch her eye, aren't they? Then where would that leave me??

Thursday 20 December

We got our Christmas tree tonight. Dad insisted on standing it in a bucket of water for an hour like he always does, to help stop the needles dropping off it by Christmas Eve, then we dragged it into the house and plonked it by the front window. After Mum had hoovered up the trail of pine needles from the back door to the lounge, we placed the lights round it and switched on. Nothing. An hour later, after Dad had gone through every bulb and checked the fuse, and Mum had hoovered up some more needles, the lights were switched on and bathed us all in a Christmassy glow of red, green, and white.

We dug out the tinsel and baubles and threw out an old mince pie that had somehow found its way into the box, and set about decorating the tree with such enthusiasm that it was twinkling like Paris Hilton jacked up on Red Bull by the time we'd finished with it! HRBH put the fairy on top of the tree and got covered in needles, then Chairman Meow brushed past it on his way onto the window sill and got covered in needles, so that he looked a bit like a green hedgehog!! Dad started grumbling about the mess and said we'd be having an artificial tree next year, but then he says that every year so we all ignored him.

Sent Han a text just before I went to sleep and told her we'd put our tree up. She just sent me one back saying, 'Nice'. Sending nondescript messages like that does nothing to make me feel better about stuff!

Friday 21 December

Last day at school, and I wish I could say it was a happy one. We were allowed to go home early, so Han asked me over to hers. As we were walking to her house, I stupidly tried asking her about the text she'd sent to me by mistake again, and then I asked her if any of her ex-girlfriends were on Facebook (I know, I know!) and she got dead snappy with me! I said I was just intrigued at how many people she knew on there and she said, 'For God's sake, Clem! Enough, already! Facebook, Facebook, Facebook! It's all you bloody talk about at the moment.'

I kinda just mumbled 'Sorry' to her, although I wasn't really sorry, and she said, 'How many times do I have to tell you that it's just friends from the past, friends of friends, friends off music forums I chat on. You know all about those, don't you?'

I nodded meekly and, 'cos I felt a bit stupid, I tried to take her hand as we were walking along the road, but she let it drop again, which kinda upset me.

She said, 'Do you think I'm cheating on you, or something? 'cos that's what it feels like,' and I just said, 'Of course not!' but I don't know how convincing I sounded.

She kinda looked hurt and said, 'Good, 'cos I'd never do the dirty on you, not in a million years, so can you just change the record over it?'

We walked to her house in silence after that. There were so many things I wanted to say, and I kept saying them in my head, but something stopped me actually saying them to her. Anyway, in the end I spent, like, only an hour at her house because the atmosphere between us was so strained I made an excuse to leave and come home again.

The sad thing is, she didn't try to stop me.

Saturday 22 December

Alice sent me a text at 7 o'clock this morning to wish me a Happy

Christmas (!!) She was at the airport 'cos she's going to Germany with her parents to eat schnitzel and frankfurters, or whatever it is they eat in Germany at Christmas. She's so lucky! All we do is the same thing every year: have turkey and sprouts and then Great Aunt May on Boxing Day (to visit—not to eat).

I suddenly felt really sad. Mainly, I suppose, because I didn't know Alice was going away for Christmas 'cos she never told me. We used to tell each other everything, and that's all over now. I s'pose that's what happens when your best friend makes declarations of love to you, like, totally out of the blue. How can you ever go back to being as you once were when that happens? You can't. And I think that's what's happened to me and Alice.

Anyway, I didn't want to just text her a Happy Christmas wish, so I rang her. She sounded a bit awkward, like she always seems to these days when I speak to her but we at least managed to have a bit of a chat about nothing in particular. She asked me if I was okay, 'cos she said I didn't sound my normal self, and I felt tears welling in my eyes. I wanted to tell her about Han, but I didn't really feel like I could.

She said, 'Are you sure you're okay?' and I said, 'Kinda,' and she said, ''Cos if you want to talk that's cool. My flight's delayed and my parents have conveniently buggered off into the Duty Free lounge and left me with all the bags, so I'm bored rigid.'

I giggled a bit and she said, 'That's better,' and I felt like my heart was shattering, I dunno why.

I said to her, 'Things are just a bit strained with me and Han, is all,' and she just said, 'Oh,' which was cool 'cos I didn't really expect her to say much more than that.

Anyway, I kinda told her about Han and Facebook and me wanting to know who her friends were on there, and that she wasn't telling me anything and it was making me think horrible thoughts, and even as I was saying it, I realised how ridiculous and clingy it all sounded.

Alice said, ‘Clem, anyone who’s anyone has loads of people on Facebook. Doesn’t mean they’re cheating on their boyfriends or girlfriends.’

So then I asked her how many friends she had on it. She told me she had 465.

465!!!

How??

I felt real stupid when she asked me how many I had, and I told her I only had, like 10, then I felt even stupider when I realised what a fuss I’d been making over Han and her measly 88 friends! How is it possible for one person to have 465 friends? What does she find to talk about all the time?

I could hear Alice sighing down the phone which probably meant she either thought I was being ridiculous too, or she really didn’t want to hear about mine and Han’s tiffs, and then I heard a muffled announcement somewhere in the background on her phone and she said, ‘Clem, I gotta go. They’ve just called our flight at last.’

I wished her a Happy Christmas again, and told her not to eat too much Simnel cake, but then she told me you only eat that at Easter and I felt a bit stupid again. She said, ‘Listen, Clem, I don’t confess to know Han very well, but I’ve spoken to her enough times at school to know she’s not the most open person in the world, not the most talkative, you know?’

I said, ‘She’s an EMO, they don’t do talking,’ and Alice just said, ‘Yeah, but what I do know is that she’s nuts about you. You only have to see the way she looks at you when she thinks no one else is looking to know that. I notice these things, Clem, 'cos it's only what I've done myself in the past.'

I didn't know what to say to that so just kinda mumbled 'Thanks' to Alice, and remembered just what a thoroughly nice person she really is.

She said, 'I've really gotta go. Have a great Christmas, Clem. I'll be thinking of you.'

I started to say I'd be thinking of her as well, but the phone had gone dead by then, I guess either cut off or Alice had had to dash off for her flight. I dunno.

I think I felt a bit better after speaking to Alice, but I suppose I'll feel even better still if I could shake this niggling worry from me about it all.

Sunday 23 December

Mum and Dad dragged me and HRBH over to Autumn Leaves to visit Great Aunt May today, when all I wanted to do was hang out with Han and try and get things back to normal between us.

I texted her before we went and told her I was going to see Great Aunt May and she just sent one back saying ''K. Have a good day.' Nothing else. After feeling a bit more positive yesterday, I was back to feeling crap all day. Even HRBH noticed, telling me I was 'quiet for a change. You're usually gobbing off left right and centre. Cat got your tongue today or what?'

How could I tell her? How could I tell her that I feel sick all the time at the moment, sick with feeling like things aren't great with me and Han? How can I tell her that all I seem to do is wait for Han to text me, then dread her texts at the same time? My sister has no idea what real love is, but I do.

Every tiny part of me loves Han, so why do I feel like crap all the time at the moment?

Monday 24 December

Christmas Eve! Texted Han first thing and asked her if I could come over later and give her her present. She texted me back and just said, 'Sure.'

I got a sinking feeling at getting yet another short text and really didn't know what to do. It's our first Christmas together but there's such a crap atmosphere between us at the moment, I just can't enjoy the feeling of it. I should have a warm feeling of fuzziness, of seasonal cheer, but all I seem to feel at the moment is sick.

Anyway, I decided to go over to her house after lunch. I handed her the presents I'd bought her and she handed me mine and then gave me strict instructions not to poke it. I told her (probably a bit too huffily) that I was seventeen years old and had ceased to prod my presents when I was about eleven. She just smiled, kinda tightly, I thought.

Tuesday 25 December

Woke up at 6 a.m. but thought better of getting up, bearing in mind Mum didn't get home from Midnight Communion until about 1:45 this morning. She got chatting to Brenda Shelduck in the Lady Chapel and didn't realise the time.

Sat up in bed willing it to get lighter so I could get up and start opening some presents, but then curiosity got the better of me and

I had a rifle through the pillowcase Mum had put at the foot of my bed. Remembered then that I'd put Han's present under my bed; I wanted to open it in the privacy of my own room, just in case she'd bought me something that wasn't fit for my parents to see, such as a poster of a comely lady showing off her bits, or some chocolate body paint or some such. I needn't have worried though, 'cos she'd bought me the funkiest T-shirt, like, *ever*, a Foo Fighters CD to add to my collection, a book of funny pictures and jokes about cats, and another leather necklace, a bit like the one she brought me back from Portugal.

I lay in bed with her presents scattered across my bed and imagined her opening my presents in her room too. I wondered if she was thinking about me, then wondered if she ever thought about me like I always think about her, or didn't she bother anymore? I got myself a bit spooked thinking stuff like that, so I texted her and wished her a Happy Crimbo and thanked her for her presents.

I was ridiculously pleased and relieved that she texted me back pretty much straight away, and kinda thought that, yeah, maybe she *was* lying in her room thinking about me as well, after all. She wished me 'Happy Holidays', which is a bit too American for my liking, but she's an atheist so it would be just a bit hypocritical of her if she wished me anything else, I suppose. She thanked me for her presents and then just as I was texting her back to tell her she was welcome, she sent me another one, saying that she wished we could be together. My throat tightened when I read that, and suddenly really wished we were together as well.

I got up and went downstairs and opened some presents from around the tree on my own while everyone else carried on sleeping upstairs. They did eventually deign to come downstairs, just after 10 a.m., and slumped on the sofa (still in their dressing gowns, mind you) to watch some bloody awful Christmas special on the TV.

Then Han sent me another text a bit later on to tell me that she, Dan,

Joe, and her dad were all waiting to go out for a walk, but her mum was holding them up 'cos she still had her hand up the turkey's bum (stuffing it, I hope). She also said that they'd put tinsel round Toffee's neck but were a bit worried 'cos some of the tinsel was now missing, and her dad was stressing in case they had to take her to the vet and pay extra 'cos it was Christmas Day. I looked across at Mum, Dad, and HRBH, still all in their dressing gowns, still slumped on the sofa, surrounded by wrapping paper and all yawning loudly and thought that normal families (i.e., Han's) do normal things on Christmas Day like bracing walks in the crisp winter air. What do mine do? Sweet FA!

Anyway, after Christmas lunch, most of which I managed to force down, Mum insisted on watching the Queen's speech like she normally does. I don't get why she does that each year. Normally she doesn't have time for any of the royals, but each Christmas Day, at 3 p.m. on the nose, there she is, glued to the telly, drinking in every word Her Majesty has to say like some loyal, fawning servant. Then (at bloody last!) we all took Barbara out for a long walk. I dressed her in her red bowtie and everyone we passed commented on how smart she looked!

Sent Han another text in the afternoon telling her I hoped she was having a nice day, but didn't get a reply until gone midnight.

Went to bed not feeling too full of Christmas cheer, just too full of mince pies.

Wednesday 26 December

Woke up feeling sick, but I wasn't sure if that was from worry or the four mince pies I had at midnight last night.

Dad went over to Autumn Leaves and picked Great Aunt May up at lunchtime. She's staying with us just for tonight 'cos they've got their Christmas party there tomorrow night and she doesn't want to miss it. It was supposed to be on the 23rd, but they had trouble slaughtering the turkey or something. I didn't like to ask.

I sent Han a text and told her Great Aunt May was coming over today and asked her if she wanted to come over as well, 'cos I know Great Aunt May really likes Han. She sent me one back and said she couldn't come today, but could I say hi to Aunt May from her, and could she come over tomorrow instead 'cos she'd been thinking about 'us'. My mind went into overdrive and my heart started thumping madly in my neck when I read that, so I texted her back and said, 'What about us?' and she just said, 'I'll talk to you 2moro. I'll come over around two, okay?'

So, what the hell does that all mean? She's going to dump me, isn't she? Great! After telling me yesterday she wished we could be together, now she wants to finish with me.

What a shitty end to the year.

Great Aunt May gave me and HRBH our Christmas presents when she came over. She gave me a pink makeup compress and HRBH a spanner 'for her bicycle' (she doesn't have one). It was nice of her, I suppose, but I was feeling so damned wretched about everything I could quite cheerfully have bashed her over the head with the spanner, old lady or no old lady.

Thursday 27 December

Couldn't sleep a wink for worrying about everything last night, not helped at all by the bloody neighbours over the road from us having a party until God knows what hour last night.

We weren't invited 'cos we don't really speak to them much. Mum says they're a bit 'uncouth'. I asked her once what made a particular person uncouth and she sniffed and said, 'gold jewellery and holidays in Benidorm,' and folded her arms tight across her chest, just like Great Aunt May does when she's talking about Ariadne Dawkins, who's got a room down the corridor from her at Autumn Leaves, and who looks a bit like Joan Rivers' grandmother.

Anyway, the uncouth neighbours' party went on until 3 a.m., by which time I thought I might possibly go mad from worrying about what Han was going to say to me today. Woke up looking and feeling like crap and waited for Han to come over so she could dump me.

After not being able to eat any lunch, something that didn't go unnoticed by HRBH, who made some flippant comment about my New Year's resolution being too early, I went up to my room and waited for Han.

She came over around two, looking stunning as always, and after making small talk with Mum and Dad, came up with me to my room.

We sat together on my bed and she smiled at me kinda awkwardly and I waited for her to tell me she was fed up with my clinginess, fed up with all my questions and, well, just fed up with me really.

Instead, she took my hands in hers and looked at me, like, real intently and said, 'Things have been a little, uh, how can I put it? A little strained with us, haven't they?'

I nodded, too afraid to say anything in case I started crying.

Then she said, 'I've been a bit of a shit and I'm sorry.'

I just nodded again, then I said, 'I think it's my fault, so I'm sorry too.'

She said, 'Your fault?' so I said, 'Yeah, all that Facebook stuff I kept going on and on about, badgering you for answers.'

She grinned at me and said, 'Yeah, and I didn't handle it so well, so that was my fault too,' and we both giggled.

She leant over and kissed my forehead and said, 'I can promise you, Clemmy, there are NO exes on my Facebook. I have a grand total of two exes, neither of whom I would piss on if they were on fire. I certainly have no desire to know what either of them is doing, so why would I want them as my friends?'

I bit my lip and felt completely stupid. I just said, 'But why were you being so secretive about it all, then?' and she said, 'I wasn't being secretive, silly, I just didn't think it was that important, and that was stupid of me. Of course it was going to be important to you. So, I'm sorry. I'm sorry I was so flippant about it, and I'm sorry I went weird with you over it. I should have handled it better.' She thought for a minute, then said, 'And you know how stubborn I can be. Maybe, I dunno, maybe a part of me was deliberately not telling you stuff, just 'cos I'm a stubborn cow like that sometimes.'

I kinda shrugged and grinned sheepishly at her, then she said, 'I swear to God, Clemmy, there's no one on there that you have to be worried about. It's you I want, you I love. Just you. Always has been, always will be.'

She looked at me and said, 'Do you trust me?' and I nodded meekly at her. Then I looked down at my hands and mumbled something about just being really scared that she was keeping stuff from me, at which point she held my face in her hands and planted kisses all over me, saying, 'OMG, Clemmy! I didn't realise you were so cut up about it all! If I'd known you were worrying about it I'd have talked to you more about it all! I'd have, I dunno, I'd have shown you my stupid bloody Facebook page so you could have seen for yourself!'

So I said I hadn't wanted to say too much about it to her 'cos I was frightened she'd get annoyed, then I kinda laughed and said about how ridiculous I sounded.

Han smiled and said, 'You have no idea, do you?' so I said, 'No idea about what?'

So she said, 'No idea about just how much I love you. 'Cos I do, Clem, very much. You're everything to me; the sun, the moon, the stars, everything. Forget anything that happened before I met you 'cos it doesn't matter. I only started living the day you came into my life.'

When she said that I felt REAL stupid!

She's just sent me a text tonight telling me how much I mean to her and now I'm lying in the dark just reading it over and over again, with a stupid, loved-up grin on my face.

Friday 28 December

Woke up to, like, a hundred texts from Han telling me how much she loves me and how much she needs me. Now that's what I call a good way to start the day!

Got my appetite back (funny, that) so had a cold turkey sandwich for breakfast. HRBH made some puerile comment about my New Year's resolution breaking already but I was way too happy to respond to her childish witterings.

Han loves me and I love Han, and there's no greater feeling in the world (although getting my appetite back at last comes a close second!).

Saturday 29 December

Han came round after lunch and we had another heart-to-heart in my room. I told her I was sorry again, and she said she would 'never, like, EVER do anything to hurt me' 'cos all she wanted to do was 'love me and look after me.'

She looked at me with more love in her eyes than I think I'd ever seen before and I felt a right prat for doubting her and getting myself so wound up over a dumb website that I'd never even heard of two months ago!

Mum was in town buying some glitter for Aunt Marie and Uncle Bob's party on Sunday (don't ask!) and Dad was busy down in the lounge wrestling with the fairy lights which had fused *yet again*, so I figured Han had said enough, and locked my door so I could make sure I could show her just how much I loved her too.

After we'd shown each other for the third time in a row and we'd finally got our breath back, Han told me I was 'the most important person in her world, like, *ever*' and I vowed never to doubt her ever again.

I tell you what, though, this bloody dating lark is tougher than I thought!

Sunday 30 December

Watched something on the news today when they do this review of everything that's happened over the last year. I have to say, it's been a bit boring in Britain, really. The most exciting things they could come up with was Tony Blair retiring to Barbados or wherever he's going to disappear to, the Grumpy Gnome taking over from him, and England losing in the Rugby World Cup finals. Is this all we have to show for the last twelve months? Surely something more earth-shattering must have happened? I think if I was the telly news reader having to come in to announce that, I would have taken a sickie. Not worth getting out of bed for, that!!!

My year, on the other hand, has been pretty darned good. It's just a pity I can't go on the telly and tell everyone just how good it's been, 'cos I tell you, sometimes I feel like shouting it all to the rooftops!

Han had gone to visit some relative near London today so I was at a loose end all day. I was dead bored by the evening, despite Han sending me regular text updates, so I decided to start to think about my New Year resolutions for next year and made myself a list. They won't last more than a week, probably, but it passed a pleasurable hour while I was waiting for Mum to serve us the remains of the Christmas turkey for tea. I resolve to:

1. Love Han with all my heart forever and ever (that won't be difficult).
2. Think before I say anything to her about matters of the heart (she's so sensitive).
3. Try and like her choice of music more (but I draw the line at Metallica).
4. Be more patient when Great Aunt May comes to stay.
5. Stop winding HRBH up over her diets.
6. Work hard for my exams next year.
7. Try to like Ryan more.
8. Clean Uncle Buck's cage more often. The smell of rabbit piss makes my eyes water.

I think that's all! I know I can stick to numbers 1, 2, and 8 but I can't guarantee I'll stick to the others. Certainly not number 5. I'm only human after all.

Monday 31 December

Mum and Dad are off to Aunt Marie and Uncle Bob's annual shindig tonight. Thank God I don't have to go this year, dear diary, for I have been cordially invited to spend the evening having a civilized meal with Han and her parents, which means I don't have to be a part of the annual humiliation that is Mum getting arse-holed on Campari and kissing any man who has the misfortune to stray into her path.

2 a.m.
Had a really grown-up and sophisticated New Year's Eve meal at Han's tonight. What a difference from last year! We had three courses (we usually have only two at ours—and that's depending whether or not Mum can be arsed to rustle us up a pudding) with a respectable delay between each course so we could have polite conversation. If it wasn't for the fact I was wearing ripped jeans and a sweatshirt with 'Pimp My Ho' written on it, I could quite have imagined myself in some sort of Jane Austen novel, squeezed into a corset and nibbling on roast swan or some such. We made it to midnight, then watched Big Ben bong, toasting each other with Cava, which was a bit dry and made my eye wink. Han's mum and dad just hugged me rather than kissing me, which I was glad of! Her mum's okay but her dad's got a beard and I'm always worried he might have the remains of his dinner lurking in it. Then me and Han snuck out into the garden and stole a kiss round the back of the shed. We stood arm in arm and looked up at the moon, and Han whispered, 'Thank you for the best year of my life, Clemmykins,' which made my tummy turn to mush.

Then she said, 'Just always remember what I told you the other day, okay? I love you *so* much, you know that? I'd be nothing without you,' and I thought I'd never felt happier.

Han's dad dropped me back home at around 1 a.m., and when he'd parked up, he squeezed my hand and thanked me for being such a good friend to his daughter. He told me that 'he and Jeanette had been worried about Han fitting in at her new school, but that they were both so relieved she'd found such a good friend as me'. I smiled weakly at him and felt a rush of guilt inside. I bet if he knew the truth it'd be my throat he'd be squeezing, not my hand.

Tuesday 1 January

Another diary! Yay! I really do promise to keep this one neater than last year's! I also promise not to assume Mum is going to get hammered every New Year from now until eternity, as she actually arrived home at a reasonable hour last night. She was slightly merry, granted, and her right eye kept looking at her left eye, and there was the faintest of faint whiffs of Campari on her breath—but she was completely empty-handed! Result!

So, another day, another year! What a year it's been! 365 days of fun, angst, excitement, nervousness, sofas, and LOVE! I went out with a boy for all of three weeks, got over my J obsession, had my best friend tell me she fancied me and…I was lucky enough to fall in love with the most perfect, lovely, funny, beautiful girl in all the world. Who'd have thought it, hey?

It seems crazy to me that just a year ago I was so unhappy and so confused about who I was, confused about my feelings for J, confused about who I wanted to be, or who I *thought* I ought to be. A year later and here I am. So I finally accepted that I'm gay (and boy, didn't I take my time coming to THAT conclusion??!!) and now I've admitted that to myself, and actually *fallen in love*, I feel happier and more settled than I've ever been.

And who'd have guessed just a year ago that I would have ended up so complete? That this gorgeous Goth—sorry, EMO—who loves me as much as I love her would walk into my life, turn it upside down and yet make it so perfect and complete? Life's just wonderful and it's all down to that one girl…

I'm going over to Han's this afternoon. She says she's going to buy me something special to celebrate the New Year, and to celebrate our love for each other.

OMG! I hope it's not a tattoo!!!

About the Author

KE Payne was born in Bath (the English city, not the tub), and after leaving school she worked for the British government for fifteen years, which probably sounds a lot more exciting than it really was.

Fed up with spending her days moving paperwork around her desk and making models of the Taj Mahal out of paperclips, she packed it all in to go to university in Bristol and graduated as a mature student in 2006 with a degree in linguistics and history.

After graduating, she worked at a university in the Midlands for a while, again moving all that paperwork around, before finally leaving to embark on her dream career as a writer.

She moved to the idyllic English countryside in 2007 where she now lives and works happily surrounded by dogs and guinea pigs..

Soliloquy Titles From Bold Strokes Books

365 Days by K.E. Payne. Life sucks when you're seventeen years old and confused about your sexuality, and the girl of your dreams doesn't even know you exist. Then in walks sexy new emo girl, Hannah Harrison. Clemmie Atkins has exactly 365 days to discover herself, and she's going to have a blast doing it! (978-1-60282-540-6)

Cursebusters! by Julie Smith. Budding-psychic Reeno is the most accomplished teenage burglar in California, but one tiny screw-up and poof!—she's sentenced to Bad Girl School. And that isn't even her worst problem. Her sister Haley's dying of an illness no one can diagnose, and now she can't even help. (978-1-60282-559-8)

Who I Am by M.L. Rice. Devin Kelly's senior year is a disaster. She's in a new school in a new town, and the school bully is making her life miserable—but then she meets his sister Melanie and realizes her feelings for her are more than platonic. (978-1-60282-231-3)

Sleeping Angel by Greg Herren. Eric Matthews survives a terrible car accident only to find out everyone in town thinks he's a murderer—and he has to clear his name even though he has no memories of what happened. (978-1-60282-214-6)

Mesmerized by David-Matthew Barnes. Through her close friendship with Brodie and Lance, Serena Albright learns about the many forms of love and finds comfort for the grief and guilt she feels over the brutal death of her older brother, the victim of a hate crime. (978-1-60282-191-0)

The Perfect Family by Kathryn Shay. A mother and her gay son stand hand in hand as the storms of change engulf their perfect family and the life they knew. (978-1-60282-181-1)

Father Knows Best by Lynda Sandoval. High school juniors and best friends Lila Moreno, Meryl Morganstern, and Caressa Thibodoux plan to make the most of the summer before senior year. What they discover that amazing summer about girl power, growing up, and trusting friends and family more than prepares them to tackle that all-important senior year! (978-1-60282-147-7)